REQUIEM'S SONG

REQUIEM'S SONG

DAWN OF DRAGONS, BOOK ONE

DANIEL ARENSON

Copyright © 2014 by Daniel Arenson

All rights reserved.

This novel is a work of fiction. Names, characters, places and incidents are either the product of the author's imagination, or, if real, used fictitiously.

No part of this book may be reproduced or transmitted in any form or by an electronic or mechanical means, including photocopying, recording or by any information storage and retrieval system, without the express written permission of the author.

ISBN: 978-1-927601-35-8

LAIRA

On Laira's tenth birthday, the crone dragged her outside to see her mother burned at the stake.

Laira blinked in the weak morning sun. She had not seen daylight in so long. For five days they had kept her in her tent, alone in shadows, alone in fear, the sounds of the trial—shouting, pleading, weeping—rising outside. Now silence filled the camp. Now, finally in daylight, Laira only wanted to return to the darkness.

Other tents rose across the yellow grass, similar to hers, their animal-skin covers stretched across cedar poles. In the distance rolled a red forest, a place of berries and the whispers of secret men, and beyond the trees rose the faded blue mountains where the elk roamed. A murder of crows circled above, cawing, and Laira felt her head spin and she nearly fell. She clutched her doll, a wooden little thing she had named Mustardseed. The crone's talon-like hand tightened around Laira's arm, dragging her forward; Laira felt like a doll herself, helpless and small.

"Keep walking and don't close your eyes," said the crone, a shaman named Shedah. Her arms were knobby like old carob branches, and her fingers ended with sharp, yellow nails that nicked Laira's flesh. Other fingers—torn off the hands of dead men—hung around Shedah's neck in a lurid necklace of bone and dried flesh, charms to ward off evil spirits. The crone was ancient beyond measure—some claimed her two hundred winters old— and so wizened her eyes all but disappeared into nests of wrinkles. Her gums were toothless, her nose beaked, her body withered, and yet she was still so strong, strong enough that Laira thought the crone could snap her arm in two. All Laira could do was keep walking, guided by the old woman.

"I won't close my eyes," Laira whispered.

Shedah cackled. "If you do, I'll rip off your eyelids and make you watch. So be a good little maggot."

They kept moving through the camp. The tribe's totem pole rose ahead—the great bole of an ancient cedar, carved with images of bison, eagles, and leaping fish. Near its crest flared a gilded mammoth tusk, long as a boat, attached to the pole with rawhide thongs. The cross of wood and ivory towered above the tents—the god Ka'altei, a deity of meat and fire. Wherever they set down this pole marked their territory, a beacon for all other tribes to fear.

Around the pillar brooded its guardians—the rocs, fetid birds the size of mammoths. Oil dripped down their black feathers, and their long, naked necks turned as Laira approached. Their cruel beaks—large enough to swallow men—clacked open and shut, and their talons, which were longer than human arms, dug into the soil. Their eyes watched Laira, gleaming orbs like circles of bronze. Were they not tethered to the totem, Laira thought they'd leap toward her, tear out her entrails, and feast.

The tribesmen stood everywhere, dour, staring, clad in fur and leather and holding spears. Some stared at Laira balefully. One hunter, a burly man with a scraggly red beard, spat at her. Others gazed in pity. Clad in a robe of patches, a druid woman whispered ancient prayers, reaching toward Laira but daring not approach. In Laira's old home across the sea, men now wove wool and cotton, built houses of stone, and shaved their beards, yet here in the north—in the Goldtusk tribe—lived an older, prouder, rougher people, warriors of fur and stone and hair. War paint covered their leathery skin, and tattoos of totem animals coiled around their arms.

The crone kept tugging her forward, and Laira wanted to use her curse—the secret disease of her family, the power that would let her escape this tribe, let her free her mother, let her kill them all. Yet she dared not. Mother had used the dark magic; now the woman would burn.

Past campfires, the totem pole, and a mammoth carcass buzzing with flies it rose—the pyre.

Upon the pile of wood and kindling she stood tied to the stake—Laira's mother.

For five days in her tent, Laira had shed many tears, yet none would now flow. The crone who dragged her forward paused, and Laira stood in the dead grass, staring, feeling dead herself, feeling empty.

Mother wept.

Her face was so beaten Laira barely recognized her. It looked less like a face and more like a slab of bloodied meat. Tears poured from bruised, bloodshot eyes to flow down lacerated cheeks. When Mother spoke, her voice was slurred, thick with blood and shattered teeth.

"Don't make her watch. Turn her aside. Please . . . Laira, my sweetness, please, close your eyes."

Laira bit her lip so hard she tasted blood. She wanted to run away, but how could she? She wanted to close her eyes, but Shedah had promised to rip off her eyelids. The crone gripped both her arms now, fingers digging, hard as bronze, and Laira wondered if those fingers could shatter her bones, rip off her limbs, kill her right here with the pain. Mother wept upon the pyre and Laira wanted to do *something*—to use her curse, to scream, even to weep, some act of defiance or emotion . . . but she only watched.

"Behold the reptile!"

The voice, high-pitched and raspy, tore through the camp like a blade through flesh. Goose bumps rose on Laira's skin.

Wincing, she turned to see him—the man who ruled the Goldtusk tribe, the man who would sentence Mother to death, the man who filled Laira's nightmares.

"Zerra," she whispered.

The chieftain limped toward them, tall and swaying like a wicker effigy in the wind. He wore patches of fur, leather boots, and necklaces of bone beads. His prized possession, a bronze *apa* sword, hung upon his belt. The blade was leaf-shaped, double-edged, and as long as a man's forearm, sprouting from a semicircular crossguard. In some of the villages across the river, men now forged metal, plowed fields, and raised huts, but Zerra had always scorned them. His were the old ways, the ways of hunting and gathering, of tents and campfires, of blades taken from corpses rather than forged in smithies.

More than his towering height, his sword, or his mane of grizzled hair, it was Zerra's face that frightened Laira. Half that face was gone, burned into something wet, raw, and dripping. Mother had given him that wound—or at least, the creature Mother had become, a monster of scales, fangs, and fire.

The disease, Laira thought and shivered. *The curse that had us banished from Eteer, our old home across the sea. The curse that lets my family turn into reptiles. Into monsters. Into . . . dragons.*

"Zerra, listen to me!" Mother cried from the pyre. "Banish us. Banish us to the escarpment. We will not hurt you. We—"

"You will burn and scream for me," Zerra said, his left eye blazing from his melted flesh. "You are lower than one who lies with pigs. You will squeal."

You screamed, Laira thought. *You squealed.*

She had seen it five days ago. She had dreamed it every night since. She knew those nightmares would fill her forever. The memory pounded through her, shaking her bones.

While the men had hunted upon their rocs, Mother had taken Laira into the woods to gather berries, nuts, and mushrooms. Mother's amulet gleamed around her neck, a silver talisman bearing the sigil of Taal, a god of their old home across the sea, a god unknown to any others in this northern hinterland. Past a grove of birches they had found a pond, a place of water lilies, golden leaves, and mist. It was a secret place, a perfect place. A place for dark magic.

The curse always itched within Laira and her mother. The disease forever cried for release. They stepped into the pool, submerged themselves in the water . . . and shifted.

Hidden underwater, Laira opened her eyes, and between algae and the roots of lilies, she saw Mother change. White scales flowed across her body, the color of moonlight, and wings unfurled from her back. Her body grew, becoming almost as large as a roc, slick and graceful and thin. Laira changed too, letting the curse raise golden scales across her. Her wings stirred the water, and she blasted sparks from her mouth.

Their claws rested on the pool's floor. Their tails braided together. Their heads—long, scaled, and horned—rose to the surface. Nostrils and eyes emerged into the air. Men called it a curse, but to Laira it felt so good. This felt more like her natural form than the scrawny, raven-haired girl she was at their camp. Scaled and winged, a golden dragon, Laira felt whole. She felt true. Looking around the forest, she tried to imagine flapping her wings and flying, seeing mountains, forests, and rivers from high above, so high nobody could hurt her.

"Why must we hide?" she asked, sticking her snout over the water. Lilies tangled around her teeth. "They say that other cursed ones live at the escarpment in the north. They say it's safe. They say Zerra's own twin brother hides there, cursed with the same disease."

Mother blasted smoke from her nostrils. Her eyes narrowed. As a dragon, her voice sounded deeper, stronger, almost musical. "There are no others, Laira. That's only a myth.

The world is cold and large and empty. The lone wolf perishes. The pack survives. The tribe of Goldtusk is our home, and Zerra is a kind master."

"A master who would slay us if he knew our secret!" Laira said. "I hate hiding. I hate this curse. Why did you have to give me this disease? You infected me." Tears burned in her eyes. "If I must be a dragon, let me fly. Let me be free. I won't cower in the water."

Anger flowed through Laira, rattling her scales, and flames filled her maw. With a cry, she beat her wings. She rose from the pool, water and algae dripping off her scales, claws scratching at the air. Mother gasped and stared from below. Laira knew the rule—only become a dragon underwater, in darkness of night, or in deep caves, never in the open. They had been caught shifting in their last home, a place Laira could hardly remember, and they had barely escaped. But Laira didn't care. Laira was done caring. She hated hiding and she would fly.

She beat her wings, rising higher, soaring between the trees until she crashed through the forest canopy with a shower of orange leaves. The cold wind streamed around her and Laira laughed. This was freedom. This was who she was. They called it a disease but she felt healthier than ever, not a monster but a noble spirit of fire.

"Laira!"

She looked down to see Mother rising from the forest—a slim white dragon with blue eyes.

"I can fly!" Laira shouted and laughed. "I can fly to the escarpment. I can find the others. I know they're real. I—"

"Laira, come back here!" Mother shouted, flying toward her.

The white dragon reached out her claws, grabbed Laira's leg, and tugged. Laira screamed and tried to free herself, and her wings beat, and—

Shrieks pierced the air.

Laira fell silent.

Mother spun around in the sky, stared east, and cried out in fear.

"Rocs," Laira whispered.

The great birds, larger even than dragons, covered the sky, fetid things like oversized vultures. Their heads were bald, their necks gangly, their black feathers damp with the oil they secreted. Their talons reached out, and upon their backs rode the hunters of the Goldtusk tribe.

At their lead, riding upon a massive roc that dwarfed the others, rode Zerra.

"The curse of the reptile rises!" cried the chieftain, his hair billowing. He raised a flint-tipped spear in his hand; feathers and scrimshawed raven skulls adorned its shaft. "Behold the weredragon."

Mother hovered and snarled, hiding Laira behind her. She faced the advancing horde. Dozens of rocs flew toward them.

"Fly down into the forest," Mother said softly, still facing the foul birds; it took Laira a few heartbeats to realize Mother was talking to her. "They haven't seen you yet. Land among the trees, become human again, and return to the camp."

"We have to flee!" Laira said.

"They're too fast," Mother replied. "They will catch us if we flee. Into the forest, go! I'll hold them off."

The rocs shrieked, drawing nearer. Their stench filled the air, thick as fog, and their cries split the sky, slamming against Laira's eardrums.

Laira shook, hesitating, wanting to fight too, wanting to drag Mother to safety, wanting to fly north and find the other dragons fabled to exist . . . but she simply obeyed.

She flew down past the leafy canopy. Before she hit the ground, she heard screams above. Fire blazed overhead and blood rained. Laira landed by the pool, shifted back into human form, and gazed up at the sky.

She trembled. She wanted to cry out but dared not. Past the branches, she caught only glimpses of the violence. She saw Mother blowing fire, a blaze greater than any pyre, tinged blue and white with horrible heat. She saw Zerra ignite, scream, and burn upon his roc. And then only smoke, talons cutting into scales, and pattering blood on fallen leaves.

A human again—ten years old, scrawny as a twig, and clad only in her buffalo pelt—Laira ran.

She ran through the forest, across the meadow, and into their camp. She ran until Shedah—wizened, cackling, covered in moles—grabbed her. She screamed in the crone's grasp as the hunters returned with their catch. Mother was now in human form, beaten and bloodied, tied with ropes. She was trying to shift into a dragon again; scales appeared and disappeared upon her body, but whenever she began to grow, the ropes dug into her flesh, shoving her back into human form. Men tossed Mother onto the ground, kicking, striking with sticks, and Laira wanted to run to her, she wanted to shift into a dragon and save her, but she only raced into her tent, and she only trembled.

For five days she cowered as Shedah guarded the tent, sealing Laira in the shadows.

And now she stood here, staring, all her tears spent, watching her mother upon the pyre, watching Zerra lift a torch and bring it toward the pile of wood and kindling.

"Please," Laira whispered, and finally her eyes dampened. "Please, Zerra, please don't kill her. Please."

The chieftain slowly turned toward her. He stared, the ruined half of his face dripping pus and blood. Slowly a smile spread across his face, displaying crooked teeth.

Requiem's Song

"One day, little worm . . ." he said, voice like wooden chips rubbing together. "One day I will find the curse in you too, and you will scream like this."

With that, Zerra spun back toward the pyre and tossed his torch into the kindling.

Oil soaked the straw, twigs, and dried leaves. They burst into flame with the speed and ferocity of dragonfire.

Mother screamed.

The fire spread across her, blazing skyward, licking skin off muscle, flesh off bones. And still Mother screamed, writhing in her bonds, begging, wailing.

And Laira screamed too.

She tried to close her eyes, but Shedah grabbed her eyelids with rough fingers and held them open. She tried to break free, to run to her mother, to flee into the forest, but the crone held her fast.

"Mother!" she cried. "Mother, please!"

Please, she prayed silently. *Please die. Please stop screaming.*

Yet she would not. The screaming and writhing continued within the inferno, the fire eating Mother's flesh as if slowly savoring a meal. The smell of cooking meat filled the camp, as savory as spiced game. The flames tore through the ropes, and Mother fell from the stake to land in the blazing kindling. She managed to roll off the pyre, to run several steps through the camp, a living torch. She soon collapsed, rolling and whimpering. Zerra stood above the charred mockery of life and laughed.

"Yes, reptile." The chieftain smiled thinly and the firelight blazed against his own wound. "You burned me. Now you will forever burn in the depths of the Abyss."

When finally Mother was silent and still, Shedah spat a green glob, huffed, and released Laira.

She stood for a moment, staring at the corpse of her mother. It still burned, crumbling away into charred ashes. Laira

13

wanted to embrace the corpse. She wanted to save her, to beg the shaman to heal her. But she knew: Mother was dead.

Men tossed rugs over the corpse, stamped out the flame, and bound the remains with ropes. They hung the charred, blackened thing from the tribe totem, a sacrifice to Ka'altei. Mother swung in the wind, banging against the carved pole, shedding ash. She barely looked human, just burnt meat upon bones. The rocs beneath the totem rose, reached up their talons, and snapped their beaks, but they dared not yet eat. The great vultures looked back at Zerra, their master, begging.

"Eat, my friends." Zerra nodded. "Eat, hunters of the sky. She is nice and crunchy."

With shrieks and flying feathers, the birds leaped up, grabbed the hanging corpse, and tore it apart. The beasts tossed back their beaks, guzzling down legs, arms, the head, then fought one another for the torso and its dangling, smoking entrails.

Laira turned and fled.

She ran between the tents, tears in her eyes.

She wanted to keep running—to flee the camp, to head across the open fields, to enter the forest and never emerge. Other weredragons lived in the world; she knew that they must. But Mother's words returned to her.

There are no others. The world is cold and large and empty. The lone wolf perishes. The pack survives.

She ran back into her tent, raced toward her pile of fur blankets, and grabbed her doll. She clutched the wooden girl to her chest, and her tears flowed.

"We must never shift again," she whispered, rocking the toy. "I promise you, Mustardseed. I promise. We'll never become dragons again."

She shivered, the fire still burning in her eyes, the screams still echoing in her ears. She would remain. She would keep her disease secret. And she would grow strong.

"We'll become hunters, Mustardseed." She knuckled tears away from her eyes. "We'll grow big and strong and become hunters like Zerra, and he'll never be able to hurt us. Ever. I promise."

Outside rose the laughter of men, and the smell of burnt meat wafted into the tent. Laira lay down, held her doll close, and shivered.

RAEM

Prince Raem stood above the prisoner, khopesh raised, prepared to swing down the sickle-shaped sword.

"Look at me," Raem said softly. "Look me in the eyes."

Bound and bruised, her neck upon the block, the prisoner shivered. When she raised her eyes, they shone with tears.

"Please," the woman whispered. "Please, my lord, I beg you."

"Do not look away from my eyes." Raem's voice was still soft.

He always insisted his victims looked him in the eyes as his blade descended. Many called him a noble ruler for it. They said that Prince Raem, Son of Nir-Ur, held life so sacred he used no executioner but only condemned those truly worthy of death—those he could look in the eyes as he swung the sword himself, their guilt clear beyond doubt.

Raem had always found those claims amusing. Truth was he simply enjoyed the work, and when they stared into his eyes during the act, it felt more intimate—the ultimate connection of souls. It was better than bedding a woman, better than creating life.

Taking life, he thought, *is the most intimate connection you can make with another living soul.*

"Please." The woman trembled. "I will never shift again, I promise. I am cured. I can no longer become a dragon. I—"

Raem swung down his khopesh.

The curved, bronze blade drove through her neck with a single blow and thumped against the wooden block.

Raem nodded.

"Good!" He took a cloth from a nearby bench and wiped the blood off his blade. "Single blow again."

Around him in the courtyard, the spectators—nobles, priests, and slaves—applauded politely. A wrinkly old scribe, clad in but a loincloth, scratched the departed's name onto a clay tablet.

Raem was pleased. The last execution had not gone as well. The man's neck had been too thick, and Raem had slammed his sword down five times before cleaving it; the man had lived through the first three blows. Every moon now, Raem found more of the diseased creatures infesting the city—men and women with reptilian blood, able to become great, winged beasts. Every moon now, blood coated his khopesh.

"The reptiles infest our city!" he told the crowd of onlookers. They stood upon the cobblestones, shaded by fig and palm trees. "Taal, Father of All Gods, teaches that the human body is sacred and pure. Followers of Taal do not pierce or tattoo their skin. We do not go fat or frail. We preserve the body." Raem sneered. "The curse of weredragons is the greatest abomination unto our lord. To shift into a dragon—grow scales, horns, and claws, deforming the human form—is heretical."

The people nodded in approval, their necklaces of faience beads chinking. A merchant in purple robes, his beard curled into many ringlets, even raised his fist and cried out in his passion; the man had turned in his own wife, a filthy weredragon, only last year.

"A plague has descended upon our kingdom," Raem said, standing above the decapitated body. "Hundreds in our city are sick with the dragon disease, able to morph at will. Hundreds more hide their curse. But I, Raem son of Nir-Ur, Heir to the Seran Dynasty, Prince of Eteer, will find them. And I will purify our kingdom."

They cheered. They cried out Taal's name. They raised bone, stone, and tin figurines of the god—a slender man with a lowered head and forward-facing palms. Staring at the crowd, Raem wondered how many more of his followers—from nobles to slaves—hid the diseased in their homes.

Raem clenched his fist to remember that night years ago, the night he had learned that his own wife and daughter were ill. He had caught them shifting into dragons deep in the city cisterns, hiding their shame in darkness.

I will find you someday, Anai, my dear wife, he thought, trembling with rage. *I will bring you back to me, my daughter, my precious Laira. And you will suffer.*

Raem slid his khopesh though his belt. He walked away from the decapitated corpse, leaving his servants to clean up the mess. His sandals whispered against the cobblestones, and he inhaled deeply, savoring the smell of blood mingling with the aroma of fig trees, palms, and grapevines. As he moved through the courtyard, men and women bowed before him: nobles in garments of silk, silver disks, and gemstones, their feet clad in sandals; priests in flowing black robes hemmed in gold, their beards long and curled; and eunuch slaves in loincloths, metal collars around their necks. Only his soldiers did not bow; they stood between the columns that surrounded the courtyard, holding round shields and curved blades, and bronze helmets hid their faces.

Bronze, Raem thought, admiring the gleam of sunlight upon the metal. The humble, seaside tribe of Eteer had discovered the precious metal only a hundred years ago. Within a generation, their primitive tools—made of flint and wood—had vanished. Now Eteer was a great city-state, its sphere of power spreading across farmlands, the coast, and deep into the sea—the greatest civilization in the world, a light in the darkness, law in chaos, might rising in a weak world.

And soon I will rule this kingdom.

He stepped between two columns, leaving the courtyard, and craned back his neck. He stared up at his home.

The Palace of Eteer rose several stories tall. Blue bricks formed the bottom tier's walls, inlaid with golden reliefs of winged bulls, rearing lions, and proud soldiers in chariots. Columns lined the upper floors, carved of indigo stone, their capitals gilded. Balconies thrust out, holding lush gardens of palm trees, blooming flowers, and vines that cascaded like green waterfalls. Upon the palace roof grew a forest lush with trees and birds. This palace was the greatest building in the world, a monument of life and power.

And all it would take, Raem thought, *is a single dragon to burn it. And so no single dragon must live.*

He approached a towering stone archway, its keystone engraved with the winged bull—the god Kur-Paz, protector of the city, a deity of plenty. Cedar doors banded with bronze stood open within the archway, their knockers shaped as phalli, symbols of fertility and fortune. Leaving the courtyard, Raem stepped through the archway and into a towering hall. A mosaic spread across the floor, depicting sea serpents wrapping around ships. Columns supported a domed ceiling painted with scenes of cranes and falcons. As Raem walked, his footfalls echoed.

When he passed by a limestone statue, he paused, turned toward it, and admired the work. He had ordered this statue—a likeness of himself—carved only last year. The stone prince was an accurate depiction—tall and broad, clad in ring armor, the face stern. The jaw was as wide as the forehead, and small eyes stared from under a great shelf of a brow. The head was bald, the chin protruding. Raem was a towering man, and this statue—life-sized—towered over most who walked by it. The shoulders were wide, the arms thick—a body built for the battlefield, a body the god Taal would approve of. Though fifty years of age, Raem kept himself strong, training with his blade every day. He had seen nobles go soft in their palaces, far from battles and fields, pampered with endless feasts, plays, and other luxuries of wealth. Raem refused such decadence. He would keep himself as strong as the gruffest soldier in his kingdom's army.

He reached a staircase and climbed through the palace, passing by many halls and chambers. Finally, five stories up, he emerged onto the roof.

He stood upon the edge and inhaled deeply, filling his nostrils with the scent of the gardens around him, the city below, and the sea beyond. Eteer, center of the Eteerian civilization, spread along the northern coast. Home to two hundred thousand souls, here was a hive of limestone houses topped with white domes, gardens leafy with palm and fig trees, and cobbled streets lined with cypresses. Walls surrounded the city and ran along the shore, topped with battlements.

The greatest wonder of Eteer, however, was not its massive size, its fabled gardens, or its towering walls, but the city's port. A canal drove into Eteer, ending with a ring of water large enough to surround a town. Other cities built ports that stretched into the sea; Eteer brought the sea into the city. Dozens of ships navigated this man-made canal, their sails high and bright. In hulls and upon decks they carried the treasures of distant lands: spices, copper and tin ore, exotic pets, collared slaves, and tales from across the world.

Eteer was a stronghold of might, a city none could conquer—not the southern city-states with their own bronze blades, not the rising desert tribes in the western desert of Tiranor, and certainly not the fur-clad barbarians of the north.

Nobody could harm this place, Raem knew . . . nobody but dragons.

"And so they will die," he said, gazing upon the countless roofs and streets below.

"Do not be so quick to deal death, my son." The voice rose behind him. "Only Taal, Father of All Gods, may doom us mere mortals to our eternal rest or damnation."

Raem frowned, anger filling his throat like bad wine, and turned away from the view.

Gardens covered the palace roof, lush and flowering, the greatest in a city fabled for its greenery. Olive trees grew from wide clay pots, twisting and ancient, their leaves deep green and their fruit aromatic. Vines hung from terraces, their grapes deep purple. Flowers of every kind bloomed, and finches fluttered among leafy branches. Cobbled paths ran through the gardens, lined with statues, and a stream ended with a waterfall that cascaded down the palace wall to a pool below.

Nearly invisible among the plants, clad in a simple green robe, stood Raem's father, King Nir-Ur of House Seran.

At seventy years of age, Nir-Ur still stood straight and tall, though deep creases filled his face, and his beard was long and white as milk. His eyes, glittering under bushy brows, were as blue as the sea. A headdress of golden ivy and lapis lazuli crowned his head of snowy hair. In gnarled hands, he held a small clay tablet engraved with cuneiform prayers.

Raem was a child of war, a soldier who had commanded armies in battle, a man of bronze and blood. His father was a weaker sort of ruler, a man who valued his gardens, his jewels, and the music he played upon his lyre.

A weak king, Raem thought, staring at the man. *A weak father.*

"The cursed ones are a threat," Raem said, clutching the hilt of his khopesh. "A threat I will not let grow. Not in this kingdom that I love. I will not cower upon rooftop gardens while the disease spreads through our mighty city, an abomination unto Taal." He sneered at the clay tablet the king held. "You are a man of words. I am a man of blades."

The old king sighed. "Walk with me through the gardens, my son."

Not waiting for a reply, the old man turned and began to head deeper into the rooftop gardens, moving down the pebbled path.

"Let us walk through the *city*!" Raem reached out and grabbed his father's shoulder. "I care not for strolls through a garden. March with me house by house, door by door. We will break bones. We will cut off fingers. We will interrogate the people until we find every last cursed, diseased creature. I will behead them myself."

The king turned back toward him. The old man's eyes dampened. The display of weakness disgusted Raem.

Nir-Ur spoke in a soft voice. "A curse? A disease? Raem . . . why do you name it thus? Perhaps it is a gift from the stars; the dragons rose in our kingdom once the dragon constellation began to shine. Your own wife. Your own daughter, the innocent Laira. They could have stayed with you, Raem, if only you had accepted their magic, their—"

Raem struck his father.

He struck so hard the old man fell to the ground. A family of cardinals fled. The clay tablet shattered.

"A gift!" Raem shouted, standing above his fallen father. "How dare you speak thus. My wife is impure, an abomination. So is Laira. When I discovered their filth—when I saw them shifting into reptiles in the shadows—they fled me like cowards. Accept them? When I find them in the northern, barbaric hinterlands, I will drag them back in chains, and I will lock them in Aerhein Tower, and I will watch them wither. They will beg for death before the end. Still the people of this city mock me. I hear them speak behind my back, talking of the prince who married a reptile, who fathered a reptile."

Blood trickled down the king's chin. Lying on the path, he stared up with watery eyes. "A reptile? Laira is your daughter, she—"

Raem spat. "I have only two children. Sena is strong and pure, a proud heir to the throne. Issari is a beautiful, chaste young woman, a princess for the people to worship. Both are pure of body and spirit. They inherited my blood. But *Laira?* She inherited my wife's disease. She is a creature. When I find her, she will suffer."

The old king struggled to rise, arms shaking. When he coughed, blood dripped onto the path. He managed to raise his head, and finally some anger filled his eyes.

"You are a fool," Nir-Ur said, no longer the kindly old man walking through his gardens but a twisted wretch.

"The only foolishness, Father, is letting our kingdom weaken." Raem raised his sword. "I have led armies and vanquished the desert tribes of Tiranor, the southern city-states who would rival our kingdom if left to grow, and the northern barbarians across the sea. I strengthened these walls, and I placed a bronze khopesh in the hand of every soldier in our kingdom. I did this for Eteer's glory—not to see the reptiles rise, to see this dawn of dragons undo my work. They would be the death of us all if they bred." He trembled with rage. "I will eradicate the curse."

Blood trickling down his chin, King Nir-Ur pointed at his son, and his eyes hardened with cold rage. "Then, my son, you are no longer my heir. Raem, I disavow you. I—"

Raem's bronze sword sliced into his father's chest, passing between ribs.

"And I will eradicate any who stand in my way," said Raem, tugging the blade back with a red curtain.

His father stared at him, eyes wide. Blood dripped from his mouth and down his chest. He tried to speak but only hoarse gasps left his mouth. The old king—frail, weak, his time done—fell.

"Raem," the old man managed to whisper, clutching his wound. "Your own son . . . your heir . . . Prince Sena has the gift."

Raem stared down at the dying man, and rage exploded through him. "Even with your last breath, you lie."

His father reached out and touched Raem's leg. Tears streamed down his creased cheeks. "Accept your son. You already lost a daughter. When you learn what Sena is . . . accept him. For our family. For—"

Raem swung his sword again.

The blade sank into the king's neck, and the old man spoke no more. Nir-Ur collapsed onto his back, fingers curled like talons, dead eyes gazing upon the birds he had loved.

"You were a traitor," Raem whispered, and suddenly a tremble seized him. "You were a lover of weredragons. You spoke heresy."

He looked down at his slain father. Raem had faced barbarian hordes in battle. He had slain dozens of men, maybe hundreds, and the scars of wars covered his body. He had never flinched from bloodshed before, but now he shook, and now his eyes burned, and now he felt very young—a humble boy in the courts of a rising kingdom, so afraid, so alone in a palace of shadows and echoes. A boy with a secret. A boy with a shame.

He turned away.

He all but fled the rooftop gardens.

He raced through his palace, bloody sword in hand, ignoring the startled looks of scribes, slaves, and guards.

I exiled my wife and firstborn child. I killed my father. I must see my two remaining children, the noble Sena, the beautiful Issari. His breath shook in his lungs. *I must see the purity that remains.*

When he found Sena, he would pull the boy into an embrace. He would tell his son: You are noble, you are strong and pure, and I will never be a weak father to you, for you make me proud.

Down several staircases and halls, he reached the tall bronze doors of his children's chamber. Without knocking, desperate to see his son and daughter, Raem barged into the room.

He froze.

His heart seemed to fall still.

His breath died.

The chamber was large, nearly as large as a throne room. A mosaic featuring birds, beasts, and fish covered the floor, and blue columns topped with golden capitals supported a ceiling painted with suns and stars. Stone figurines—carved as hunters, cattle, boats, and chariots—stood in alcoves. The chamber's giltwood beds, tables, and divans had been pushed against the walls. In the center of the chamber, nearly filling even this vast room, stood a dragon.

The dragon sported blue scales—blue as the sea outside, blue as the columns, blue as the god Taal's banners. The beast's horns were long and white, and its eyes seemed young, afraid.

Raem's youngest child, the beautiful Princess Issari, stood before the dragon. Her raven braid hung across her shoulder, and a headdress of topaz gemstones and golden olive leaves crowned her head. Clad in a slim, white gown hemmed with golden tassels, she had her hand upon the dragon's snout.

"Father," the princess whispered. She withdrew her hand and stepped backward.

"Father," said the dragon, speaking with the same fear . . . and changed.

The beast's wings pulled into its back. Its scales, horns, and claws vanished. It stood on its rear legs and shrank, becoming a young man clad in white.

"Sena," Raem whispered. His eyes watered. "My son . . . you are . . ."

Raem trembled. He could barely see; the world turned red with his rage. He raised his sword, and he shouted, and his children fled from him, and all the palace, and all the city, and all the kingdom seemed to collapse around him.

LAIRA

On her twentieth autumn, Laira knelt in the mud, scrubbing her chieftain's feet.

"Clean them good, you maggot," Zerra said and spat upon her. "I think I stepped on some boar dung. Fitting for a piece of shite like you."

The chieftain—clad in furs, his face leathery, his shaggy hair wild—sat upon a fallen log peppered with holes. Mud squelched below them, and patches of yellow grass covered the surrounding hills like thinning hair on old scalps. Few trees grew here, only a few scattered oaks and elms crowned with red leaves. Mossy boulders lay strewn like the scattered teeth of a giant. It was a place of mist, of wind, of mud and rock.

The Goldtusk tribe had been traveling south for two moons now, seeking the warm coast for the coming winter. There would be fish there, herds of bison, and geese to hunt, a place of plenty for the cold moons. Zerra boasted that the weak villagers, those who built walls and plowed fields, suffered in the snow, while he—leading a proud tribe that followed ancient ways—would give his people warm air and full bellies even in the winter.

Yet Laira knew the southern coast would offer her no relief. There too Zerra would all but starve her, feeding her only scraps—fish bones, rubbery skin, sometimes the juice of berries to lick from clay bowls. No plenty for her, Laira, the daughter of a dragon. In the south too, he would allow her no tent; she would sleep outside as always in the mud, tethered and penned with the dogs, nothing but her cloak of rodent furs to shield her from the wind and rain.

So many times she had dreamed of escape! So many times she had clawed at her bonds, trying to sneak out in the night! Yet she had always stayed, fearing the wilderness—the hunger and thirst of open land, the roaming tribes that fed on human flesh, and the wild rocs and saber-toothed cats who patrolled sky and land. And so she remained, year after year, a broken thing.

She looked up at her chieftain now, and perhaps it was the filth on his feet, and perhaps the thought of southern suffering, and perhaps it was that today she was twenty—whatever the reason, today she stared into his eyes, a feat she rarely dared, and she spoke in a strained voice.

"If I'm shite, wouldn't I just make your feet dirtier?"

For a long moment, Zerra stared down at her, silent. Ten years ago, Laira had watched her mother—a beautiful white dragon—burn the chieftain. Zerra's wounds had never healed. Half his face still looked like melted tallow, a field of grooves and wrinkles, the ear gone, the eye drooping. The scars stretched down his neck and along his arm. He was missing two fingers on his left hand, gone to the dragonfire.

But his scars were not what frightened Laira. After all, her own face was ravaged now too. Zerra—still seeking vengeance—had seen to that. She had seen her reflection many times; Zerra insisted she stare into whatever clear pool they passed, forcing her to see her wretchedness.

A few years ago, he had beaten Laira so badly he had shattered her jaw. Today her chin and mouth were crooked, pushed to the side, and her teeth no longer aligned. It not only marred her appearance but left her voice slurred; she always sounded like she were chewing on cotton, and her breath often wheezed. One time she had tried to pull her jaw back into place, only for the pain to nearly knock her unconscious. And she so remained—crooked, mumbling, a pathetic little wretch Zerra kept alive for his amusement.

"You look like a mole rat," he would tell her, scoffing whenever she walked by. Often he would shove her in the mud, toss game entrails onto her, or spit in her face, then mock her ugliness. "You are a small, weak maggot."

Small and weak she was. Years of hunger had damaged her as much as his fists. The chieftain only allowed her to eat whatever bits of skin and fat remained after the hunt, and whenever anyone had tried to give her more, he had beaten them with stick and stone. The long hunger left Laira fragile, as weak as a sapling in frost. She hadn't grown much since that day ten years ago, that day her mother had died. Though a woman now, she stood barely larger than a child, her growth stunted, her frame frail. Her head often spun when she walked too much, and her arms were thin as twigs. Zerra enjoyed mocking her weakness, shoving her down and laughing when she could not rise. He claimed she was weak because of her curse, the disease he was determined—but could not prove—she carried.

To complete her misery, the chieftain sheared her hair every moon, leaving her with ragged black strands and a nicked scalp. He clad her not in warm buffalo or bear fur like the rest of the tribe, but in a ragged patchwork of rat pelts. He had pissed on that garment once and refused to let her wash it. "That is how I mark what is mine," he had said. "And you are mine to torment." The tattered cloak still stank of him.

Her only redeeming feature, Laira thought, was her eyes. On their own, they were perhaps ordinary. But in her gaunt face, they seemed unusually large, a deep green tinged with blue. Whenever Zerra forced her to stare at her reflection—to see her slanted chin, her crooked mouth, her sheared hair like ragged porcupine quills—Laira would focus on those large green eyes. *They are my mother's eyes,* she thought. *And they are beautiful.*

And so no—it was not Zerra's scars that frightened Laira today, for she was no prettier. It was the rage in his eyes—the rage that promised another beating, that promised days of hunger, that promised he would hurt her, break her, make her regret every word and beg for mercy.

I need not fear him, Laira thought, staring up into his eyes. *My father is a great prince in a distant kingdom. My mother told me. I am descended of greatness. I—*

She was so weary with hunger—she had not eaten in a day—that she didn't even see his fist moving. It slammed into her head, knocking her into the mud.

She lay for a moment, dazed. Her head spun. She wanted to get up. She wanted to fight him.

I can turn into a dragon, she thought. *I did it once. I can do it again. I can burn him. I—*

The vision of her mother reappeared in her mind, interrupting her thoughts—a memory of the woman burning at the stake, screaming.

I promised. I promised I would never shift again.

A weight pressed down on her wrist and Laira whimpered. Through narrow eyes, she saw Zerra stepping on her, smirking, and she thought he would snap her bone, tear off her hand. He wiped his other foot upon her face, smearing her with its filth.

"You're right," he said. "You are worse than shite. Your mother was no better." He snorted. "I know what she told you. She claimed she had bedded some southern prince, that she spawned a princess. But you are filth. You are only a princess of worms. You will never leave this place. And someday . . . someday I will uncover the reptilian curse in you too, and you will burn like she did."

He kicked her stomach and Laira doubled over. Through floating stars of pain, she saw him walk downhill toward their camp.

She lay wheezing and trembling. With her crooked jaw, she couldn't even cough properly. She should be thankful, she knew.

Requiem's Song

He had not broken her bones this time. He had not cut off her ears, which he had often vowed to do, or burned her body, another common threat. He had shown her mercy today.

"I must be strong," she whispered. "I am the daughter of a prince."

She closed her eyes, trying to remember that distant kingdom across the sea. Laira had been only three years old when Mother had fled with her, coming to this northern land, for the cursed ones—those who could become dragons—were hunted in Eteer too. In a haze, Laira saw faded images, perhaps memories, perhaps the stories Mother had told. Towers in sunlight. A great port that thrust into a city of countless homes. Walls topped with soldiers and lush gardens that grew atop the palace roof. Laira had seen villages here in the north; Zerra sometimes stopped at these small settlements, trading meat and fur for bronze and ale. But their old city across the sea . . . that was a place a thousand times the size, its houses not built of mud and straw but of actual stone.

"I want to go back home," Laira had once begged her mother. "Please. I hate the cold north. I hate this tribe. I want to go home."

Mother had only hushed her, kissed her brow, and smoothed her hair. "We cannot. We bear a secret, a magic of dragons. We had to flee Eteer, and Zerra is kind to us. Zerra gave us a new home. Hush now, Laira, my sweetness."

Laira had blinked away tears and clung to Mother. "Is my father still there?"

Mother had rocked her. "Yes, my child. Your father is still there, a great warrior prince." She showed Laira her amulet, the silver sigil of Taal, the god of the south. "This is the amulet he gave me, an amulet to protect us. You are descended of royalty. Never forget that, even here, even in our exile."

Yet what was royalty worth, Laira thought, if she could not return? Cursed with reptilian blood, they had fled the distant land of Eteer. Yet how was Goldtusk any safer? Mother had died here. Laira suffered here.

"Should I flee this tribe as Mother fled her old kingdom?" Her eyes stung. "Dare I fly to that fabled, secret place . . . the escarpment? The hidden land where they say other dragons live?"

Tears streamed down Laira's bruised face, mingling with the mud. Others like her . . . humans able to become dragons . . . cursed, outcast, afraid. Men whispered of them. They said that Zerra himself had a twin brother, a weredragon, a *leader* of weredragons. Could it be true? Or was the escarpment just a myth as Mother had claimed?

Laira sighed. If she fled this tribe to seek a legend, she was likely to die. The escarpment lay many marks away; a single mark was a distance too far for her to cross alone, let alone many. In this world of harsh winters and roaming beasts, even a dragon could not survive alone. Her mother's words echoed in her mind from beyond the years.

There are no others, Laira. Only us. We are alone. And Goldtusk is our home.

"Goldtusk is my home," Laira whispered.

She pushed herself up onto wobbling arms. Bedraggled and covered in mud, she stared downhill toward their camp. The tribe's tents rose across the misty valley, made of animal hides stretched over branches. Their totem pole rose among them, carved with animal spirits, topped with the gilded mammoth tusk they worshiped, the god Ka'altei. Deer, hares, and fowl roasted upon campfires, and the tribesmen, clad in fur and leather, tended to the meat.

The tribe's source of power, a flock of rocs, stood tethered outside the camp. Great vultures the size of dragons, they gathered around a mammoth carcass, tearing into the meat with sharp beaks. Those beaks were large enough to swallow Laira whole. As she watched, the tribe hunters—tall, strong, and sporting jewelry of clay, bronze, and even gold—walked toward the beasts. One by one, they mounted the rocs and took flight, brandishing bows and roaring hunting cries.

"The hunters are strong and proud," Laira said to herself, watching as they soared. "They are the nobility of Goldtusk. They are never beaten, never spat upon, never afraid."

She rose to her feet, hugged herself, and stared at the hunters flying into the distance, their rocs shrieking.

"My old kingdom is forbidden to me," Laira whispered. "The escarpment is but a myth. But I am the child of a warrior prince. I am noble and I am strong." She clenched her small fists. She would become what she had vowed the day her mother had died. "I will be a huntress."

* * * * *

That evening, the hunters returned upon their rocs, singing the songs of their totems. The great birds shrieked, beating their rotted wings, holding game in their talons: deer, boar, and buffalo. With splatters of blood, they tossed the carcasses down between the tents. Soon great campfires burned, and the game roasted upon spits, filling the camp with delicious aromas.

The women returned too, placing down baskets of berries, nuts, and mushrooms collected from a nearby grove. Though not as honored as the hunters, the gatherers too were praised; tribesmen blessed their names and reached into their baskets, feasting upon their finds.

Songs rose and ale, traded in what villages they passed, flowed down throats. One tribeswoman played a lyre, and people clapped and danced. Teeth bit into the roast meat and grease dripped down chins.

Laira spent the feast serving the others. She sliced off slabs of meat and rushed to and fro with clay bowls. She collected what bones the diners tossed into the dirt, bringing them to the camp dogs in their pen. She kept scurrying to the nearby stream, returning with buckets of water, then filling cups and serving the thirsty.

Never did she eat herself. When once she only sniffed at a bone, Zerra made sure to march over, slap her cheek, and tell her that bones were for the dogs, that she was merely a maggot. She kept working, belly growling and mouth watering.

When the feast ended, she could rummage through the mud. She would always find a few discarded nuts, bones, and sometimes even animal skin. As Laira worked, slicing and serving and rushing about, she made sure to drop little morsels—when nobody was looking—into the mud. She would dig them up later, and she would give her belly some respite.

As the sun set and the stars emerged, Laira drew comfort from the sight of the new stars, the ones shaped like a dragon—the Draco constellation. Mother would tell her that these stars blessed them, gave them a magic others thought was a curse. Laira glanced up and prayed silently.

Please, stars of the dragon, look after me. Give me strength to hide your magic. Give me strength to fly.

The feast died down. Men lay patting their full bellies, women nursed their babes, the rocs fed upon carcasses, and the dogs fought over scraps. Laira still had much work to do. She would be up half the night, collecting pottery and washing it in the river. But for now, she had a more important task.

Hands clasped behind her back, she approached her chieftain.

Zerra sat upon a hill overlooking the totem pole. Several of his hunters sat around him, drinking ale, gnawing on bones, and belching. When the men saw her approach, they lowered their mugs and narrowed their eyes. Zerra grunted and shifted upon the boulder he sat on.

Requiem's Song

"Return to your work, wretch." He spat. "Wash our pottery and clean up our scraps, then sleep among the dogs where you belong."

Laira took a shuddering breath. She thought of her mother's eyes. She thought of the stars above. She thought of her distant home, a mere haze of memory. She raised her crooked chin—the chin he had shattered—and tried to speak in a clear, loud voice. That voice was slurred now, another victim of Zerra's fist, but she gave it all the gravity she could.

"I can do more than clean and serve, my chieftain." She squared her narrow shoulders. "Allow me to serve you better. One of your hunters has fallen to the fever. One of your rocs, the female Neiva, is missing a rider. Tomorrow let me mount Neiva. Let me hunt with you."

For a moment the men stared at her, eyes wide.

Then they burst out laughing.

Zerra tossed his empty bowl at her. It slammed into her face and shattered. She gasped and raised her fingers to her cheek; they came away bloody.

Not waiting for more abuse, Laira turned and fled.

She spent that night trembling as she worked—scrubbing dishes in the stream, cleaning fur tunics, and collecting bones for the dogs. Her blood dripped and her belly felt too sour for food. When finally her work was done, she curled up among the dogs. They licked her wounds, and she held them close, and her eyes dampened.

"I am a daughter of a prince," she whispered into their fur, trembling in the cold. "I am blessed with forbidden magic. I will be strong. I will hunt."

When dawn broke, the tribe moved again. They packed up their tents. They mounted their totem on wheels. Their hunters flew above upon rocs, shrieking in the wind, while the rest of the tribe shuffled below through the mud.

Laira brought up the rear as always. Sometimes, walking here at the back, she had dreamed of slinking behind a tree, running to the hills, even shifting into a dragon and flying away. But the rocs forever circled above, and if she lingered too far behind, Zerra would swoop down and lash her with his crop. And so she walked on, weak with hunger, her head spinning, following the others. She had not eaten more than morsels in days, and her belly rumbled, but there was no food to be found. When they crested a hill lush with grass and bushes, she picked a few mint leaves and chewed them, staving off the hunger for a while. When she saw worms in the dirt, she managed to grab one. She swallowed it down quickly before disgust overwhelmed her.

That evening she served the camp again, preparing food, cleaning, washing. And again she approached Zerra.

He sat upon a fallen log thick with mushrooms, gnawing on a bison rib. Laira stood before him, half his size, a weary little wisp of a thing. She raised her chin, straightened her back, and said, "Let me hunt."

He clubbed her with the bone, then laughed as she fled.

"I will be a huntress," she vowed that night, huddling with the dogs. Among them she found a bone with some meat still on it, and she ate the paltry meal. "I am the daughter of a prince. I am blessed with forbidden magic. I am strong and I will hunt."

Because hunting did not only mean honor, a rise in status, and perhaps true meals and no more beatings. Lying among the dogs, Laira stared up at the dragon stars.

Hunting meant flying.

She had never forgotten the beating of her wings, the feel of open air around her. She had flown only once as a dragon, the day her mother had died, but the memory still warmed her in the cold.

"If I cannot fly as a dragon again," she prayed to those stars, "let me fly upon a roc, a proud huntress of my tribe."

For six nights she approached Zerra, demanding to join the hunters. For six nights he scoffed, tossed bowls or bones or stones her way, and laughed at her pain.

On the seventh night, she waited until he retired to his tent.

That night she approached that tent, the greatest one in the camp, a towering structure of tiger pelts and cedar branches topped with gilded skulls. Fingers trembling, Laira did something she knew could mean death, could mean burning at the stake.

She pulled back the leather flap and she stepped into her chieftain's home.

He sat upon a flat stone, polishing his leaf-shaped sword with oil and rag. None in the Goldtusk tribe knew the secrets of metal; only the loftiest warriors owned jewelry of gold or knives of copper. Most still tipped their arrows with flint. A sword of pure bronze, captured from the corpse of a great champion from the northern villages, was the most valuable artifact the tribe owned aside from their gilded tusk. It signified to all that Zerra was mightiest of his tribe.

But I come from a kingdom of bronze, Laira told herself. *Mother told me that thousands of warriors there wield bronze khopeshes—great swords shaped as sickles—and that my father leads them all. I will be brave. I will not fear this man.*

Before he could rise to his feet and strike her, she spoke.

"Why do you hurt me?"

He froze, risen to a crouch, and stared at her. He said nothing.

Her voice trembled and her knees felt weak, but she would not look away. She stared into his eyes—one baleful and blazing, the other drooping in the ruined half of his face.

"I did not burn you," she said, voice slurred from the wounds he had given her. "My mother had the curse. She could become the reptile. And she paid for her sins. I am not diseased." Her eyes stung and she clenched her fists, refusing to cry before him. "You beat me. You starve me. You make me sleep with the dogs. But I am no reptile. I am not my mother. I have served you well, and whenever you beat me down, I stood up again. Whenever you hurt me, I grew stronger. My face is ruined now as yours is. And our spirits are both strong." She took a step closer. "In the mud, in the dog pen, in puddles of my own blood, I proved my strength to you. Let me show you this strength upon a roc, a bow in my hand. I will hunt with you, and I will prove that I'm worth more than scrubbing your feet." She took another step, raised her chin, and stared at him with all the strength she could summon. Her tears were gone. "I will kill for you."

Slowly, his joints creaking, he rose to his feet. He loomed over her; the top of her head did not even reach his shoulders. He stank of ale, sweat, and his old injury.

"You have the curse." His voice was low, full of danger. "You lie, maggot. Your mother had the reptile in her veins. You carry it within you too."

"I do not!" She raised her chin, staring up at him, refusing to cower. She would show him her strength in this tent. "You lie to yourself so you may hurt me. I cannot fly as a dragon, but I will fly upon a roc." She raised her fist. "I am small and weak; you made me so. But my spirit is as strong as bronze."

Quick as a striking cobra, he reached out and clutched her throat.

She gasped, unable to breathe.

"Your spirit is strong?" He leaned down to bring his face close to hers. His breath assailed her. "I could just . . . tighten my grip. And your neck would just . . . snap. Like a pheasant bone. You are a woman, and all women are weak."

She sputtered, struggling for air, forcing down the urge to strike him. His grip loosened just the slightest, and she whispered hoarse words.

"I am a woman, yes, my chieftain. And I have a woman's strength." Even as he held her throat, she tugged at the lacing of her cloak. The patchwork of rat furs fell to the ground. "I have a woman's gifts to give."

He released her throat, and she gasped and held her neck, sucking in deep breaths. He took a step back and admired her. She stood naked before him, chin still raised.

She was not comely, Laira knew. Years of hunger had left her body frail. She had not the wide hips or rich breasts the men liked to carve into their images of stone. Red marks covered her skin—the scars of the leeches Shedah, the tribe's shaman, often placed upon her. The crone would mix the blood in potions she drank; she claimed that the blood of a princess gave her long life. Shedah lingered on in her mockery of life, and the leechcraft left Laira bruised and added to her fragility.

And yet, despite her meager size and marked body, lust filled Zerra's eyes. Men such as him, hunters and conquerors, were easy to please. They saw every woman, even a scrawny and broken thing like her, as lands to conquer.

"I will give you this body," she said. "But my chieftain . . . you must give me a roc."

He stared at her for a long moment, and strangely she no longer trembled. She was no longer afraid. She did not feel exposed. She felt, for the first time in years, in control of her life.

This body, she thought, *is the only power I have left.*

He doffed his own cloak and removed his tunic. He stood naked before her. The scar that covered half his face—the burn of dragonfire—spread down half his body, twisting his arm, chest, and leg, and even half his manhood bore the marks.

He grabbed her arms.

He took her into his bed of animal hides.

As he thrust into her, nearly crushing her with his weight, she closed her eyes and bit her lip. He pressed against her, slick

39

with sweat, and the pain drove through her, and she clenched her fists and thought of the sky. In her mind she was a dragon again, a beautiful animal of golden scales and long claws, too strong to hurt, too proud to tame. She flew upon the wind, free and noble and far from home.

JEID

Jeid Blacksmith stood above the grave of his daughter, head lowered and fists clenched.

A boulder marked the hilltop grave, overgrown with ivy and moss. An oak shaded it, and autumn leaves covered the soil, a crimson carpet. Below the hill rolled valleys of mist, scattered birches, and rocks engraved with the runes of ancient men. No rune, however, marked this makeshift tombstone. If the men of nearby villages knew that here, under this earth, lay a fallen weredragon, they would dig up the bones, they would smash them with stones, and they would pray to their totems to curse the soul of the creature.

"But you were no creature to me," Jeid said, jaw tight and eyes dry. "You were my daughter, Requiem. And you were blessed."

Weredragons, they called him and his family—cursed beings, monsters to burn. Jeid had fled their villages long ago. He had given his family a new home, a new name.

His head spun and he fell to his knees. The wind gusted, blowing dry leaves into his shaggy hair and beard. Jeid was a strong man, a blacksmith with thick arms and a barrel chest, but now, here, before his fallen daughter, he felt weaker than old tin.

"I named our new home after you." He placed his hand between the fallen leaves, feeling the soil, feeling her soul below. "Requiem. And we are no longer weredragons. We are *Vir Requis*, people of Requiem." His eyes stung. "I swear to you, your name will live on—a tribe to last for eternity."

But you will not be here to see it.

Jeid lowered his head, his despair overwhelming. That day returned to him again—as it returned every time he came here. It had been years ago, but still the pain felt raw, still the wound bled inside him.

He had fled his smithy, his village of Oldforge, the only home he'd known. Blessed by the stars—cursed, the villagers called it—he could grow wings, breathe fire, take flight as a dragon. He had passed this gift to his children.

"You called us monsters, brother," he whispered. "You called us cursed, Zerra."

His twin—cruel, envious, full of venom—had railed against Jeid's so-called illness. And so Jeid had fled, taking his children with him. Requiem had been only a toddler, barely old enough to shift into a dragon herself. For a long time, they had wandered the wilderness, finally finding a home upon the escarpment, a hidden crack in the world, a place of secrets, of exile. Jeid had thought that would appease the villagers. He'd been wrong.

On this day years ago—the autumn equinox—Jeid had taken Requiem, a sweet child with soft brown locks, on a flight. Requiem had been but a small dragon, no larger than a deer, wobbly as she flew. They glided upon the wind, laughing, counting the trees below. It was freedom. It was joy. It was the best day of Jeid's life, and it turned into the worst.

"Look, Dada, food!" Requiem cried, pointing a claw below. The small, blue dragon laughed and dived.

"Requiem, wait!" Jeid called after her.

She ignored him, squealing with laughter as she swooped. The lamb stood upon the field below, groggy, lost from its flock and not fleeing. Before Requiem even reached it, the lamb fell over, dead before the small dragon's mouth closed around it.

"Requiem, wait!"

But she ate the meat.

And she cried.

Requiem's Song

And she shook and vomited and begged her father for help.

She lost her magic and lay in the grass, a human girl, skin pale, clutching her swollen belly.

Shaking with rage and fear, Jeid carried her back to the escarpment. He and his father, the wise healer Eranor, spent two nights feeding her healing herbs, praying for her, holding her. And yet the poison spread. On the third night she died.

And now, years later, Jeid knelt above the grave, and that grief burned with no less intensity.

"I miss you, Requiem," he whispered, touching her tombstone. "You've been gone for years, and I promise you. I will make our tribe strong—for your memory, for your name. Requiem will survive."

A voice, soft and trembling, rose behind him.

"Are you . . . are you Jeid? Jeid the weredragon?"

He spun around, fists tight, tears in his eyes.

A young woman stood there, soot staining her face. She had long, black hair and wore cotton in the manner of villagers. A tin bracelet adorned her wrist, and she held a shepherd's crook. Tears filled her eyes and her full, pink lips shook. She seemed vaguely familiar—perhaps a face he had seen years ago when she'd been a child, when he'd still lived among others.

Jeid growled. "You are from the village of Oldforge across the river. I recognize the cotton you wear. Leave this place. This is my territory. Leave or I burn you."

She trembled. "Please. Please . . . I need help. I am Ciana. Are you the weredragon?"

He straightened. "I am Vir Requis. That is our name." He took a step closer, fists still clenched. "The kind you hunt."

Ciana blinked away tears. "My . . . my brother is a were— a Vir Requis. They're going to burn him. Please. Please. I came to you for help. They have him tied to the stake. They say they'll burn him at sundown." Tears streamed down her cheeks, and she reached out to him. "I don't have the magic. I came to find you. If you can become a dragon, if you are truly Jeid Blacksmith, Chieftain of Dragons . . . help him. Save him."

Jeid stared, frozen.

Another Vir Requis.

His heart throbbed and his legs felt weak.

For years he had dreamed, prayed, flown across the world to find others. For years, he had come to this grave, vowed to his daughter to build a tribe in her name, a tribe of others like them—who could turn into dragons, who were hunted, feared, poisoned, killed.

For years, he had found no others.

"You lie!" He stepped closer, teeth bared. He raised his fist as if to strike her. "There are no others. There are no more Vir Requis in this world. Just me. Just my family. Just us that you hunt and kill."

Ciana did not flinch. She met his gaze steadily, and some strength filled her damp eyes.

"There is another. But if you let him die, Jeid, your family will truly be the last." Gingerly she reached out and touched his arm. "Come with me. Save him. Please." Fire lit in her eyes. "Become the dragon again. Grow your wings, sound your roar, and take flight."

Another Vir Requis . . .

His head spun. Could it be—another like him? Afraid? Alone?

He growled.

He stepped away from the girl.

And so I fly again.

With a deep breath, Jeid shifted.

Copper scales rose across him, clattering like a suit of armor. Wings burst out from his back with a thud. Fangs sprouted from his mouth and claws grew from his fingers. He tossed back his head and roared, and his fire blasted skyward in a pillar. Standing before him in the grass—now so small next to his larger form—Ciana took a step back and gasped.

Jeid beat his wings, rising several feet aboveground. The blast of air scattered leaves, bent the old oak's branches, and fluttered Ciana's hair. Snorting smoke, Jeid reached out, lifted the woman in his claws, and soared.

He caught an air current and glided, wings wide. Since Requiem had died, he had dared not fly in daylight. Too many still wished to fell dragons from the sky. Warriors of the villages bore arrows coated with poison. His twin, the cruel Zerra, now wandered the wilderness, leading a pack of a hundred rocs, oversized vultures that feared the escarpment but would gladly hunt a lone dragon in open sky. Yet now Jeid flew in the sunlight, blowing his fire, roaring for the great hope, the dream of Requiem, his most sacred prayer.

We are not alone.

Behind him rose the escarpment—the cliffs of stone and trees and hidden caves, his fortress. The misty hills and valleys rolled below. Ahead stretched the River Ranin, the border of his territory, and there beyond, nestled along the bank, was his old home. The village of Oldforge.

Fifty-odd buildings rose along the riverbank. Most were simple huts of clay, branches, and straw, humble homes with a hole in each roof to vent the smoke of cooking fires. Vegetables grew in backyard gardens, and pigs rooted in pens. Several boats floated upon the river, tethered to posts.

The largest building, and the only one built of stone, was the smithy. It rose taller than two men, topped with a dome. Jeid's grandfather himself had built this smithy. Once Jeid had forged tin and bronze there, had raised his children there. Today those who had exiled him lived within those walls.

The villagers filled the pebbly village square, clad in fur, cotton, and canvas. Mud coated them and their hair hung long and scraggly. A great pyre rose among them, and upon it, tied to a stake, stood a young man.

Another Vir Requis.

Jeid howled, filled his maw with flames, and dived toward the village.

The villagers saw him, pointed, and shouted. They fled the square, scattering into their homes, leaping behind barrels, and grabbing what makeshift weapons they could—humble farm tools of bronze and tin, many which Jeid himself had forged before his exile.

"Flee and you will live!" Jeid bellowed, his voice louder than hammers striking anvils, and the blast of his wings tore thatch off roofs and knocked down fences. "Face me and burn."

He blasted down flames.

The fiery pillar slammed against the square, scattering sparks and sending pebbles flying. A nearby tree caught fire. His wings pounding like drums, Jeid—large as his old smithy, a burly beast of scales like the metal he'd forge—landed before the pyre. He roared and whipped his tail, and the last villagers scattered.

Tied to the stake, the young man gazed at him, face sooty, eyes wide.

Another Vir Requis, Jeid thought, eyes stinging. His breath shook. *We are not alone.*

"I will free you," Jeid said, voice a low rumble. "There is a safe place for you. A place for dragons. A tribe called Requiem." His voice choked. "You have a home."

He stretched out his claws, ready to sever the prisoner's ropes.

The young man moved so quickly Jeid barely saw it. His expression changing to hatred, the prisoner brought his hands forward, letting his ropes fall. He held a bow and arrow.

Requiem's Song

Before Jeid could retreat, the arrow flew.

The bronze arrowhead drove into Jeid's neck.

The dragon howled. He sucked in air, prepared to blow fire.

Around the square, a dozen men leaped up from behind barrels, a well, and bales of hay. They too held bows and arrows. They too fired.

The projectiles slammed into Jeid. Some shattered against his scales. Others pierced his soft underbelly.

The pain drove through him, burning through his bloodstream. He felt poison flow, dragging him down, pulling him into blackness. Ilbane covered these arrowheads, the juice of crushed leaves grown in the northern hills. Harmless to most, the sap was poisonous to dragons, stiffening muscles, blazing through veins, turning bones heavy as rocks. Jeid tried to beat his wings, but they wouldn't move. He tried to blow fire, but only sparks left his mouth.

He turned his head, lashing his claws, trying to cut the men. And there he saw her—Ciana, the young woman who had found him on the hill. Her tears were gone. She smiled crookedly and raised a bow.

Finally Jeid recognized her.

You were friends with my son. He gazed at her with blurred eyes. *Years ago. You were only a youth . . .*

Her arrow drove into Jeid's chest.

He fell, cracking stones beneath him.

"Kill the beast!" Ciana shouted, face twisted with rage. "Slay him!"

Jeid's eyelids fluttered. His wings beat uselessly against the ground, unable to support his weight. The poison held him down like chains.

I will fly to you now, Requiem, he thought, seeing his daughter's face. *We will fly together again.*

Through the mists of pain, he saw Ciana walk toward him, drawing back another arrow, this one aimed at his eye. But then she faded, and he only saw Requiem, his dear daughter, angelic and pure . . . writhing in pain. Poisoned. Dying.

No. I cannot die too.

His eyes burned.

His daughter laughed.

I must live for you, Requiem—for Requiem, the daughter I lost; for Requiem, the tribe I must build.

As Ciana laughed, nocking another arrow, Jeid managed to lift his head.

He blasted his fire.

The flames roared across Ciana, crashed past her, and slammed into the pyre where the false prisoner still stood. With a blast that pounded in Jeid's ears, the pyre burst into flame. Men screamed and ran, burning, living torches.

The fire raced toward Jeid.

He pushed himself up.

He was weak, almost blind, maybe dying.

He beat his wings.

He rose a few feet, crashed back down, and rose again. More arrows slammed into him. He howled, soared higher, and flew. His claws banged against a house, knocking down the roof, and he crashed onto a hilltop beyond. For a moment he rolled downhill, tearing up grass and soil. With another flap of his wings, he was airborne again, flying across the river.

They screamed behind him. Arrows whistled around him, and one slammed against his back.

He kept flying, the land a haze of blue and green below, and Requiem laughed, and the mist engulfed him, but still he flew.

For you, my fallen daughter, he thought. *For you, Tanin and Maev, my living children. For you I still fly.*

Requiem's Song

The escarpment rose ahead from the mist, a great wall of stone draped with vines and moss. Jeid dipped. He nearly crashed. He beat his wings and rose higher, flying above the cliffs until he reached the canyon upon their crest. It gaped open below, a hidden place, a safe place, a home called Requiem.

He crashed down.

He fell into the canyon, slammed against boulders, and lay still. His wings splayed out around him like the sails of beached boats.

"This is why I must fly," he whispered. "They hunt us. They kill us. Requiem must stand. We must find the sky."

Through the haze, he saw them rush forth—his father, beard long and white, and his living children, shouting in muffled voices, fading . . . all fading into colors and shadows and light.

RAEM

My son is cursed. Raem felt as if the world were crashing around him. *My son, my heir, my pure prince . . . is a weredragon.*

"Father, please!" the boy said, reaching out to him. "I'm sorry. I'll never shift again. I . . ."

Nineteen years old, Prince Sena Seran had the noble looks of his family: raven hair, green eyes, a proud jaw. Slim and tall, he wore a white robe hemmed in gold, and a bronze dagger hung from his belt.

He is beautiful, Raem thought, frozen in place, torn between rage and anguish. *I already lost a daughter, and now I lose a son.*

Raem—taller, broader, stronger than his son—stepped forth and swung his fist, driving it into Sena's cheek.

The boy crumpled, falling to the floor with a yelp and gush of blood.

"Father, please!" cried Issari. "He didn't mean to do it. Please don't kill him."

Raem looked across the curled-up, bleeding prince and stared at his youngest child, Princess Issari. At only eighteen years of age, she was blooming into a beautiful young woman. She was everything Laira, his eldest, should have been—a proper princess. Her black hair hung across her shoulder in a braid. Her green eyes filled with tears. A white gown covered her slim body, and a headdress of golden olive leaves and topaz gemstones glimmered upon her head.

"You are my only child now, Issari," Raem said. "You are the only pure thing our family has left."

Before she could react, Raem knelt, grabbed his disgraced son, and pulled the prince to his feet. He twisted the boy's arm behind his back and manhandled him out of the room.

"Father!" Issari cried, racing toward them. "Father, please. Please forgive him. He'll never shift again."

All traces of sadness had left Raem; rage now consumed him. Ignoring his daughter, he dragged his son along a hallway. The boy's bleeding nose left a trail behind them. Guards stood at attention between the hallway's columns, still and stiff, faces hidden inside their helms.

"Do you know what you did, my son?" Raem asked, voice shaking with his fury. "You spat upon Taal, the god of purity. You are an abomination." He twisted his son's arm so hard it nearly snapped. "You are filth."

He dragged the boy out of the palace. He shoved him into the courtyard, past the fig and palm trees, and toward the spot where only that morning Raem had executed a woman. Ignoring the prince's whimpers, Raem shoved the boy's neck down onto the chopping block.

Sena tried to speak, to beg. The boy looked over his shoulder, eyes full of tears, face covered in blood.

"Father, I'm sorr—"

Raem struck him again, a blow that bloodied Sena's mouth and chipped a tooth. The prince gurgled on blood, hiding his face, and Raem kicked him in the ribs. He shoved the boy's head down against the wood.

"You will not call me your father." Raem drew his khopesh from his belt. "You are no son of mine." He raised the semicircular blade, so enraged he could barely breathe. "By the god Taal, I condemn you to—"

"Father, no!"

The cry rose behind him, and Issari leaped onto his back. The princess clutched his arm, holding back his sword. Her tears fell onto his shoulder.

"Please!" the princess begged. "Send him into exile like Laira or imprison him in Aerhein Tower. But please, Father, please . . . don't kill him. For me."

Raem spun around, staring at the princess. Her cheeks were flushed and wet with tears. She trembled, clutching at him, whispering inaudible words. In a world of evil—his father's treachery, his wife and eldest daughter's exile, and now his son's abomination—Issari was a ray of piety. The young woman was a single, pure light in a dark world. Raem felt some of his rage dissipate.

"Oh, my daughter," he said. "Your heart is still too soft. But I will strength it. I will hammer your heart like a smith hammers bronze. You will be my heir now. Your grandfather is dead; he fell in the gardens. Your brother is diseased. Only you and I remain now, holding this fragile kingdom together."

Fresh tears budded in Issari's eyes. "Is Grandfather . . . ? He's . . ." She covered her face with her palms.

Raem yanked her hands away. "Dry your tears! Today you must be strong. I will honor your wish. I will spare your filthy brother's life. But he will not taint this kingdom again."

He grabbed the boy, lifting him off the block. Sena seemed too dazed, too hurt, to resist. Blood filled his mouth and poured from his nose. His arm hung at a strange angle, perhaps dislocated, and his face was pale. Even if he wanted to shift now, to become a dragon and fly into exile like his mother and sister had, he was too hurt to summon his magic.

Leaving his daughter behind, Raem manhandled the prince across the courtyard, down a stone path, and toward Aerhein Tower.

Requiem's Song

The steeple rose outside the palace, towering and ancient, one of the first buildings to rise in all of Eteer. Many years ago, the first king had raised Aerhein Tower to gaze upon the city, an eye watching the coast. Today it served as Eteer's most infamous prison, a place for its greatest enemies to languish. This place had imprisoned usurped kings, treacherous generals, and now a disgraced prince.

Blood trailed as Raem pulled his son up the winding staircase. They climbed round and round, the sunlight falling through arrowslits. Whenever Sena faltered or tried to beg, Raem struck him again, beating his face into a red, swollen mess.

When they reached the tower top, Raem shoved the door open, revealing an empty chamber. The bricks were rough and stained with old blood. Messages from previous prisoners were carved into the craggy walls. Chains hung from those walls, and only a single window, small and barred, let in light.

"You will remain here until your last day," said Raem. "The kingdom will forget you. So will I. So will your sister. Eventually you will forget yourself, remaining but a starving, mad thing clawing at the walls, and even then you will linger. You became a creature in your chamber, and so I will turn you into a creature—a frail, mad mockery of a man. You have shamed me, Sena, and now you will suffer for your sin. Death would be a kindness to you. I give you instead damnation."

A new burst of vigor filled Sena. He howled wordlessly, seeming unable to speak through his bloodied mouth, and tried to race toward the door. Another blow sent him sprawling.

Lying on the floor, Sena tried to shift. Scales began to rise across him. Wings began to sprout from his back, his body began to grow, and fangs lengthened in his mouth.

Raem kicked, driving his foot against his son's scaly face.

With an anguished cry and splatter of blood, Sena lost his magic. His eyes rolled back and closed. He slumped down, unconscious.

Moving methodically, Raem grabbed chains from the walls. He bound his son's wrists and ankles, then wrapped more chains around his torso.

"When you wake, you may try to shift again," Raem said. "As you grow, you will find that these chains tear you apart." He snorted. "Goodbye, reptile."

Fists clenched at his sides, his son's blood covering him, Raem left the tower.

He reentered the palace. He descended dark, narrow staircases, moving past wine cellars and armories, climbing down and down until he reached the deep cave under the palace, that gaping belly of water—the city cistern.

Columns rose here in many rows, supporting a vaulted ceiling. Water filled the chamber, running deep and black, enough for a city to drink. It was an old, oft-forgotten place, one of the oldest chambers in the city-state of Eteer. It was a place to be alone.

This is where I found them, Raem thought. *This is where I found my wife, Anai, and my daughter, Laira. Here is where they came to shift.*

That day returned to him, perhaps the worst of his days. He had secretly followed them here. He had seen them become the reptiles, swim in the water, fly to the ceiling.

He had confronted them with rage, screamed, even shed tears. He had drawn his sword, prepared to slay them, and they had fled, flying away from this city, flying to the northern lands of barbarians.

Raem trembled. "And now I've lost a son too."

He could no longer contain his despair; it welled inside him, all consuming. Eyes stinging, he entered the water.

He clenched his fists, ground his teeth, and squeezed his eyes shut.

He releases the rage.

The curse swelled.

Scales flowed across Raem, black as the darkness. Horns grew from his head, and claws sprouted from his fingers. His wings burst from his back, banging against the columns, and his tail lashed in the water. Fire sparked between his teeth.

A dragon in the deep, he lowered his head, trembling, clanking, diseased, ashamed.

"You infected me too, Anai," he said, voice rising from a mouth full of fire. "But I will hide it. I will end it. I will stop this disease from spreading. And I will kill anyone who stands in my way."

He released his magic.

He became a human again, a mere man, a sick man, floating in the water.

He climbed onto a ledge of stone, trembling with his shame. He pulled off his shirt of bronze scales and the cotton tunic he wore beneath it. He unbuckled his thick leather belt.

Upon the ledge, Raem clenched his jaw and swung the belt over his back. The leather connected with his flesh, tearing into the skin.

Raem bit down on a cry.

I am filthy, he thought. *I am a sinner. I will purify myself.*

He lashed the belt again. Again. The blows kept landing, driving the shame away. When he was done, when the purity was restored, he curled up on the stone floor. He bit his fist. He took short, ragged breaths, and again he smelled it, that beautiful smell that could always soothe him. Blood.

TANIN

He stood on one foot, juggling his bronzed raven skulls, but the onlookers only yawned, shifted their weight, and fluttered their lips with bored snorts.

Standing on the creaky wooden stage, Tanin gulped. It was a chilly autumn day, the sky overcast and the wind biting, but Tanin felt as if he stood within the flames of the Abyss. He needed to win this crowd over—and quickly. Only the top performers in the harvest festival won the coveted prize: a purse of seashells from the distant southern coast. Seashells could be bartered for food, ale, medicine—and, Tanin thought, maybe a little dignity.

As the crowd began to wander off, Tanin cleared his throat.

"Ah, but juggling is not all I can do!" he announced. "I can sing while I juggle."

He launched into a baritone song—a tale of a buxom lass from a wandering tribe, her hair as thick as mammoth fur, her legs as long and pale as tusks, her breasts as large as—

He dropped one skull, losing his place in the song. For a moment he wobbled on one foot, then completed his embarrassment by crashing down onto the stage. His remaining raven skulls clattered away in all directions. He quickly raced around, scooping them up, and tried to resume his performance despite jeers from the crowd. One man in the audience, a beefy brute with red cheeks, burst into laughter.

Tanin sighed. *Another village, another humiliation.*

This village—a little place called Blueford—lay south of the Ranin River. While most folk north of the sea still lived in nomadic tribes, hunting and gathering across the plains and forests, a few villages now grew along the river, none older than three or four generations. The recent invention of bronze, a metal Tanin himself used to forge with his father, meant plows could now till soil. Food could be grown, not merely collected from wild plants. Nails could hold together fences, and animals could be penned, not hunted. Many of the tribes, Tanin knew, mocked the villagers for abandoning the old ways, for growing soft and lazy.

Banished from his own village a decade ago, Tanin himself preferred open spaces and solitude. But villages would barter. Villages would offer seashells, food, and even precious metal in return for juggling and singing—at least on days when he didn't end up on his backside, his skulls rolling around him. And so Tanin kept traveling along the river, juggling and singing his rude songs.

His sister, Maev, had it even worse. She traveled from town to town with him, wrestling, boxing, and earning her keep with fists and kicks. She joked that he fell on his arse for seashells while she kicked arses for them. He often countered that her face—covered with bruises and scrapes from her many fights—ended up looking like an ape's swollen backside.

My sister and me, he thought with a sigh. *Two lost souls—outcast, afraid, always only days away from starvation.*

Blueford—a village like any other. Looking off the stage, Tanin saw a collection of clay huts topped with straw roofs, a few gardens, fields of rye and wheat, a smithy, and corrals of cattle.

It looks like the village Maev and I were born in, he thought. *The village that banished us. This place would banish us too if they knew our secret . . . our curse.*

At the thought of his shame, Tanin stumbled upon the stage, falling again with a cascade of clattering skulls. The crowd jeered.

"Get off the stage!" someone shouted. "Let the dancer on, you lout!"

Sitting on the stage, his legs splayed out before him, Tanin turned his head to see a dancer standing in the grass, awaiting her turn to perform. She met his eyes and gave him a shrug and sympathetic smile. Seeing her only amplified Tanin's humiliation.

By the stars, she's beautiful, he thought. The young woman—she seemed about twenty, five years younger than him—wore only thin bits of cotton over her tall, curvy figure, and tresses of red hair cascaded across her shoulders. Her eyes were green, her nose freckled, and Tanin felt his face redden.

Just the type of woman I'd want to impress, he thought. *And I'm sitting here like a—*

"Clumsy sack of shite!" someone shouted from the crowd. "Off the stage!"

A gob of brown, gooey mud sailed from the crowd to slam against Tanin's face. At least he hoped it was mud and not one of the many cow pies dotting the village. Wishing he could vanish in a puff of smoke like the magician who had performed before him, Tanin all but fled the stage, slipping over a bronzed skull and crashing down into the dirt.

He moved through the crowd, any trace of lingering dignity gone, and wiped the mud off his face. The crowd cheered behind him, and Tanin turned to see the red-haired woman step onto the stage and begin her dance. She swayed like reeds in the wind, jingling bells in her hands. Tanin gulped to see the seductive movements of her near-naked body. It had been so long since he'd held a woman, even talked to one—aside from talking to his sister, that is, but Tanin often thought her more an enraged warthog than a woman. Watching the dance, he imagined holding this dancer, kissing her lips, and seeking in her arms some respite from loneliness. As she swayed, she met his eyes across the crowd and gave him a knowing, crooked smile. Tanin felt his face flush.

Requiem's Song

I'm a fool, he thought. She knew what he was thinking, yet after his travesty of a performance, surely she only mocked him. *Besides, if she knew my secret, knew who I really am, knew why I was banished from my own town . . .*

The shame grew too great to bear. Tanin turned and walked away.

Leaving the stage behind, he walked through the village. The harvest festival was in full swing. Farmers displayed their largest gourds, turnips, and cabbages upon tables for judges to measure. Shepherds haggled over prize bulls. Gardeners swapped wreaths of wheat and flowers for meat pies and mugs of ale. Several dogs ran underfoot, tails wagging furiously as they begged for treats.

Grunts, curses, and the thud of fists on flesh rose from within a ring of cheering men. Tanin approached, peered through the crowd, and a saw a pit of mud. In the dirt, his sister was pinning down a hairy man twice her size, pounding his face with her fists. All around, the crowd raised their own fists, cheering for her. A brusque woman, her powerful arms tattooed with coiling dragons, Maev could have been beautiful if not for the black eyes, fat lips, and cuts that always marred her face. Blood dripped down her face today, and more blood matted her long blond hair, but she smiled as she pummeled her victim.

"The Hammer!" cried the crowd, chanting the name Maev had chosen for her fights. "The Hammer!"

Tanin sighed and turned away. He hated seeing his sister fight like this in every village they passed through. Whenever he tried to sway her away from another battle, her rage turned on him.

I juggle, fall on stage, and sell my dignity to survive, Tanin thought. *She sells blood.*

Grimacing, he walked away. That evening he would nurse his sister's wounds. For now, he sought distraction in the festival.

Leaving the wrestling pit behind, he approached a dirt square where a puppeteer hid inside a wooden booth, putting on a show. A group of parents and children were watching the puppets, and Tanin paused among them.

One puppet, a wooden girl with long hair of golden wool, walked across the little stage, picking fabric flowers. A second puppet lurked behind her—this one was stooped, hook-nosed, and pale, its eyes beady and red, its warts hairy. Children squealed to see the ugly man, crying out to the golden-haired doll, warning her of the danger lurking behind.

The wooden girl seemed to hear the shouts from the audience. She froze, then spun around to face the lurking man behind her. With a flurry of ribbons and a puff of smoke, the twisted puppet vanished. Where it had stood now roared a wooden dragon, painted black, its eyes red.

"A weredragon!" shouted the wooden girl.

The crowd gasped and cried out. "A weredragon! Be careful!"

Tanin's heart sank. He hadn't thought the day could get worse, but seeing this play soured his belly more than his failed performance.

We are monsters to them, he thought, balling his fists at his sides. He shut his eyes, remembering that night—that night his old home, a village like this, had discovered his family's secret.

His father, Jeid Blacksmith, a beefy man with a shaggy beard. His sisters, headstrong Maev and little Requiem. His grandfather, the wise druid Eranor. And him—Tanin, only a youth in those days. A family cursed. Diseased.

"Weredragons!" the people had cried to them, firing arrows, tossing stones. His own uncle, the cruel Zerra, had stood among them. "Weredragons!"

Today, ten years later, as Tanin stood here in this new village, the voices calling toward the puppet mingled with the voices in his memory.

"Weredragon, weredragon!"

He opened his eyes and took a shuddering breath. In the puppet booth, a new doll—a noble warrior clad in armor, bearing a little spear—raced across the stage and slew the carved dragon. The crowd cheered. The wooden girl rose to her little feet and kissed the hero—a happy ending, a monster vanquished.

"But we're not monsters," Tanin whispered. "We're not."

A voice rose in the crowd. "Oi! Juggle boy!"

Tanin blinked, banishing his memories, and looked to his side. He lost his breath, his heart burst into a gallop, and he felt his cheeks flush. The dancer was walking toward him, her red hair cascading like a fiery waterfall. She swayed as she moved through the crowd, her scanty outfit doing little to hide her form, and gave him that crooked smile of hers.

He cleared his throat. "Hello, dancing boy! I mean, girl. I mean—obviously you're a girl." He glanced down at her body, then froze and quickly raised his eyes. "I mean—not obviously. Not that I care. I mean, whether you're a boy or a girl, or—"

She reached him and placed a finger against his lips. "Shush, juggling boy. You're only digging yourself a deeper hole."

Tanin sighed. "I'm as clumsy with words as I am with juggling."

She laughed. "But I think you're cute. I'm Feyna." She gave a little curtsy.

"My name is Tanin." His heart leaped. Cute indeed!

For years now, wandering from town to town, Tanin had tried to forget the girl he had loved in his youth—the girl who had broken his heart, who had turned against him after learning his secret.

She called me diseased, he remembered, wincing. *She shouted for her father to kill me—the dirty weredragon, the monster she had kissed.*

Tanin looked at Feyna's green eyes, her bright smile, and her tresses of red hair, and his heart rose again. Maybe this day, this new life, wouldn't be so bad. Maybe there was some hope for him—for acceptance, for love.

Music was playing at a stage nearby. *Ask her to dance,* Tanin told himself. *Ask her to drink some ale.* He gulped. *Ask to walk together in the fields or—*

As he was stumbling with his tongue, Feyna pointed at the puppet show and gasped.

"Oh, look, Tanin!" she said. "A weredragon." Upon the stage, the heroic doll was now battling two wooden dragons, slashing them with its sword.

At once, Tanin's heart sank again. "Anyway, how about a dance or—"

But she seemed not to hear him. Her face changed—turned bitter, disgusted. She shuddered. "Foul creatures, weredragons. Even as dolls they chill me. They say they drink the blood of babies. Thank goodness our town has arrows to shoot down those monsters."

"They're not monsters!" Tanin said before he could stop himself. He instantly regretted those words.

Stupid! he told himself. *Do you want another village to shoot arrows at you, chase you into banishment?*

Feyna turned toward him, narrowed her eyes, and tilted her head. "Not . . . monsters? Have you met one? My father saw a weredragon only this moon—a great beast in the village of Oldforge. The creature burned ten men." She sneered. "One of those men was my uncle. I hate weredragons and would slay them all myself if I could."

That creature was my father, Tanin thought. *He burned them after they tried to kill him, after they pierced him with ten arrows.*

But he could say nothing. How could he? He turned away, feeling ill.

"I have to go." He began to walk away, eyes stinging.

I have to leave this village, he thought. *I have to keep going, to keep traveling, to keep looking for others like me.*

His throat felt too tight and his eyes burned.

Her voice rose behind him. "The juggler! He loves weredragons!" She laughed bitterly. "A weredragon lover among us!"

Men began to grumble around Tanin. One cursed and spat at his feet. Tanin kept walking through the crowd.

"Weredragon lover!" cried one woman, pointing at him.

"Maybe he's a weredragon himself!" shouted another man, an old farmer with white whiskers.

Tanin increased his pace, but more people began to mob him, and one man grabbed his shoulders. At his side, Feyna was pointing at him, shouting that a weredragon had killed her uncle, that the juggler knew of weredragons and was protecting them, was maybe even a weredragon himself. The faces danced around Tanin, and he tried to worm his way through the crowd, but they grabbed him, and a woman shoved him, and—

"What is the meaning of this?"

The authoritative voice pierced the air. A man yowled and fell, clutching a bloodied nose. Another man grunted as a boot flew into his belly. Shoving her way through the crowd, sneering, came Tanin's little sister.

"Maev!" he said.

Her one eye was swollen shut, and a bruise covered her opposite cheek. Blood stained her knuckles, and mud caked her body and long, golden hair. As she balled her fists, her dragon tattoos twitched upon her arms. She was a couple of years younger than Tanin, almost as tall, and ten times as fierce.

When she reached him, Maev grabbed him and stared at the crowd, daring anyone to approach. The people stepped back, blanching. Tales of the Hammer, the traveling wrestler with the dragon tattoos, had spread to most towns across the Ranin River. Most of these folk had just seen Maev pummel her latest opponent—a burly wrestler with arms like tree trunks—in the mud pit.

"Was my dolt of a brother blabbering about weredragons again?" Maev snorted and rolled her eyes. "The fool keeps going on about them. He's got a doll of one at home—like a little girl—and doesn't realize the damn creatures are monsters. Soft in the head, he is." She tugged Tanin's collar and sneered into his ear. "Isn't that right, brother?"

Tanin tried to shake himself free, but she wouldn't release him. Abandoning any hope of saving his dignity today, Tanin nodded.

"Uhm, yes. Sorry about that." He nodded. "Damn weredragons. Horrible creatures." The words tasted like ash in his mouth.

The crowd dispersed slowly. Feyna gave him a disgusted glare before walking off to flirt with a tall baker's boy.

"You almost got us killed," Maev said. She released Tanin's collar and shoved him several paces back.

"She . . ." His voice dropped to a whisper. "She saw Grizzly. She called him a monster."

Maev groaned. "I call our big lummox of a father a monster too. So what?" She punched his chest. "You can't go around getting us into trouble like this all the time. All right? What happened in Oldforge was bad enough. You and girls. Always you and girls . . . almost getting us killed."

Her words stabbed him.

You are diseased! his old beloved had shouted.

Father, kill him!

Still those old voices echoed, that old pain.

Tanin sighed. "Let's leave this place. I want to go home."

His sister sighed and mussed his hair. "Oh, you stupid clump of a brother." She showed him the purse of seashells she had earned—the prize from her fight. "We'll barter these in the next village over. Just keep your mouth shut there, all right? Once we get the herbs Grandpapa wants, a new belt for me, and some new fur pelts for Grizzly, we'll go home."

They left the village. They walked through fields of wild grass, geese honking above, until the sun began to set and the village disappeared in the distance. The stars stone above and distant mountains rose, deep black under the indigo sky.

In darkness, Tanin and Maev—outcasts and wanderers—summoned their magic.

Wings grew from their backs. Fire filled their bellies. With clanking scales, they rose into the sky, creatures, cursed ones, monsters . . . dragons. They flew in silence. They flew in darkness. Rain began to fall, and Tanin closed his eyes.

"Someday," he whispered into the wind, "I'll find others. Someday I'll know that we're not alone. Someday the world will know that we're not beasts to hunt."

At his side, his sister—a green dragon, her scales gleaming in the moonlight—looked at him, her eyes sad. She gave him a playful tap of her tail and blasted a little fire his way, just enough to singe his scales. He groaned and they flew onward into the shadows.

ISSARI

Issari Seran, Princess of Eteer, tightened her ragged cloak around her shoulders and entered the seediest, smelliest part of her city.

Back in the palace, Issari had gazed from balconies upon the port of Eteer, the great city-state, center of her family's civilization. From there, in safety and luxury, it had seemed a magical place. The canal thrust in from the sea, ending with a ring of water like the handle of a key. Ships sailed here every day, bringing in wares from distant lands: furs from the northern barbarians, spices from the desert tribes in the west, and even silk from the east. Issari had always imagined that walking along the port would reveal a landscape of wonder: merchants in priceless purple fabrics, jesters and buskers, and many tales and songs from distant lands.

Now, walking for the first time along this port she had seen so often from her balcony, she found a realm of grime, sweat, and stench.

Issari saw no merchants bedecked in plenty, only sailors with craggy bare chests, scowling faces, and hard eyes that seemed to undress her. She saw no jesters and musicians like those in the palace, only ratty men offering games of chance played with cups and peas, a chained bear battling rabid dogs, and topless women selling their bodies for copper coins.

My own face is engraved on some of those coins, Issari thought, shivering as she watched a sailor toss a few coppers toward a plump prostitute whose three children clutched her legs.

"How much for a trick?" one sailor called out, trundling toward Issari. He stank of cheap spirits, and yellow stains coated

Requiem's Song

his breeches. He grabbed his groin. "I got me two coppers. I say you ain't worth one."

His smell—a miasma of urine, vomit, and fish—assailed Issari. Her head spun and she took a step back. "I . . . I'm not . . ."

. . . *a prostitute,* she wanted to say, but she couldn't bring the word to her lips. She had heard of such loose women, but she had thought them only tales to stop rebellious daughters from running away.

"Come on!" The drunken sailor stumbled toward her, reaching out talon-like fingers. "Let's see what's under your robes."

"Stand back, sir!" Issari said, trying to keep her voice steady, but she heard it tremble.

She took another step back, and she hit somebody. Something clattered and curses rose behind her.

Issari spun around to see a stout woman standing over a fallen tin dish. Live crabs were fleeing the vessel to run along the boardwalk.

"I'm sorry!" Issari said, kneeling to lift the animals. "Let me help—"

The woman scowled, spat out a curse so vile Issari blushed to hear it, and smacked Issari on the head.

"Watch where you're going, princess!" the woman said and slapped her again.

Princess? Issari gulped and trembled. Was her cover blown? She had disguised herself, donning a ragged old robe, hiding her raven braid under a shawl, and even caking her face with dirt. How did this woman—

"Go on, get lost, you whore!" the woman shouted and tried to smack her again.

Some relief filled Issari to realize that "princess" here was an insult, much like the others the stocky woman was now hurling her way. Issari fled, racing away from the woman, the scurrying crabs, and the drunken sailor who was busy tugging his groin while ogling the two women.

Tears budded in Issari's eyes as she moved through the crowd. She had never imagined any place like this could exist in her kingdom, let alone so close to her home. When she craned her neck and stood on tiptoes, she could even see that home—the blue and gold palace with its rooftop gardens—rising upon a distant hill. Issari had been away for only a couple of hours, but already she missed that home so badly she wanted to weep.

Making her way closer to the water, she steeled herself, rubbing her eyes and tightening her jaw.

I must be strong, she told herself. *My brother needs me. I came here to save him, and I can't do that by crying or whimpering at a few smacks or taunts.*

She stepped toward the edge of the canal. Many boats moored here at piers, and others sailed back and forth, entering and leaving the port. Some were the simple reed boats of fishermen, their single sails barely larger than her cloak. Others were proud, oared merchant vessels, built of sturdy wood, their hulls bedecked with paintings of the winged bull—Kur-Paz, the god of plenty. Slaves sat in them, chained to the oars, their skin bronzed in the sun. Not all were Eteerian ships; Issari saw vessels of foreign lands too. The northern barbarians sailed wide, oared cogs engraved with animal totems. Issari shivered to see these foreigners—they were gruff folk, clad in fur and leather, their beards bushy.

These men will sail back north, Issari thought, looking at the foreigners. *They will return to the open, cold wilderness . . . where Laira hides.*

Issari's eyes moistened.

"Laira," she whispered.

She could not remember her older sister. Laira had been only three when she fled with Mother into exile, escaping Father's wrath. Issari had been only a babe.

"But if you're out there, Laira, you're twenty now," Issari whispered. "You're tall and strong, and you can become a dragon, and you can save our brother. I know you can."

Issari lowered her head to remember visiting Aerhein Tower. She had climbed the winding staircases, approached the door, and peered through the keyhole. Sena had knelt in chains, his face so bruised and swollen Issari had barely recognized him. Issari had begged the guards—towering men all in bronze—to enter the cell, to comfort her older brother, but they had shoved her back. When the guards had told her father of her visit, the king had struck her.

Issari raised her hand to her swollen cheek, still feeling the blow. "I cannot save you from the tower, brother," she whispered as she watched the ships sail by. "But a dragon can. Mother can. Laira can."

For the first time in her life, Issari wished she too were cursed. Why couldn't she have inherited Mother's disease? So many times these past few days, Issari had tried to shift, focusing all her energy on the task. She had screwed her eyes shut, leaped into the air, and willed herself to become a dragon. A dragon could fly to the tower top, smash the window's bars, and fly away with Sena to freedom. Yet try as she might, Issari was pure of body, a blessing unto Taal, the god of beauty and the human form. She carried not the reptilian blood like her mother and siblings, and so Sena languished.

A blow hit the back of her head.

Issari winced and scurried a few paces away, half-expecting to see Father here. If he caught her in this port, he would imprison her too.

But it was only a towering, gruff sailor. The man had a leathery face, one eye, and a chest tattooed with leaping fish. Upon his shoulder, he carried a basket of squid and shrimp.

"Stop standing here, gaping like a fool," he said and raised his hand to smack her again. "Men are working here. Get back to whatever brothel you fled from."

As Issari stepped back, the man walked by her, moving along the boardwalk. Several other sailors walked behind him, spitting and snorting. One glob of spit landed right on Issari's foot, and she winced and gulped down her disgust.

"I . . . I heard a tale!" she said, speaking in a high, hesitant voice. "I heard that the prince could become a dragon, that he's imprisoned in a tower. Will you be sailing north? They like stories in the north, and—"

But the men only trundled by, carrying hooks, ropes, and baskets, ignoring her.

Issari tightened her lips. She knew her task. She had to spread the news. She had to make sure all the northern barbarians across the sea knew of Sena. She had to let Laira know.

Because you'll come for him, Issari knew. *You'll fly back home, strong and brave, a great golden dragon. Maybe you'll have an army of dragons with you. And you'll save our brother.*

She walked farther down the boardwalk, moving between fishermen sorting their catches, a legless child begging for coins, and a leper begging for prayers. She approached a few sailors, trying to tell them the news, but they were too busy hauling supplies, mending nets, or even drinking booze to notice. After a few more slaps, kicks, and spits, Issari's spirits sank.

Maybe it was hopeless. She had been a fool to come here. Surely her father had noticed her absence by now. Would he beat her? Would he chain her too?

Her wandering brought her to the root of the canal. Here before her stretched the open sea. Dozens of ships sailed in the water—merchants, fishermen, and military vessels with proud banners. The smell of salt, fresh fish, and dates hanging from a nearby tree filled her nostrils. Seagulls flew overhead, their cries sounding like mocking laughter. Issari stepped onto the stone wall that separated her from the coast, leaned across the battlements, and stared at the sand, the seashells, and the water that spread into the horizon.

"You're somewhere over that horizon, Mother and Laira," she whispered. "How can I deliver you this news?"

Perhaps she should smuggle herself onto a ship, sail north, and walk through the wilderness, asking of her family in every village and tribe. And yet how could one girl find two souls? The north was vast, they said, its people scattered. There were no kingdoms there, no roads, no writing, no civilization—only endless, empty spaces and patches of life.

Issari turned away from the sea. She was prepared to head back home when she heard laughter to her left.

She turned her head and saw a small stone building. At first she had not noticed it; it nestled between a few olive trees, tucked away a little distance from the canal. Laughter rose from within, and she even heard a man singing. Hope kindled in Issari.

"A tavern," she whispered.

She tightened her robe around her, fixed the shawl that hid her hair, and entered the building.

A crowded room greeted her. Sailors, merchants, and soldiers sat at a dozen wooden tables, drinking and eating. The smells of ale, fried fish and garlic, and stewed figs filled Issari's nostrils, intoxicating and delicious. Tin engravings of fish, ships, and even a dragon hung upon the walls, and candles burned in sconces. A stone tablet stood near the bar, engraved with the slim, cuneiform characters of Eteer—a wine menu. Stone jugs of the wines—each large enough for Issari to have hidden inside—stood along the walls, painted with scenes of racing chariots, men hunting deer, and the wars of gods.

"And the sea serpent had three heads!" one sailor was saying, standing on a table. "Three—I counted them. And when I chopped one off, it grew two more."

Other sailors roared in laughter. "You're drunk, you are. Sea serpents with growing heads?"

Across the room, standing over a table topped with scattered mancala pieces, a merchant was patting his ample belly and telling his own tale. "And they say the Queen of Tiranor is so fair, a thousand ships sailed to fetch her the Jewel of Alari, but no jewel is as bright as her eyes."

A dozen more stories were being told around the room. This was the place Issari had sought—a hub of songs, tall tales, and gossip of distant lands.

She approached the bar, handed over a copper coin—it showed her father on one side, the winged bull on the other—and purchased a mug of wine. She winced, expecting a foul drink, but the wine was surprisingly good, as fine as the wine Father sometimes let her drink in the palace. After a few sips to steel her resolve, she turned toward the crowd and spoke in a high, clear voice.

"I have a story!"

Nobody seemed to hear her. The sailor kept speaking of the sprouting heads, the merchant kept extolling the distant queen's beauty, and others gossiped of King Nir-Ur's recent death and the rise of Raem Seran to power.

"They say Raem stabbed his father right in the gut, they do," said one soldier, his cheeks flushed and his eyes watery. "Killed the old man in the gardens, they say. They fought over how to deal with them dragons been cropping up."

The man's friends glowered. "Lower your voice! That's no proper talk." Soon the group was arguing.

Issari stood on tiptoes and raised her voice. "I have a tale of dragons! They say Prince Sena Seran, son of King Raem, is cursed with dragon blood."

At once the tavern silenced.

All eyes turned toward her.

Issari gulped, dizzy at the sudden attention. Praying nobody recognized her—the city folk had only seen her high upon her balcony, clad in finery—she spoke again.

"Prince Sena himself turned into a dragon! King Raem imprisoned him in Aerhein Tower, they say. He's keeping his own son in chains, so the prince can never shapeshift again."

As quickly as the tavern had grown silent, it erupted with new sound. Men pounded on the tables and demanded to know her name, to know where she had heard the news. Others nodded vigorously, saying they had indeed heard whimpers from the tower. Some claimed they had even seen Sena as a blue dragon, flying in the night; they swore they could recognize the prince even in dragon form.

Issari smiled tremulously. The seed was planted.

When she walked along the boardwalk, heading back toward the palace, she already heard the rumor spreading. Sailors, loading their ships, laughed about the Dragon Prince in his tower, awaiting rescue like a damsel. Fisherman whispered to one another, pointing at the distant palace, speaking of the creature the king kept hidden away. Ships sailed out into the open water, carrying the news, a story too scandalous, too horrible, too dangerous not to spread like wildfire.

When Issari was back in the palace, she entered her chambers—those chambers so empty without her brother—and stepped onto her balcony. Clad again in a fine tunic hemmed with gold, her raven braid upon her shoulder, she leaned against the railing and stared across the city to the distant sea.

"If you're out there, Mother," she whispered, "if you hear these tales, Laira . . . come back. Come back as dragons. Come back with claws, fangs, and fire . . . and save him."

LAIRA

In the cold dawn, Laira mounted a roc, dug her heels into the beast, and soared into the sky on her first hunt.

The wind whipped her face, Neiva's wings beat like drums, and Laira laughed upon the gargantuan vulture. She shouted wordlessly and raised her bow above her head.

"Goldtusk!" she cried, soaring so fast her ears popped and her head spun. "Blessed be the gilded ivory of Ka'altei!"

Around her, the other hunters raised javelins and bows and roared their prayers, calling out the name of their tribe and gods. All were men—beefy, clad in furs, wild of hair and beard. Bone beads hung around their necks and tattoos of their totem animals adorned their arms. Some riders sported tin rings in their ears, lips, and brows, the precious material stolen from the villages that knew the secrets of metallurgy. A few of the hunters were mere boys, the youngest among them thirteen.

I am twenty, old already, and this is my first hunt, Laira thought. *Yet this is not the first time I've flown.*

Heart wrenching, she remembered the only other time she had taken flight—a cold autumn day so long ago. As she soared now upon her roc, Laira could almost see her mother again, a proud white dragon on the wind. She could almost smell Mother's burning flesh, hear her dying screams, see the rocs feast upon—

No, Laira told herself. *Do not raise that memory now. Now you must be strong. Now you must prove you are a great huntress, as great as the men.*

She took a deep, shuddering breath. Between her legs an ache still lived, the pain of Zerra's thrusts, but as the roc moved below her, that pain faded into a comforting throb. It kept her alert, alive, hungry for the hunt. They left the camp far below upon the hill. Their tents, their tribesmen, their dogs, and even their totem pole seemed like toys from up here. Soon the camp vanished into the hazy distance, and Laira saw only the open wilderness: fields of swaying grass, fiery autumn forests of birches and maples, a rushing river, and distant blue mountains under white clouds. Geese and crows flew below her, and clouds streamed at her sides.

This is freedom, Laira thought. *I missed this.*

"Prove yourself today, and I will bed you again!" Zerra cried, flying his roc near hers.

His was a great beast, a terror named Ashoor, the largest roc in the tribe. Every flap of the animal's oily black wings blasted out stench. Its gangly neck thrust out, ending with a bald head and cruel beak. Zerra was no prettier than his mount; his burned half faced her. Laira winced to remember his body pressing against her last night, wet and sticky.

"I will prove myself," Laira shouted back from atop Neiva, though the thought of him invading her again made her queasy, and pain flared in her belly. She had allowed him into her once; would hunting game today not be enough? Would he demand this price before every hunt? Bile rose in Laira's throat, but she swallowed it with a snarl.

I will prove myself the greatest hunter, and he will learn to respect me . . . to fear me.

Zerra smirked. He seemed ready to speak again when cries rose ahead from the other hunters.

"Mammoths! Mammoths upon the plains!"

Laira turned her head back forward, narrowed her eyes, and bared her teeth. She drew a stone-tipped arrow and nocked it. A herd of the great, woolly creatures raced across the plains below, making their way toward the cover of the forest. Laira spotted a dozen adults and several cubs; even the smallest was large enough to feed many men. The other hunters cried out wordlessly, nocked their own arrows, and swooped toward their prey.

"Neiva, go!" Laira shouted and dug her heels into the roc.

The dark bird, as large as a mammoth herself, shrieked, clawed the air, and began to dive.

Fur and feathers flashed.

Zerra and his roc swooped in beneath Neiva, blocking her descent.

The two rocs—a slim female and a burly male—slammed together. The beasts screeched and feathers flew.

"Zerra!" Laira shouted. In shock, she loosed her arrow. It drove down, just narrowly missing the chieftain's head.

In the space of a heartbeat, thoughts raced through her mind. There had been an accident. She had flown her roc wrong. She had proven herself a failure. No—Zerra had meant to block her! He was sabotaging her. He—

Grinning, Zerra rose higher upon his roc, and the beast's talons reached out.

Laira screamed as the talons closed around her. She drew another arrow from her quiver. Wielding it like a sword, she tried to stab Ashoor, but the fetid beast's talons pinned her arms down. She screamed. Ashoor tugged, tearing Laira off her mount, and she kicked the open air.

Riding upon the beast, Zerra leaned across the saddle and spat. The glob splattered on Laira's face. Amusement filled the chieftain's voice as he spoke.

"We will now see, little piece of pig dung, if you can truly fly. Ashoor—release!"

As Laira screamed, Ashoor tossed her into the open air.

She tumbled through the sky.

She plummeted.

"Neiva!" she cried, flailing. "Neiva!"

She could see her roc above. The bird tried to dive and catch her, but Ashoor blocked her passage. The two rocs battled in the sky.

"Zerra!" she shouted, plunging down, the wind whipping her and stealing her voice.

She looked around, her cloak fluttering madly. She could see the other rocs; they now flew too far away, diving against the mammoths below. They did not see her fall, and Laira understood.

This had been a trap.

He invited me on this hunt not because I bedded him . . . but for this.

"Fly, weredragon!" the chieftain shouted, swooping above her. "Shift into a dragon and fly! I slew your mother for the curse. I know it fills you too." He laughed, the wind in his hair. "Fly or hit the ground and my roc will feast upon what's left."

She looked down. The ground was only instants away. Heart thudding madly, Laira raised her bow and arrow.

If I die, you die with me.

She fired. The flint-tipped arrow scratched along Zerra's roc, then vanished above, doing the chieftain no harm. The movement tossed Laira into a spin. She tumbled, earth and sky roiling around her. Her brain felt like water swirling around a shaken bowl. Whenever she faced the ground—spin after spin—it was closer. Her bow tore free from her grasp and vanished into the wind.

I will die here, she thought, eyes stinging. *He killed me. Goodbye. I—*

No.

Her eyes stung.

No.

She would not die here. Not like this.

If I die, I die in fire.

Requiem's Song

The ground rushed up toward her, Zerra laughed above, and for the first time in ten years, Laira—hurt, broken, grieving, a shell of a woman—summoned her magic.

Scales flowed and rattled across her, golden like the dawn. Fangs sprouted in her mouth and her body ballooned. Wings burst out of her back with a thud. Her claws grazed the grassy plains, her wings beat, and Laira soared, a dragon roaring fire.

The grass flattened under the beat of her wings, and she veered as she ascended, dodging Zerra and his roc. She burst into open sky, scattered flames, and roared—a roar that shook her body, that cut the sky, that burned in her eyes and soul—the roar of a girl exiled and cursed, of a girl who had watched her mother die, of a huntress who had given her body to her tormenter and now might give her life.

Zerra's roc soared in pursuit. Farther away, above the fleeing herd of mammoths, the rest of the hunters shouted and flew toward her, nocking new arrows.

Attack them! cried a voice inside Laira. *Blow your fire and slay them all!*

A second voice shouted out, *Flee! Flee into the forest, run, hide!*

Flying toward her, Zerra fired an arrow. It shattered against her scales, blasting pain like one of his fists. Within another breath, he would slam into her.

Fight! Hide!

Laira roared, spewed flames, and turned to fly toward the forest.

Her flames rained down behind her. She glanced over her shoulder to see Zerra skirt the inferno and fly higher, unscathed. The rest of his hunters joined him. With battle cries and firing arrows, they flew in pursuit.

"Take her alive!" Zerra shouted. "Capture the reptile so she may burn before Ka'altei!"

Laira turned her eyes forward and beat her wings with all her strength.

She wobbled, dipped, and cried out.

She had not become a dragon since her mother had died; and even as a girl, she would shift only in secret caves and pools, afraid and ashamed and returning to human form within moments. She had never flown like this in the open, and every beat of her wings made her sway and nearly fall.

Arrows whistled. Several slammed into her, shattering against her scales. One arrow—tipped with flint—found its way under a scale and drove into her flesh like a splinter under a fingernail. She yowled but kept flying.

She streamed over the grassy plains. The mammoths trumpeted and ran below. She shot over them, ruffling their fur, and turned her neck back toward the chasing rocs. A hundred flew there, riders howling atop them—the men she had grown up with, the only men she knew, the men who would burn her now.

So I burn you.

She blew a curtain of fire. The inferno blazed across the sky, a storm of heat and smoke and crackling wrath, shielding her from the pursuit. She turned back toward the forest and kept flying. Behind her, she heard the rocs screech as they passed through the wall of fire.

Hoping the smoke and flame still hid her, she dived and crashed through a canopy of birches and oaks, scattering dry leaves. She slammed down onto the forest floor, her claws driving into the soil and shredding a twisting root. The rocs screamed above, and their wings bent the trees.

Laira released her magic. Her wings pulled into her body. Her scales melted into her skin. Her body shrank, leaving her a woman again.

She ran.

Behind her, she heard trees shatter and rocs shriek. She glanced over her shoulder to see the beasts barreling through the forest, slamming into boles, tearing up roots. The riders dismounted and fired arrows. The projectiles slammed into the trees around Laira, and one grazed her arm, drawing blood.

"Grab her!" Zerra shouted, his face red with rage.

I have to hide. I have to vanish between the trees.

She ran, arms pumping, breath ragged. She leaped over a fallen log, tripped, and rolled down a slope. Rocks jabbed her, cutting her skin, but she swallowed her cry. She slammed into a jutting root, leaped up, and ran again. The trees were thick here, and grass and reeds rose shoulder-high. Panting, Laira leaped into the brush. Brambles cut her. A thorn drove into her neck, and she winced and almost cried out. She crawled, feeling like a flea upon a shaggy dog's back. The hunters' cries rose behind her, and she kept moving, foot by foot, breath by breath.

They can't hear you. They can't see you. Just keep moving.

If she lived, she did not know what she would do. She could never return to her tribe; she knew that. She would have to survive alone in the wilderness, to find a new home before winter, to—

"Find the weredragon!" Zerra shouted behind.

He was close now. Laira bit her lip, banishing her thoughts. For now she had to focus only on fleeing, only on surviving every new breath. The grass, brambles, and reeds were thick and spread out for many marks. If she just kept crawling, the hunters would never find her.

Just keep moving, Laira, she told herself, bleeding and dizzy but crawling on. Her heart thrashed and her fingers trembled. *Just keep breathing.*

The sounds of pursuit faded behind. The hunters were still shouting, but they sounded farther away now; she could barely make out Zerra's words. She was weak with hunger and the crone's leeches, and her head would not stop spinning, but Laira forced herself to move onward, breath by breath, heartbeat by heartbeat. She crawled around an oak and along a stream, moving between the reeds, and hope sprang within her. She wasn't sure where to flee to, but right now, she just needed to find a quiet place, to nurse her wounds and think.

She heard shrieks and the batting of wings. Shadows raced above the trees, and Laira breathed out a sigh of relief.

"They're leaving," she whispered. She could just barely glimpse the swaying canopy past her cover of reeds and grass. "They're flying away."

She flipped over and lay on her back, feeling weaker than a trampled, dying worm. She gazed above between the blades of grass, seeing only shards of the sky. She only had to lie here, to wait, and they would fly away, and she would be free. Tears stung her eyes.

I will not burn like my mother.

But the wings kept beating.

The rocs were not leaving; they were circling above.

They no longer shrieked, and when the wind died, she heard it. Sniffs. Snorts. Silence and sniffs again. Fear shot through Laira.

They're smelling for me.

She had seen rocs sniff back in the camp, raising their beaks whenever meals cooked, but she hadn't known they hunted by smell. Their circles were growing smaller, closing in on her. Their sniffs rose louder, as discordant as stones crashing together.

"Down there!" rose a hoarse voice above—Zerra's voice. "Grab her!"

Laira leaped up and shifted.

She rose from the forest, a golden dragon blowing fire.

Her flames spurted upward, and the rocs scattered . . . then swooped. Arrows slammed against Laira. One drove into her shoulder and she yowled. She sucked in breath, prepared to blow flames again, when the rocs crashed into her.

Laira screamed.

Talons crashed through her scales, digging at flesh. A beak drove into her shoulder, shedding blood, and an arrow shot through her wing, tearing open a hole.

Fly! cried a voice inside her. *Fight through them! Fly to—*

With a howl, Zerra charged upon his roc, and his spear dug into her shoulder, and Laira couldn't even scream. Pain blasted through her. Her eyes rolled back, and all she could do was whimper.

In the agony, her magic left her.

She tumbled through the sky again, a mere human, a mere girl, afraid and alone.

Before she could hit the treetops, talons wrapped around her. Her eyelids fluttered. She thought it was Zerra's roc that carried her. She thought she heard the chieftain marks away, voice muffled, slurred, his words impossible to grasp. She thought that countless other rocs flew around her, a sea of dank wings, scraggly necks, and cruel riders. Their blackness spread. She saw nothing but oily feathers, blazing yellow eyes, and blood.

MAEV

The tattooed fist drove into Maev's face, and the world blazed with blood and white light.

Her back hit the ground.

"Gorn! Gorn!" The crowds spun around her, chanting her assailant's name. Their faces were twisted with bloodlust, red in the torchlight. "Finish her!"

The fist drove down again, connecting with her temple, and blood splattered across the ground. Maev felt herself losing consciousness. She spat out a glob of saliva and blood.

Pain is strength, she told herself, repeating the mantra that had always run through her. *Pain is life. Pain drives you.*

She raised her arms. The fists fell left and right, blows that nearly shattered her bones. She blocked them. She screamed as her blood flew.

"Gorn! Gorn!"

Somewhere in the distance, her brother called out to her, the only voice in this crowd that wanted her to live.

"Maev! Get out of there!"

She blinked. Her one eye was swollen shut. The other peered between strands of her matted blond hair. She looked up at the man above—more a beast than a man, she thought. His face was leathery and covered with tattoos. Sweat dripped off his nose, and blood—shed by her own fist—fell from his mouth, splattering against her. He growled, pinning her down with his knees, driving his fists against her arms. A blow drove past her defenses, connecting with her cheek, and she could see no more, only white, only pain.

I can become a dragon, she thought in a haze. *I am Vir Requis. I can fly, blow fire, kill him.*

Through the blood in her mouth, she smiled.

But where is the fun in that?

She roared.

I am Maev Blacksmith. I am the Hammer. I will rise and triumph.

Screaming and spitting out blood, she kicked, flipped, and knocked Gorn over. The brawny man slammed into the earth. Maev was a powerful woman, but he was twice her size. She liked the sound he made falling. At once, she leaped upon him, wrapped her thighs around his neck, and twisted his head painfully downward. His spine ridge rose, ready to crack, and she rained blows upon him. Her fists drove into his kidneys, hard and fast as her old smithy's hammers. She was raised a blacksmith's daughter and she fought with the fury of metal hitting metal.

He screamed beneath her. Maev twisted harder, stretching her legs back, twisting his head, trying to rip it clean off. She managed to grin at the crowd. They surrounded the dirt square, pounding fists into palms, calling out.

And now they were calling her name.

"Hammer! Hammer!"

With a twist, she grabbed Gorn's arm. She yanked him sideways, rolled across him, and landed hard in the mud. His arm gave a delightful *pop* as it dislocated from its socket.

Maev rose to her feet and licked the blood off her lips. She spat on him. "Had enough, little boy?"

His face was swollen and bloody, and his arm hung at an odd angle. Groaning, the man rose to his feet. Maev was tall and strong; she had inherited her father's height and his powerful arms. She was no delicate gatherer of berries; she was a warrior, her muscles wide, her body lean and fierce. And yet Gorn towered above her, twice her width, and managed to grin. He spat out a tooth with a shower of blood and saliva.

"I'm going to rip your guts out with my own hands," he said. "And I'm going to feed them to you."

He swung.

Maev ducked and his fist flew over her head. She kicked, hitting his belly. As he doubled over, Maev leaped, driving her fist upward. It connected with his chin, knocking his head back. A left hook drove into his temple, splitting open skin, and for an instant his face turned to wobbly jelly.

He stood before her, teetering.

She drove her fist forward again. Her knuckles slammed into his nose, shattering it. It hurt like punching a brick wall.

It was enough to send him down like a sack of turnips.

He crashed to the ground and did not rise.

Maev placed her foot upon the fallen man, then raised her bloodied fists and shouted out hoarsely. "I am the Hammer! I pound flesh!"

She could barely see through her swollen eyes. The unconscious man's face was a fleshy mess, all lumps and cuts. Maev knew that she looked no better, and she spat out more blood. But she could see enough. She could see the crowd of villagers cheering.

What was this village's name? Maev didn't even remember. Too many villages, too many fights. Gorn woke and began to moan; his friends dragged him out of the square, leaving a trail of blood. As Maev made her way through the crowd, villagers patted her on the back, offered her clay mugs of ale, and cried out her name.

She wiped back strands of her yellow hair. It was slick with blood—a mix of hers and his.

Requiem's Song

"Give me my prize," she demanded, head spinning. She thrust out her bottom lip and raised her chin. "Give me what I earned or I'll pound every last one of you."

The village elder approached her, clad in canvas, his belly ample and his cheeks rosy. He held forth the silver amulet. When he tried to place it around her neck, Maev grabbed the jewel, spat onto his feet, and stuffed it into her pocket.

"I don't wear no jewelry." She glared at the elder through her one good eye; the other saw only blood. "I can barter this in the next village over. It would get me some good mutton—better than the shite you serve in this backwater." She pushed her way through the crowd, following her nose. "I smell stew and ale! Feed me and give me enough booze to knock out a horse."

Ahead rose craggy tables of logs held together with nails. Other logs served as benches, and the villagers sat here, eating steaming barley bread, gnawing on legs of lamb, and washing down the food with frothy ale. Maev stumbled toward a table, desperate for a hot meal and cold drinks—free fare for the victor, and she was in no position to turn down free meals.

Before she could reach the table, however, a familiar figure leaped forward, blocking her way.

Maev groaned. "Get out of here, Tanin, or I'm going to knock your face into the back of your skull." She raised a fist. The knuckles were raw and bleeding.

Her brother gazed at her with a mixture of sympathy and disgust. A tall man of twenty-five years, he sported a head of shaggy brown hair. He had inherited his father's bearlike hair, while she had the smooth, golden hair of their late mother. His eyes, like hers, were gray tinged with blue.

"By the stars," Tanin said. "Your face is as swollen and ugly as a troll's swollen arse." He winked. "Getting it beaten up doesn't help either."

She grunted and pulled out her medallion. "A troll's swollen arse with a silver prize." She pushed past him. He was taller but Maev knew she was stronger. "Now don't come between me and ale, or you'll look the same."

She reached the tables. Men moved aside, patting her on the back, and she thumped into a seat. Ignoring the villagers, she reached across the table, grabbed a leg of mutton, and took a huge bite. The hot meat melted in her mouth, and juices dripped down her chin, stinging her cuts. Somebody handed her a tankard, and she drank deeply. The frothy ale was cold in her throat but warmed her belly.

A drunkard who sat beside her—his droopy red mustache floated in his ale—yelped as Tanin yanked him aside. Her brother, that oaf of a juggler, replaced him on the bench. He pointed at Maev and glared.

"How much longer do you think you can do this?" he said. "This is . . . what, your one hundredth fight by now? Over a hundred for sure."

"Not counting." She stared at the table, chewing her meat.

"And how many more fists can you take to the face?" Tanin leaned forward, forcing himself into her field of vision. "You can't keep doing this."

She shoved his face away and gulped down more ale. Blood dripped from her forehead into the drink. "Somebody's got to support this family. If it's not smith work, it'll be fist work." She thrust out her bottom lip, chin raised in defiance. "I was a good smith when Grizzly still had his shop. But I'm a better fighter."

His voice softened. "There are other ways. My juggling earns us some food."

She snorted. "Your juggling does nothing but land you on your arse to the sound of jeers. Other ways, brother? Not for us. Not for our kind. Not for people with our curs—"

"Hush!" He paled. "Not here."

She looked around but nobody seemed to be listening. The villagers were too drunk, too busy eating, or too busy comforting the sour Gorn; the brute was sitting across the table, his face puffy and lacerated.

"Nobody's listening. Nobody cares." Maev reached for a turnip and chewed lustily. "This is how we survive, dear brother. Let Grizzly lead us. Let Grandpapa heal our wounds. And let me pound faces and earn us a living."

The truth she kept to herself. *Because fighting like this eases the pain,* she thought, her eyes stinging. *Because fists and kicks drown the memories . . . the memories of banishment, of a lost younger sister, of who I am.* And so she fought, soaking up the bruises and cuts, hiding the wounds inside her.

Tanin sighed, head lowered. "We weren't meant to fight like this—with fists, with kicks." He lowered his voice to a whisper and held her shoulder. "We were meant to fight as *dragons*." His face lit up. "To fly. To blow fire. To bite with fangs and lash with claws."

Maev glanced around again, but if anyone heard, they gave no notice. "Well, last I checked, dragons are hunted with arrows, rocs, and poison." She shrugged. "Maybe I can't fly. Not if I want to live." She pounded the table. "But my fists are still strong. Now let me be. I'm eating. Go find some pretty shepherd's daughter to try to charm."

She turned her back on Tanin and tried to concentrate on her food. Yet her thoughts kept returning to the fight—to all her fights. Whenever she lay bloodied, fists raining down upon her, she wanted to shift into a dragon. Whenever she paced her canyon hideout, her brother and father and grandfather always nearby, she wanted to shift into a dragon. When she slept, she dreamed of flying. It was the magic of her family—some said the curse. All bore the dragon blood, the blood the world thought diseased.

Weredragons, they call us, Maev thought. *Monsters to hunt.*

She bit deep into a leg of lamb stewed in mint leaves, then chewed vigorously as if she could eat away the pain. Years ago, dragon hunters had killed her sister; they had poisoned sweet little Requiem in the fields. Everyone in the family dealt with that pain privately, desperately. Her father, Jeid Blacksmith, that huge grizzly bear of a man, had named their canyon home Requiem. He called it a new tribe, a safe haven for their kind, as if others existed in the world. Her grandfather, kindly old Eranor, dedicated himself to his gardens of herbs. Her brother cracked jokes, mocked her, mocked everyone; she knew it masked his pain.

And I, well . . . I fight. Maev looked at her torn knuckles. *I hurt myself to drown the pain inside me.* She sighed, looking around at the drinking villagers. *If anyone here knew my true nature, they wouldn't just fight me with fists. They'd try to kill me.*

A snippet of conversation tore through her thoughts. She tensed, narrowed her eyes, and cocked her head.

". . . a real weredragon!" somebody was saying—a villager with red cheeks and a bulbous nose. "Shapeshifter. Cursed with the reptilian disease."

Maev growled and made ready to leap to her feet. At her side, she saw Tanin grimace and reach toward his boot where he kept a hidden dagger.

They know, Maev thought, heart pounding. *They heard us talk.* She rose to her feet, expecting the poisoned arrows to fly, and sucked in her magic.

"Ah, Old Wag, you're drunk!" said another villager, an elderly man with bristly white muttonchops.

"I ain't!" replied the bulbous-nosed man. "I heard the tales, all the way from Eteer across the sea. They say the prince of Eteer himself, a lad named Sena, is a weredragon. His father, the king, locked him up in a tower, he did." Old Wag roared out laughter, spraying crumbs. "Like a princess from a story."

Maev slowly sat down again, loosening her fists. At her side, she saw Tanin ease too. He slipped his dagger back into his boot.

"The Prince of Eteer?" Maev said, letting her voice carry across the table. "Eteer's just a myth." She snorted. "A land of stone towers, of men bedecked all in bronze, of thousands of souls living in a town the size of a forest?" She spat. "Ain't no such place in the world."

The villagers looked at her, scratching chins and stroking beards.

"Eteer's real enough," said the old man with the muttonchops. "My cousin, in the next town over, he's been there himself. Trades there, he does. He ships in furs and brings back jewels and spices and metal tools. Aye, a land of stone towers it is, of walls taller than trees." He gestured around at the village; a few scraggly huts rose around the muddy square. "There's more to the world than the north. We here, we're a mole on the arse of the world. But Eteer now—that there's a golden crown."

Old Wag leaped onto the tabletop, spraying mud from his boots across plates and knocking over a mug of ale. "And there's a weredragon there! It's true, it is. Traders talking all about it. My old nan swears she heard it from one who saw the beast. A blue dragon flying over the sea. Locked in the tower now, he is, chained in his human form. Can't hurt no decent souls like that. His own father put him there." Wag nodded emphatically. "If my son were a weredragon, I'd lock him up too."

Men roared with laughter. "Your son can't even work a grinding stone, let alone become a dragon!" one woman called out. "Head of mush, that one has."

Maev looked at her brother. He stared back at her, eyes somber.

"Maev," Tanin whispered. "Tell me you're not thinking of . . ."

She grabbed his hand and tugged him up. She pulled him away from the table. Ignoring calls from the villagers, she walked around the well, between two huts, and into open fields.

The stars shone above, crickets chirped, and an owl hooted. Fireflies danced above the tall grass. After the heat and noise and smells of the village, it felt good to walk here in darkness. They moved through the grasslands, heading deeper into shadows, for they were Vir Requis, creatures of the night.

"There is another," Maev whispered, eyes watering.

In the darkness, she heard Tanin groan.

"The drunken talk of fools," he said. He shoved aside the tall, wild grass, moving through the darkness. "People also say dragons eat babies, drink the blood of virgins, and piss molten gold. So they say a prince in a far-off land is a dragon." He barked a laugh. "What are you going to do, fly all the way across the sea, find this mythical land of Eteer, and look for a tower?"

Maev sighed and looked up at the stars. The Draco constellation shone there, comforting her, easing the pain of her wounds.

"Fifty years ago, these stars began to shine," Maev said softly. "Grandfather was among the first in the world to become a dragon. The stars gave him this magic." She smiled to remember his stories. "And he gave it to our father. And that great grizzly bear passed it on to us. If the stars blessed our family, perhaps they blessed another family too. Perhaps they blessed Prince Sena of Eteer. And if it's true . . . if he's imprisoned . . . we have to save him." She clutched her brother's hand. "We have to bring him home."

They kept walking in silence, listening to the crickets and rustling grass. When they were far enough from the town, Maev closed her eyes and summoned her magic. It flowed through her, warmer than mulled wine, easing the pain of her wounds. She beat her wings, rising into the air, a green dragon in the night. At her side, more wings thudded, and she saw her brother soar too, a red dragon with long white horns.

Silent, keeping their fire low, they rose and caught an air current. They glided through the night, heading away from the villages that hunted their kind . . . heading toward that distant mountain, that new home, that place of safety and warmth in a cold world.

ANGEL

She crouched in the darkness, a queen of rock and fire, and licked the blood off her long, clawed fingers, savoring the coppery heat, shuddering as the hooks upon her tongue lapped the goodness, and she unfurled that tongue, stretching out a dripping serpent, and Angel howled in the depths in her hunger and lust.

"It is sweet, my children, my terrors," she hissed. Saliva dripped down her maw to steam against the stone floor. The cracks upon her body widened, leaking smoke and fire. "The blood nourishes. The blood is darkness."

Her meal writhed before her, all but drained, a gray husk of a thing. Once it had been three; she had molded them together, cutting and sewing, stitching twins like dolls, bloating the beast with embers and meat and sweet drippings of fat, letting it fester, letting it grow. Now she drank from her twisted creation, her living wineskin of meat and marrow. She drove her head down, thrusting her hollowed teeth through its skin, and sucked, sucked, lapped the sweetness, the red and black, the heat and stickiness. Its many arms twitched, and its mouths, sewn together, whimpered and begged, and its eyes blinked and wept where she had placed them, and still Angel drank, leaving it an empty shell, a shriveled thing, only skin over bones.

"Yes, my dears." She licked the creature, her conjoined twins, her meals in the darkness. "You will live. I will fatten you again, and you will grow, and more will join you. I will sew you into a great feast."

It begged her for death, tears pouring. She laughed. She shoved it aside, leaped, and scuttled through the depths. Her

Requiem's Song

leather wings beat, wafting smoke and stench, and her four arms flailed, ending with claws, cutting into the stone. Around her they lay, the creatures she had sewn together. The largest was a hundred strong, bodies morphed into a writhing hill, sacks of blood and rot, meals to last through her long, ancient banishment.

Upon their anguished faces she ran, cutting into them, digging, spurting, scattering flesh, until she scampered up the craggy cavern wall. Her wings stretched wide, and the blood coursed through her, heating her, and flames blasted from her cracked body of stone. She let out a howl of lust, a cry that echoed through the chamber, for blood was not enough, and filling her belly could never sate her, for her loins burned with the greatest heat, crying for release, begging to feast like her maw had feasted.

She left her chamber of blood, her hall of husks, her place of feeding, and she scuttled through the tunnel, a creature of fire, until she burst into a new hall, fell, spread her wings, rose, crackled in an inferno. Her flames blasted out, and she shrieked until her voice echoed, and the fire rose from her loins to crawl across her cracked belly, her stony breasts, her four arms of rock and her claws of metal.

Before her they knelt, shuddered, sang, cowered, begged, shrieked, mocked, prayed—her soldiers of the Abyss, her endless twisted things to praise her, to worship her, to thrust into her in a vain attempt to satisfy her lust, for only human flesh could silence her craving. She gazed upon them. Creatures of oozing flesh, their skin peeled away, their muscles dripping, their bones white and wet. Creatures of stone like her, their bodies cracked and dry and leaking smoke. Creatures of fat, slithering, sliding, seeping, leaving their wet trails, stuffing their folds of fat with worms and maggots and snakes and all things that crawled and burrowed. Creatures hooded. Creatures naked. Creatures inside out, organs glistening. Creatures of smoke, of horn, of scale, of rot. All filled the chamber before her, from beasts thrice her size to rotting, clattering centipedes that crawled around her legs, their segments formed of human heads.

All praised her.

She was Angel.

She was fire and light and a beacon of darkness.

"Kneel before me!" she cried, voice slamming against the stone walls, this place far under the world, this trap, this prison. "Worship me and fill me. Send one forth."

They rustled, clattered, squealed, and groaned beneath her feet. Angel screamed, her cry shattering flesh below, breaking bones, snapping eardrums, scattering blood. She pointed a dripping claw, selecting one, a mummified thing, its head long and topped with a disk of bone, its mouth rustling with maggots, it belly sliced open to reveal nests of snakes. It moved toward her on hooves, and Angel lowered herself on her four elbows, and she howled when the creature thrust into her with its barbed tool, and she dug into the stone, and she spewed flame from her maw as he took her. Around her in the cave, smelling her sex, the other creatures of the Abyss clawed and grabbed one another, copulating in pools of drool and rot, howling to the stone ceiling, filling the chamber with stench and whimpers and groans.

Yet it was all for naught. Even as her paramour took her, she knew no filling of her craving, and she knew no life would quicken within her, for thus was her curse. Thus was her banishment, her prison, to forever crave a child, to forever feel the emptiness in her womb, for only the seed of living men—of the flesh that moved above the rock—could fill her with life, with a rotting, pulsing spawn.

When the summons hit her, Angel hissed and raised her dripping maw.

A summons? After so long?

She screamed.

She sprayed lava from her mouth, and she pulled herself off the beast that mounted her, and she beat her wings.

"A summons! I am called!"

She flapped her wings, scattering the stench of the pit, churning smoke and fire. Flames burst across her, and the calling burned her. She shut her eyes, opened her arms, uncurled her claws.

"Speak, sack of flesh! Speak, creature overground!"

Astral arms pulled her, sucking her up into the stone, tugging her through tunnels. She laughed, wind shrieking around her, rock cracking against her. It had been so many years, so long since the creatures above had summoned her, weak and small and tempting, so beautiful, so warm.

Inferno blazed, and the world cracked, and when she opened her eyes again, Angel stood in a new place, an old chamber, the hall of the kings aboveground.

She laughed, spreading her wings wide, scattering her fire. The sparks landed upon tapestries, burning them, filling this place with her heat. Here was the Hall of Eteer, the throne room of the kings who ruled above her own rotted kingdom. Many times they had called her here in days of old, ancient lords of sunlight, and she had spoken with them, treated with them, and sometimes snatched them into the depths to sew into her sacks of blood.

A new king sat before her upon the throne, younger than the last one, tall and broad. His head was bald, his skin bronzed from sunlight, and true bronze—that metal she had taught the smiths of Eteer to forge—covered him as armor.

Angel hissed at him, sending out her tongue to taste him, licking, exploring. She cackled, drool spilling from her, burning holes into the mosaic beneath her claws.

"You are new," she said, smoke seeping between her fangs.

The mortal stared, face grim, and she saw herself reflected in his eyes: a woman carved of volcanic rock, cracked and red and black, flames engulfing her, her leathern wings wide, her four arms long and tipped with claws, a queen, a barren thing, a goddess of lust and hunger and emptiness.

"I am Raem Seran, son of the fallen Nir-Ur, King of Eteer." Even in her heat, and even as she hissed and spat embers upon him, he did not cower, and he did not avert his eyes. "I now sit upon the kingdom's throne. As is my right, I summon you to my service, Queen of the Abyss."

Angel cackled.

Her laughter blasted back his cloak, seared his skin, and splattered him with her steaming saliva. She beat her wings and rose higher, leaving a wake of fire. She stretched out her arms, letting him admire her nakedness, her loins like burning embers, her pulsing womb that ached for his seed.

"Serve you, King?" She spat out the last word as an insult. "Perhaps you would serve me in my pit. I will take you, copulate with you, and give you to my demons, so they might thrust into you, and you will feed us with your blood, and we will—"

"Silence!" he said, rising from his throne. "You are a queen of banishment, ruler of a prison cell. My forebears bound you to my dynasty. As is my right, I command you. You will rise. You will fight for me."

Angel beat her wings, drew near, and placed her claws upon his chest. They dug grooves through his armor and into his skin, and his blood spilled, and she licked his cheek and hissed into his ear.

"Your forebears never dared free me. If I fight, King, I will burn the world."

He reached into her flames. He grabbed her shoulders and pushed her back, not flinching even from her heat.

"You will burn only those I command you to. Weredragons infest my kingdom, diseased humans who can take dragon forms. They will be yours to slay. Raise your horde! Bring forth the creatures of the underworld. The demons of the Abyss will rise. You will live in the world once more, as you did in ancient days, and you will hunt weredragons."

Angel shrieked. Her cry cracked a column to her left. The tapestries burned all around, falling to the floor.

"For ten thousand years, we lingered in the darkness. You will free us?"

Raem shook his head. "No. I grant you no freedom. I grant you servitude in sunlight. Fight for me, Angel. You will feel the sunlight upon you. You will fly in open sky, covering my kingdom. But still you will be bound to me."

She tilted her head, snapped her teeth, and clawed at him. "I demand more! I demand . . ." She grinned, and smoke rose between her teeth to blind her. "I demand human wombs. Let my demons choose brides among your women. Let them breed with them. Let the seed of the Abyss infect mortal bellies, so that the daughters of Eteer may bear us children. Agree to this, mortal man, and I will slay your weredragons."

Raem stared at her in silence, eyes hard, lips tight.

He nodded.

Angel laughed.

She tossed back her head, stretched out her four arms, beat her wings, spread her flame, and her laughter rang and the ceiling rained dust.

"It will be so!"

She stamped down her feet, and cracks raced across the floor. Claws rose between them, widening the gaps, and mouths gaped, and tongues explored, and eyes peered, and smoke wafted. The mosaic shattered and they emerged: crawling, flying, slithering, seeping, dragging, scuttling, creatures of ooze, of fat, of scales, of horns, of dried flesh, of weeping sores. Large and small, they emerged into the hall of Eteer's king, freed, famished—the demons of the Abyss.

"We will hunt weredragons!" Angel shouted through her laughter, and they filled the hall around her. "We will mate with mortal flesh! Spread across the city, children of rot. Choose brides among the women. Sniff out reptiles and slay them. Kill and breed! Crush and bring forth life!"

They stormed through the hall, a geyser of rot, cracking the columns, crashing through doors, shattering windows, flowing into the city and the searing sunlight that had been forbidden for so long. Their howls shook the world, almost drowning the screams of the mortals.

They left the hall singed, globs of rot dripping from the charred tapestries, the floor shattered, the mosaic stones scattered like dragon scales. Still he stood before her, this new king, this human of hot skin and blood.

She placed her arms around him.

"I need no bride," she whispered and licked his face, tearing his skin with the hooks of her tongue. "You will be mine."

She tugged and they fell upon the shattered floor, limbs dangling across the open pit's ledge, and there she copulated with him, a sticky dance of stone and skin, of blood and fire, and she screamed as they merged, and she laughed and clawed the floor.

She had found freedom. She had found release for her fire. And soon . . . soon she would find dragons to burn.

JEID

"Grizzly, I am *leaving*." Maev crossed her arms, thrust out her bottom lip, and raised her chin. "I'm flying across the sea and into a bronze kingdom, and you can't stop me."

Standing in the canyon, Jeid Blacksmith stared at his daughter, rage and fear mingling inside him. He clutched his axe so tightly he thought he might snap the shaft. His arms shook. A growl rose in his throat. Finally he could not contain it; he tossed back his shaggy, bearded head and shouted wordlessly. His cry echoed within the mossy walls of the canyon, shaking the stones. This was an ancient crack in the world—boulders perched precariously atop pillars of stone, trees clinging to craggy walls, natural cairns of sharp rocks, and caves running into the depths of the earth. This natural fortress of walls, tunnels, and towers had stood here since the dawn of time. Now Jeid howled so loudly he thought the sound could shatter the old stones, burying him and his daughter forever.

Finally his wordless cry morphed into words. "No! I forbid it. You will stay here in this canyon, in safety, with me."

Maev tilted her head and narrowed her eyes. She placed her fists on her hips and snorted, blowing back a strand of her long, dark blond hair.

"You cannot stop me. I am twenty-three years old, Grizzly. When you were my age, you were already a father." She gestured at the canyon around her. Vines and moss covered the craggy walls, and boulders lay piled up around her. "I'm a Vir Requis. I can shift into a dragon. I'm not meant to hide among stone." Her eyes gleamed and she hopped to another boulder, moving closer to him. "Grizzly, there is another. I know it. Let me find him."

Jeid sighed.

She looks like her mother, but she is stubborn like me.

Jeid—tall, burly, and shaggy—sported a mane of wild brown hair, a bushy beard, and brown eyes that stared from under tufted brows. Clad in furs, he looked like something of a bear, earning him his nickname; even his own children now used the moniker.

Maev looked like her late mother. Her hair was golden, her eyes gray tinged with blue, her skin pale. But Jeid saw himself in her too—the stubborn gaze, the strong arms, the way she raised her chin, stuck out her bottom lip, and dared anyone to challenge her. He had given her those.

I never wanted this life for you, Maev, he thought. He had imagined her growing up a fair woman, perhaps a gatherer of berries or a weaver of cloth. Instead she had become a fighter, traveling from town to town to punch and kick and bite for prizes. Today a black eye marred her countenance, and her lip was still swollen, the remnants of the fights he forbade and she kept getting into. Like him, she obeyed no rules, respected no leaders, and valued stubbornness over prudence.

If she insisted on having a nap in a meadow, Jeid thought, *an approaching stampede of mammoths would not convince her to move.*

"The Prince of Eteer, a dragon?" Jeid said, waving a hand dismissively. "It's only a legend, daughter. The kingdom of Eteer itself is probably only a legend. A town the size of a forest? Houses built of stone and armies of thousands, each man bearing bronze? Towers taller than totem poles?" He hefted the shield that hung across his back. "No such place exists. These are only stories told around campfires."

Requiem's Song

Maev growled and bared her teeth. She leaped onto another boulder; she now stood only a foot away from the rock he stood on. She gave his chest a shove so hard Jeid nearly toppled over.

"A legend!" Her eyes flashed. "You know what else some claim is a legend? Dragons. And look."

With a roar, she leaped into the air and shifted.

Green scales rose across her. Her tail flailed. She flapped her wings, bending the trees that clung to the canyon walls. Rocks rolled and rearranged themselves, and even a boulder creaked upon the jutting stone pillar it perched upon. Maev ascended, rising above the canyon walls until she flew in open sky. She blasted out fire, a pillar of heat and light that filled the sky and rained down sparks.

"Maev, you fool!"

With his own roar, Jeid shifted too, becoming a burly copper dragon. He beat his wings, rose to the top of the canyon, and grabbed Maev's tail. He tugged her down into safety like a man pulling down a flapping bird. Their wings slapped against the canyon walls. Maev was a strong, slim dragon, fast as wildfire, but Jeid was twice her size, a massive beast of horns like spears, claws like swords, and scales like shields. When he pulled her back to the canyon floor, they shifted back into human forms. She stood before him, clad in fur and leather again. She panted, her cheeks flushed.

"Did you see the legend?" She spat. "Dragons are real. I'm real. You're real. Our family is real. And there are others. In the villages and tribes they speak of it—the kingdom of Eteer. Young Prince Sena is held captive by his cruel father, a father almost as cruel as you. He's locked in a tower, Grizzly! Not even a canyon where you can see the sky, but a tiny cell, chained so he can't shift." She raised her chin. "I have to save him. I have to believe there are others, not just our family. I have to fly south and save him." Her voice softened and she sighed. "You must learn to—just sometimes—let me go."

But he could not let her go. He had lost one daughter already. He had lost his sweet Requiem. How could he lose Maev too?

He pulled her into his arms. Maev was a tall woman, taller than many men, and yet Jeid towered above her; she nearly disappeared into his embrace. She laid her head against his shoulder, and her tears dampened his fur tunic.

"My daughter," he said, voice choked. "I already lost your mother to the arrows of those who hate us. I already lost your sister to their poison. I cannot bear to lose you too. What if you fly into a trap, like . . . like the trap that killed Requiem? Like the trap that almost killed me?"

"No trap can stop me." She touched his beard, and her eyes softened. "Grizzly, I am strong, fast, a warrior. You will not lose me. I will free the prince, and I will bring him back here. You've always dreamed of finding others, of building a new tribe here, a tribe of Vir Requis. And yet we've found no others. Let me find one. Let me prove to you that we are not alone."

A loud voice, speaking in falsetto, came from above them. "Oh Grizzly! I am a heroine from a tale. I rescue princes from towers, inspire bards with my bravery, and slay ogres with my bad breath."

Jeid looked up and sighed again. Upon the canyon's edge, looking down upon them, stood his son.

Two years older than his sister, Tanin sported a head of shaggy brown hair, and stubble covered his cheeks. While his father was beefy, Tanin was slender and quick. He wore leather breeches and a fur tunic, and he carried a bronze *apa* sword at his belt, the leaf-shaped blade as long as his thigh. A bow and quiver hung across his back, and a mocking smile tugged at his lips. A prankster, his only joy seemed to be tormenting his younger sister—stuffing frogs into her blankets, painting her face while she slept, and once even slicing off a strand of her hair, which Maev had avenged by giving him a fat lip.

Maev spun around and glared up at him. "I do not sound like that."

Tanin smirked and gave a little pirouette, balancing on the edge of the canyon. He kept speaking in falsetto. "I'm so lonely here, Grizzly, and I'm as homely as the south side of a northbound mule. The only way I'll ever find a mate is to travel to the edge of the world—where they haven't heard of my foul temper—and snatch one up—"

"Tanin!" Smoke looked ready to plume from Maev's ears. She leaped, shifted again, and flew up toward her brother. She landed atop the canyon, shifted back into human form, and barreled into him, knocking him down.

Jeid grunted and flew after them. When he reached the canyon's edge, he resumed human form and stomped toward the wrestling siblings. Birches, oaks, and elms grew around them, hiding them from any rocs that might dare fly above. The escarpment sloped down to the south, leading to forested hills, valleys, and finally the river where they fished for bass and trout. Beyond that river lay the towns and villages of those who hunted them—a forbidden realm.

"Enough!" Jeid bellowed. He grabbed each of his children by the collar and lifted them up. They dangled in his grip, still trying to punch one another. "Stop your bickering, children, or I'll bang your heads together like melons."

"Ow!" said Tanin, struggling in his father's grip. "What did I do?" The young man was twenty-five and tall and strong, yet in his father's grip he seemed like a bear cub.

"You will stop tormenting your sister!" Jeid said. "And you will sway her away from this nonsense."

105

He tossed both his children down in disgust. They fell into a pile of fallen leaves, rose to their feet, and brushed their woolen clothes and fur cloaks.

"Well..." Tanin stared at his feet and kicked around a pine cone. "I sort of... agreed to go with her."

Jeid's eyes widened. "You what?" he bellowed. "I expect some nonsense from Maev." He ignored her protests. "But you, Tanin? I thought you were better than this."

Tanin finally dared raise his eyes. "You taught me to be a smith, Grizzly. You taught me to forge copper, tin, and bronze." He gestured at the wide, bronze sword that hung on his hip. "And then you shifted into a dragon. You let the town see you. And we had to flee here. Now I roam around from town to town, juggling raven skulls and dancing like a trained bear—a blind, clumsy bear with gammy legs." Tanin sighed, took his bronzed raven skulls out of his pockets, and tossed them as far as they'd go. "You spoke of creating a tribe—a tribe of weredragons, a tribe called Requiem after my sister. You even gave us a fancy name—Vir Requis." Tanin gestured around him. "Well, I don't see a tribe. I see a gruff, hairy grizzly bear... and I see my father." He winked at Maev.

With a growl, Maev leaped onto her brother again, wrestling him down and punching. This time Jeid did not try to stop them. He clenched his fists, lowered his head, and the pain cut through him.

"You're right," he said, his voice so soft he barely heard himself.

The siblings, however, paused from wrestling. They stared up at him, eyes wide.

Pain clutched at Jeid's chest to remember that day, that horrible day Zerra, his own twin, had seen him shift into a dragon. Zerra had shouted the news across their town of Oldforge, raging that his brother was diseased. Jeid had fled into the wilderness that day. Zerra had left Oldforge too—he joined a roaming tribe of roc riders and dedicated himself to hunting weredragons.

To hunting me, Jeid thought.

"You're right," he repeated, voice soft. "This is my fault. I'm the one who was caught. I'm the one who doomed us to banishment. I'm the reason you live in a canyon, that you roam from town to town for food and supplies, when you should be smiths in Oldforge, a true roof over your head, starting your own families." His voice choked. "I failed you. I know this, and it hurts me every day, and—"

"Grizzly!" Maev said. She leaped to her feet and embraced him. Tanin joined her a moment later, awkwardly placing an arm around them.

"But I ask you, my children." Jeid's eyes burned. "I ask you to stay. Stay with me."

Tears streamed down Maev's cheeks. She hugged him tightly . . . but then she stepped away.

"I cannot," she whispered. "I must find others. I must. If we're banished, let us build this new tribe." She leaped into the air and shifted. Her wings scattered dry leaves and bent saplings. She took flight with clattering scales, crashed through the canopy, and hovered above. "Goodbye, Father! Goodbye!"

With that, she spun and flew southward, leaving only a wake of smoke.

Tanin stood before his father, arms hanging at his sides, his cheeks flushed. He cleared his throat and clasped Jeid's shoulder.

"I'll look after her," he said, voice hoarse. "I won't torment her much. I—"

His voice choked and he seemed ready to shed tears. With a silent nod, the young man shifted too. He rose into the air, a red dragon, and flew off, calling his sister's name.

Jeid grunted and was about to shift too, to fly after them and drag them home, when he felt a hand on his shoulder.

"Let them go, my son." The voice was deep and soft, a voice like waves on sand, like water in the deep. "Let them be."

Jeid spun around, fists clenched, to see his own father.

At seventy years of age, Eranor still stood straight, his shoulders squared. His long white hair and beard flowed down to his waist. His glittering blue eyes stared from under bushy, snowy eyebrows. He still wore his old druid robes, blue wool hemmed in silver, and he bore a staff made from a twisting oak root. Upon its top, clutched within wooden fingers, shone a blue crystal the size of a heart. Eranor, once a healer and sage in their town, had been banished with the rest of his family—the first among them to find the magic, to shift into a dragon . . . and to call it a gift.

"They—" For a moment, Jeid chocked on his words. "Those scoundrels are—"

"I know." Eranor smiled sadly and patted his son's shoulder. "They spoke to me of leaving. I gave them my blessing."

"You *what*? Father! How could you do this?" Jeid felt his face flush. He swung his axe through the air, bellowed wordlessly, and kicked leaves and rocks. "I will kill them. Why would they not come to me first, why—"

"Because they're frightened of you." Eranor swung his staff, knocking down the axe. "They don't call you Grizzly only because of your shaggy hair and beard. You terrify the poor things."

"Those poor things *should* be terrified. I'm flying after them now, and when I catch them, I—"

"Jeid, come with me." Eranor clasped his son's arm, holding him in place. "Come to the watchtower."

Jeid tossed down his axe with a grunt; it vanished into the fallen leaves. Huffing, he followed his father. They tramped between the trees, approaching the pillar of stone. It rose narrow and tall, a shard like a tower, a remnant of the ancient calamity that had fallen upon this land. Countless years ago, the druids said, half the world plunged down like a sinking loaf of bread, creating the escarpment—a great shelf of stone that ran into the horizon. When the land had collapsed, boulders fell, the canyon gaped open, and the watchtower rose from the earth like a blade. Jeid and his father climbed the stone pillar now. The top was barely wide enough for two; they stood pressed together.

Here was the highest point of the escarpment. Standing here, Jeid could see the land slope down before him, finally reaching treed hills and valleys; beyond them flowed the River Ranin. Upon the horizon, he could just make out pillars of smoke—the cooking fires of Oldforge. To his right, a waterfall crashed down the escarpment, feeding a stream.

Eranor gestured at the scenery. The wind whipped his beard and fluttered his wide sleeves. "The world."

"Yes, Father, I know what the world is."

"But your children do not." Eranor smiled sadly. "You have traveled far and wide and seen many lands. They have never gone south of the River Ranin."

The old druid turned around and pointed down. The canyon stretched beneath them, mossy boulders piled up in its depths. Vines and roots covered its walls. Several caves gaped open, leading to a network of tunnels and caverns.

"This canyon is a safe place," Jeid said, his voice still gruff. "I built a new home for us here. Even my brother fears this place. Here is our fortress. Here we are safe behind walls of stone, safe to blow fire from caves upon any roc that might attack."

He gestured around him. To a random traveler, the canyon would seem like nothing but a natural collapse of nature, a sculpture all of stone, wood, and moss. But Jeid saw a fort. Pillars of stone thrust up—watchtowers. Caves lined the canyon walls—secret holes for blasting flame. Boulders rose and fell like walls, some balanced upon one another—traps to crush invaders. In the wilderness, arrows could slay them. In the skies, rocs could hunt them. Here was safety. Here was survival.

"Aye," said Eranor, stroking his white beard. "It's a safe place for weary travelers such as you and me. But for Tanin and Maev . . . they need to believe there is more. They need to believe there is hope, that there are others like us."

Jeid lowered his head. The wind fluttered his hair around his face. He winced to remember flying back to Oldforge only days ago—of Ciana betraying him, of the poisoned arrows thrusting into him. His wounds still stung, but worse was the pain inside him.

"*Are* there more, Father?" he said softly. "I told them that other dragons fly. I told them we can build a tribe, a tribe called Requiem. I told them tales to comfort them—when they were young, afraid, banished. I told them that our family is not diseased, that we carry a gift, that others in the world are like us." He raised his eyes and stared at his father. "I told them the stories you told me when I was young. But I lied. And you lied."

Eranor raised his eyebrows. "Lied, did I? Look at your shield, Jeid. Look at the shield that you yourself forged."

With a grunt, Jeid slung the shield off his back. The bronze disk was inlaid with silver stars, forming a dragon-shaped constellation. Those same stars shone in the sky every night.

"Simple stars," Jeid said. "A coincidence."

Eranor shook his head. "You were born seeing those stars at night. But when I was young, the Draco constellation did not shine." Eranor's eyes watered. "A great gift has come to the world—the gift of magic, of dragons. I do not believe that it blessed only our family. In villages and wandering tribes, they speak of others—others who were hunted, caught, killed. Zerra hunts them; so do other tribes. But some must have escaped. Some must have survived. Your children need to believe this . . . and so do I. Even their old grandfather, white-haired and frail, must cling to some hope. Requiem might be a dream, but let us live that dream."

Requiem's Song

Jeid slung the shield across his back again. "You are many years away from being frail, Father. And I wish I could believe too. But since . . . since they died . . ." His voice choked.

Eranor nodded and lowered his head, and his white beard cascaded like a waterfall. "I miss them too. As the stars blessed us with magic, so do they harbor the souls of our departed. Your wife and daughter look down upon you. And they are proud of you."

Another story, Jeid thought. *Another comforting fairy tale.*

He wanted to believe, wanted to hope too, but Jeid could not. Hope led to despair.

He climbed down the pillar of stone. He entered his small cave in the canyon. He opened his wooden chest, pulled out Requiem's old coat, and held the soft cotton against his cheek until darkness fell.

LAIRA

In the cold autumn morning, fog cloaking the camp and crows peering from naked trees, Laira stood tied to a stake, awaiting her death in fire.

The Goldtusk tribe gathered around the pyre, watching her, five hundred souls. They wore mammoth, wolf, and deer fur, and their strings of bone and clay beads hung around their necks and arms. Mist floated between them and their breath frosted. The tribe's totem pole rose behind upon a hillock, the gilded mammoth tusk upon its crest all but hidden in the fog. The rocs stood tethered to the pole, scratching the earth and cawing, anxious for a meal; the birds had seen enough burnings to know they would soon feast upon charred flesh.

Branches, straw, and twigs rose in a pile beneath Laira's feet. She watched a grub crawl down a birch branch, only for a robin to land, suck it up, and fly off. Strangely, the sight almost comforted to her.

I will burn. I will scream. I will rise to my mother. But the world will go on. Birds will fly, grubs will die, the leaves will fall and bud again. Maybe I'm as small and meaningless as that grub.

Zerra came walking through the crowd, heading toward her, holding a torch. A cruel smile twisted his features, lipless on the burnt half of his face. His fur cloak billowed in the wind, revealing his bronze sword—the most precious weapon in their tribe. When he reached her, he held his torch close, and the heat and smoke stung Laira and invaded her nostrils. She grimaced.

"Aye, you were a sweet one in my bed." Drool dripped down his chin and he grabbed his groin. "It's almost a shame to burn you. You were as hot and smooth as your mother was. I claimed her too, did you know? Your father abandoned her for me to take." He smirked. "Mother and daughter—both mine to bed and burn."

Laira found rage filling her, overflowing her moment of stoicism.

"You lie!" She spat on his face. "My father is a great warrior-prince across the sea. He is stronger than you, and his sword is wider and longer. My mother was just as strong. She never submitted to you as I did. You will forever bear the mark of her strength upon your ravaged face."

Slowly, he wiped the spit off. His hand wet with her saliva, he struck her. The blow snapped Laira's head to the side, rattling her teeth, searing her with white light. The torch crackled only inches from her, only heartbeats away from igniting the pyre.

"Half my body is burnt," Zerra said. "I think that, after I've burned all of yours, I will pull you from the flames. I will keep you half-alive, writhing and begging for death. I will heal you. For long moons, you will scream in your tent, and we will apply ointments, bandages, prayers . . . then burn you again, only to repeat the cycle. I wonder how many burnings you will survive. I will try to make it many. You will end up envying your mother."

Laira grimaced as the torch drew nearer, singing her cheek, and her heart thrashed. She gritted her teeth.

No. I will not give up. I will fight even as the fire blazes.

She gave the ropes binding her a mighty tug. But they only chafed her wrists, keeping her arms tied behind her to the stake. She tried to kick, but the ropes dug into her ankles, and blood trickled onto her bare feet.

"Yes, struggle for me." Zerra leaned forward and licked her cheek. He brought the ravaged half of his face near her eyes. "Look at my scars, child. Soon all your body will look like this."

Laira sucked in breath, chest shaking.

Use your curse. Use your disease. She ground her teeth. *Use your magic.*

She shut her eyes, trying to ignore the pain, to focus, to calm herself and find that inner power. At first it evaded her. The magic lurked deep inside, fleeing from her mental grasp like a mouse fleeing from reaching hands.

Zerra stepped back and raised his torch. "For the glory of Ka'altei!" he shouted. "We will burn the reptile! Shaman of Goldtusk, will you bless my fire?"

Concentrate, Laira. Grab your magic.

Shedah, the crone, stepped forward. Strings of human finger bones rattled, hanging around her neck. Among them hung the silver amulet of Taal—the amulet of Laira's fallen mother, now the crone's prize. The wizened old thing, frail and covered in warts, raised her staff. The painted skull of an ape grinned atop it.

"I name her a cursed thing!" cried the shaman, voice shrill.

Laira reached down deep inside her. She found that secret pool and fished out the warm strands.

The magic flowed through her.

Ahead, Shedah reached into her leather pouch, pulled out blue powder, and tossed it onto Zerra's torch. The powder ignited, spewing orange smoke, and Zerra raised the flame high.

"The fire is blessed with the seed of Ka'altei!" he announced. "The reptile will forever blaze in his halls of retribution."

Scales flowed across Laira's body.

Wings emerged from her back.

Fangs grew from her gums and her fingers lengthened into claws.

Fly!

As her body ballooned, the ropes dug into her growing ankles and wrists, cutting into flesh, and Laira yowled. If she kept growing, the ropes would sever her feet and hands.

I still must shift, she thought as Zerra approached. *I still must fly, even without hands and feet. I—*

The ropes dug deeper, and the agony overwhelmed her, knocking the magic from her grasp.

The scales, wings, and fangs vanished. She shrank into a woman again, hanging limply from the stake.

With a thin smile, Zerra tossed the torch onto the pyre.

The kindling caught fire, and heat bathed Laira, and she screamed. The flames raced up the pile of wood, branch by branch, heading toward her feet.

What do I do? Dragon stars, what do I do?

She screamed and tugged at her bonds again. She reached for her magic but no longer found it. The fire licked her toes and she screamed. Through the haze of smoke and crackling flame, she saw the tribesmen cheer. Behind them the rocs fluttered madly, snapping their beaks, awaiting their meal. Tears filled Laira's eyes. She could barely see through the heat, and the world swayed.

"Neiva!" she shouted and managed a high whistle. "Neiva, to me!"

The smoke blinded her and filled her mouth. The fire seared her feet.

"Neiva, please!"

She opened her eyes to slits. The smoke billowed. The flames blazed. Through the inferno, she saw wings flapping, talons reaching out, yellow eyes gleaming. She had ridden this animal only once, had bonded with Neiva for only a day, yet today she was *her* roc, bound to Laira with fire—and now her roc reached into the flames. Talons closed around the stake, tugging, lifting the bole out of the flaming pyre. Laira's feet rose from the blaze.

"Fly, Neiva! Fly north. Fly!"

Laira's eyes rolled back. She blinked, forcing herself to regain consciousness. The world spun around her. Wings beat and the oily, rancid stench of the roc filled her nostrils, and it was beautiful to her, the sweetest thing she'd ever smelled. When she looked down, she saw the pyre consumed with flame. The tribesmen were scurrying below and leaping onto their own rocs.

"To the forest, Neiva!" Laira shouted. If she still had any chance, it lay among those trees.

She was still tied to the stake, trussed up and charred and bruised, a bit of meat on a skewer. She felt so weak she could just slip into endless sleep. She ground her teeth, bit down on her cheek, and forced herself to remain awake.

"I will not die," she hissed, fists clenched behind the stake she was tied to. "I will not give up. I will fight this until my very last drop of strength, and then I will fight some more."

The roc flew, shrieking, holding the stake in her talons. They glided toward the forest, a hundred rocs shrieking and chasing behind them.

The grassy hills rolled below, speckled with boulders and scattered elm trees. Mist hung in the valleys, deer ran along a riverbank, and a forest of oaks, maples, and birches sprawled in the north. Neiva flew toward those woods now, descended above the canopy, and screeched.

"Through the trees!" Laira said. "Land among them."

The roc hesitated. Clutching the stake in both talons, Neiva seemed unable to land; the canopy was too thick. With her talons free, perhaps Neiva could have parted the branches, but now she merely hovered above the trees, holding the stake. When Laira twisted her head, she saw the other rocs chasing, and their riders fired arrows.

"Drop me!" Laira cried. "Do it!"

Neiva tossed back her head, her beak opened wide, and she cried out, the sound so loud Laira thought her eardrums might snap. The roc's talons opened and the stake—Laira tied to it—tumbled down.

Laira screamed as she crashed through the canopy, snapping branches and scattering leaves. For an instant she fell through open air. The stake hit a branch, tilted, and straightened vertically; her feet faced the ground. Then, with a thud that rattled her teeth and spine, the stake slammed into the forest floor.

Laira cried out in pain, sure that her bones had shattered. Every segment in her back seemed to knock against another. She couldn't even breathe. She tried to gasp for breath when the stake tilted forward. She winced, tugging at her bonds . . . and slammed facedown into the dirt. The stake landed on her back, creaking against her spine, driving her deep into the mud. Soil filled her mouth, nostrils, and eyes.

For a moment, Laira only lay still. She saw nothing but stars floating across blackness. She didn't know if she was alive or dead. The smell of soil, worms, and blood filled her nostrils. The pain throbbed, but it felt distant, dulled. She was floating away.

No.

Her fingers curled inward.

No. Fight. Get up. Move.

Somewhere above, a hundred rocs shrieked, and hunters cried out.

Get up! spoke the voice inside her. *Move! Run!*

She growled, pushed down her shoulders, and screamed into the mud.

Her face rose from the soil, and she sucked in breath, choking on dirt and leaves. She spat. The weight of the stake pushed down on her back. She wanted to cry for Neiva again, but dared not make a sound; the hunters would hear. Somewhere ahead, she heard trumpeting and thumping feet—mammoths running among the trees. Briefly she wondered if these were the same mammoths she had tried to hunt only days ago. Now she was the hunted.

I'm burned. I'm broken. I'm bruised. I'm bound to a wooden stake that crushes me and I cannot move. I will die here.

She gritted her teeth, gulping down the despair.

So I will die fighting.

With a growl, she pushed down her knees and tugged mightily at her bonds. The ropes dug into her again, but she found that her wrists slid a short distance up the stake.

Hope kindled inside her. She could not break her bonds, but with the stake lying flat above her, perhaps she could sling her wrists and legs above its top. She would still be tied but free of the stake; she would be able to crawl, maybe even hop, forward.

Wincing, she tugged again. Her wrists and ankles slid up the wood.

The thud of wings and cries of rocs sounded above. Hunters shouted; she could make out Zerra's voice among them. The stench of the flock wafted down into the forest, a foul miasma. Laira clenched her jaw, winced, and tugged with all her might. The rope kept tearing into her flesh, but she kept tugging, inch by inch, until with a gasp, her wrists reached the top of the stake. With one more tug, she was free from the wood. She wriggled her legs free too, fell into the mud, and crawled.

The stake lay behind, but ropes still bound her limbs. She couldn't even stand up. Dry leaves stuck to the mud covering her, filling her mouth, her eyes, her nostrils. Gasping for air, she wriggled into a patch of tall grass.

"Find her!" Zerra shouted somewhere above the canopy. "Rocs, pick up her scent!"

Again Laira heard the discordant sound—like air through pipes—as the rocs above sniffed for her.

They will smell me, she thought. *They will find me like last time. They will take me back and torture me.*

She had to mask her scent somehow. She had to move faster. She crawled over a fallen log, ignoring the agony of her wounds. When she thumped down into a patch of moss, she saw an abandoned mammoth foraging camp.

The trees were stripped bare of leaves here. Prints filled the mud, and shed mammoth fur covered brambles and boulders. The animals were gone, fled from the cries of rocs; she could see a path of trampled grass and saplings. A stench hit her nostrils, making her gag; a pile of mammoth dung steamed ahead, still fresh.

"Find her!" Zerra shouted above.

Laira winced. She took a deep breath and held it. Struggling not to gag, she crawled into the steaming mound.

Her body convulsed and she clenched her fists and jaw. She wriggled around, feeling the foul slop flow around her, coating her hair, sliding down her clothes, clinging to her skin, and even filling her nostrils and ears. When she finally crawled out—sticky and covered with the stuff—she couldn't help it. She leaned her head down and vomited, and her body shook, and she almost passed out from the pain and disgust.

Trees shattered behind her as the rocs crashed through the canopy.

Still bound, steaming and fetid and coated with the mammoth dung, Laira crawled into the brush. Leaves and grass clung to her sticky skin.

Her scent was masked. Her body was camouflaged. She was battered and burnt and covered in dung, but she kept crawling, refusing to abandon hope. Behind her, she heard Zerra shouting at his men, insisting that his roc had smelled the maggot here. She heard the beasts caw. She heard them fly above, the hunters cursing, the flock confused.

"Just keep crawling, Laira," she whispered to herself. The foul waste entered her mouth and she spat it out. "Keep crawling. Never stop. You can escape them."

Through grass, under brambles that scratched her, and over stones that stabbed her, Laira kept crawling, her wrists and ankles still bound, until the sounds of the hunters grew distant behind her. And still she kept moving. She wriggled on, sticky and gagging every few feet, until she reached a declivity bumpy with stones.

She tried to crawl down to the valley below. Slick with the dung, she slipped over a slab of stone, and she rolled.

She tumbled down the slope, banging against tree roots, blinded with pain. Her elbow smashed against a rock, and she bit down on a scream. She seemed to roll forever, grass and dry leaves sticking to her, until she slammed into a mossy boulder, and her head banged against the stone.

Stars exploded across her vision. Her eyelids fluttered. She gasped, curling her fingers, struggling to cling to consciousness, but the blackness gave a mighty tug . . . and she faded.

SENA

Alone.

More than afraid, hurt, or ashamed—though he was those things too—Prince Sena Seran, Son of Raem, felt alone.

He sat in the corner of his prison cell, the top of Aerhein Tower. A barred window—barely larger than a porthole—broke the opposite wall. A ray of light shone into the chamber, falling upon him. Sena liked this time of day, the brief moment when the ray hit the wall near the floor, allowing him to sit in light and warmth. Soon the ray would move, creeping up the wall, moving over his head, leaving him and slowly fading into darkness.

But for now I have you here, friend, Sena thought, blinking into the beam. *Please don't leave me again.*

The beam began to rise as the sun moved, and Sena craned his neck, straightened his back, and tried to soak up some last moments of companionship, of sunlight, of safety. But then the beam was gone, hitting the wall above his head.

He supposed he could have stood up. Standing would make him taller, let him embrace the sun again. But he was too weak to stand most days. Too wounded. Too hungry. Too tired.

"Alone," he whispered.

He rattled his chains just to hear them answer, just to hear a sound. That was how his chains talked.

How long had he been here? Sena didn't know. At least a moon, he thought. Maybe longer.

"I'm sorry, Issari," he whispered. His chafed lips cracked and bled, and he sucked on the coppery liquid. "I'm sorry that I'm sick. I'm sorry that I shifted into a dragon. I miss you, sister."

He wondered where Issari was now. In her chamber in the palace, the gardens, perhaps the throne room? Was she thinking of him too? Sena had heard Issari several times since entering this prison. She had cried out behind the doors, calling his name, begging the guards to let her in. But they always turned her away. And Sena always tried to call out in return, but his throat was always too parched, his voice too weak.

Caw! Caw!

Sena raised his head. A crow had landed on the windowsill and stood between the bars. The bird glared at him and cawed again.

"Hello, friend," Sena whispered.

He began to crawl forward, desperate to caress this bird, to feel another living soul. The crow stared at him.

Caw!

You have freedom, Sena thought. *You have wings and can fly, yet you came here—to visit me.*

As he crawled closer, chains rattling, Sena found his mouth watering.

I can eat you.

Suddenly it seemed that this was no crow at all but a roasted duck, fatty and delicious, not perched on a windowsill but upon a bed of mushrooms and leeks. Sena licked his lips. Since landing in this cell, he had eaten nothing but the cold gruel the guards fed him once a day—a gray paste full of hairs, ants, and sometimes—depending on the guard—a glob of bubbling spit.

"But you are delicious, crow," Sena said, struggling to his feet. "You are a true friend—better than that damn light that keeps leaving me. Better than the rat that only bites me when I try to catch it." He reached out pale, trembling hands toward the crow, the shackles around his wrists clanking. "I'm going to eat you—ah!"

The crow bit him.

Sena brought his finger to his lips, tasting blood.

With a *caw* that sounded almost like a laugh, the crow flew off into the sky—back into that forbidden world, back into freedom.

Sena shook his fists at the barren window, spraying blood. It was just like that damn rat again. It was just like that damn beam of light. They all taunted him. They all pretended to be his friends. And they all left him.

He stared out the window. So many creatures flew across the sky these days. Birds. Demons. Creatures of scales, of rot, of blood, of jelly, of stone, of fire—a host of flying nightmares that cackled, grinned, sucked, spewed, swarmed, streamed, lived. Sometimes Sena thought he was delusional. Other times he thought the Abyss had risen into the world, that the endless lurid eyes and fangs were real, not just visions of his hunger but true terrors.

He shook his head wildly and knuckled his eyes, forcing himself to look away from the demons outside his window, from those taunting, cruel, cackling apparitions. They weren't real. They couldn't be real.

Alone . . . insane . . .

Sena trembled. It wasn't fair. The crow thought itself superior to him. Those winged visions of demons thought themselves superior too. If Sena had wings of his own, he could fly farther, higher, catch the damn bird, and—

But I do have wings, he thought.

Of course. He was cursed, impure, an abomination unto Taal.

I can become a dragon.

That sin had landed him in this tower cell in the first place. Perhaps it could also free him.

Wait, whispered a voice in his head. *Wait. You tried shifting into a dragon already. Don't you remember? You tried just yesterday. It hurt you. It—*

"Quiet!" Sena said, silencing that voice—that voice of the old him, of somebody who had been a prince, not a prisoner, of somebody who still clung to sanity. He hated that voice. He hated that false one, that liar.

He tightened his lips.

He summoned his magic.

Don't! cried the voice inside him. *Pain—*

Scales flowed across Sena, blue as the sky. Claws began to grow from his fingernails. His body grew larger, inflating, and—

Pain.

The chains that wrapped around him dug deep. He cried out. The metal links cut into him. His ballooning body was pressing against the bonds, and his blood spilled.

With a whimper, he released his magic.

He lay on the floor, trembling, small again, safe again, chained in the shackles that kept him human. He had always been able to shift with clothes, even with a sword at his waist, taking those objects—parts of him like his skin—into his dragon form. But these chains were foreign things, cruel, hurting.

"I'm sorry, Issari," he whispered.

The cell's doorknob rattled behind him.

Sena cowered, sure that the guards had heard him. They would kick him again, spit upon him, bang his head against the wall. He crawled into the corner as the door creaked open, raising his hands to shield his face.

"Please," he whispered.

But it was not the guards.

His father, King Raem Seran, stood at the doorway.

Clad in his bronze armor, the king stared down at his son in disgust. Sena blinked up at his father, and hope sprang inside him.

My father has come to free me.

"Father," he whispered, lips bleeding. "Forgive me. Please. Forgive me. I love you."

When Sena reached out to him, Raem grunted and kicked his hand aside.

"Forgive you?" Raem said. He sneered. "You are a weredragon, a filthy creature lower than lepers. I did not come here to forgive you." He lifted a bloody canvas sack. "I came here to show you what could have been your fate."

Raem upended the sack. A severed head spilled onto the floor, eyes still wide in frozen fear. Sena gasped and scampered away from the ghastly gift.

"A weredragon," Raem said. "My demons caught this one hiding under a bakery." He snorted a laugh. "It can be your friend. As you stare into its dead eyes, remember that you are alive, that I showed you mercy."

With that, his father turned and left the cell, slamming the door behind him.

Tears in his eyes, Sena raced toward the door. He slammed himself against the heavy oak, pounding it with his fists.

"Please, Father!" he shouted. "I'll do anything you ask. I'll never shift again. I . . . I'll hunt weredragons with you! I . . ."

His strength left him.

He slumped to the floor.

The severed head stared up at him, its mouth open, the stalk of its neck red. Sena pulled his knees to his chest and stared back into the lifeless eyes.

At least, he thought as the sunlight faded, *I'm no longer alone.*

ISSARI

She stood upon the balcony, the wind fluttering her tunic, watching the demons swarm over her city.

Eteer, center of the sprawling Eteerian civilization, had once been a city of pale towers rising into clear skies; swaying palm and fig trees; a peaceful blue sea lapping at mossy walls; and proud people robed in white, walking along cobbled streets, welcoming the ships that sailed in. Birds would sing among the trees, and the sweet scents of fruit and spices would waft upon the wind. Once, standing here, Issari would see a great mosaic of peace and beauty.

Today she saw a hive of rot and flame.

A thousand creatures of the Abyss filled the city now—crawling upon walls, festering upon roofs, and fluttering in the sky. Each of the creatures was a unique horror. Issari saw demons of scales, demons of tentacles, demons of slime, of rot, of fire. She saw creatures turned inside out, organs glistening upon their inverted skin. She saw bloated, warty things drag themselves along cobbled streets, leaving trails of slime. The heads of children, innocent and fair, rose upon the bodies of clattering centipedes. Bloated faces of dogs sneered upon the armored bodies of crabs. Conjoined twins, ten or more stitched together with demon thread, moved upon their many legs.

Some creatures were small, no larger than dogs. Others were as large as mules. Everywhere they sniffed, snorted, sought the weredragons. Everywhere they barged through doors, rummaged through temples, pulling out families, licking, smelling, rubbing, discarding.

Issari stood above, staring upon this waking nightmare, her eyes damp. Her fingers clung to the railing.

What has happened to my home?

A voice rose behind her, answering her thoughts.

"They are seeking weredragons. They are ugly, my daughter, and they frighten you, but they are purifying our city of the disease."

She turned to see her father step onto the balcony. He came to stand beside her, leaned over the railing, and watched the creatures swarm down the streets and across the roofs.

Issari spoke in a small voice. "But Father, aren't we just bringing a greater evil into our kingdom?"

Raem turned toward her, and she saw the anger in his eyes. He clenched his fists, and Issari stepped back, sure he would strike her; he had struck her many times before. But his fire died as fast as it had kindled, and he caressed her cheek.

"You are pure, Issari, the only pure thing I have left. But you are young, and you are innocent. There is no evil greater than having a pure human form and betraying it. Our lord Taal forbids tattoos, piercings, obesity, or any disgrace against the form he gave us. To shift into a reptile is the greatest abomination. These demons might look strange, but they are doing Taal's work."

Screams rose below, and Issari spun back toward the city. On a street not far away, a host of demons—red creatures with bat wings—dragged an old man from his home. The greybeard tried to fight them, but the demons clung with clawed hands. Their snouts sniffed, pressing against the man's skin.

"Weredragon, weredragon!" the demons cried. "We found a reptile!"

Issari sucked in her breath. At her side, Raem leaned forward, baring his teeth, seeming almost hungry.

The old man below managed to tear himself free. He burst into a run, only for the demons to leap onto his legs and knock him down. Then, as Issari watched and gasped, the man shifted.

A thin silver dragon beat his wings, rising into the air. Before he could clear the roofs, the company of demons leaped onto the dragon like wolves on a bison. They slammed the silver beast onto the cobblestones and laughed, clawed, bit. They tore off scales, scattering them across the street, and blood splashed. With a whimper, the dragon lost his magic, returning to human form.

Issari looked away, but Raem pushed her face back toward the city.

"Watch, daughter," said the king. "You must see this."

The demons tore the old man apart. One demon lifted a severed leg over its head, parading it as a trophy. Other demons tore out internal organs, and one began to feast upon the entrails. The demons danced with their prizes, slick with blood.

Issari winced, horror rising inside her. She closed her eyes. "This is evil, Father. This is wrong."

He gripped her wrist and his eyes blazed. "This is dominion. One cannot rule a kingdom with compassion, only with strength. With your siblings gone, you are my heir. This land will someday be yours. I will no longer pamper you. Accustom yourself to blood. When you are Queen, you too will shed blood . . . or others will shed yours."

Issari did not want to be Queen. She wished she could fly away too—like Laira. She closed her eyes, imagining that she too could shift. If she could become a dragon, she could fly off this balcony, soar so high even the demons could not catch her. She would head north, find her mother and sister, and flee this horrible city.

Requiem's Song

Yet as her father had said, she was pure. No reptile curse filled her veins. She remained a young woman, trapped upon this balcony.

She opened her eyes and mouth, about to plead with her father, to beg him to return the demons to the Abyss, when the crone stepped onto the balcony.

"So here they are—father and sister to the maggot."

Issari spun around and gasped. In the balcony doorway stood the strangest woman she'd ever seen. The crone was bent over, wizened as a raisin, and clad in animal skins. Warts covered her hooked nose, and her fingernails were long and yellow. Wisps of white hair covered her scalp, and her mouth opened in a cruel, toothless grin.

Is this a demon? Issari wondered, heart racing.

"Who are you?" Raem demanded, taking a step toward the crone. "How did you pass the guards?"

The wizened old creature cackled. She reached out twig-like fingers to rap his armor. "You are a man of metal, of might, of many demons. But Old Shedah still has some tricks." She spat right onto the balcony floor, then turned toward Issari. "Well . . . and look at this one. A fair, ripe fruit, she is." The crone reached up to stroke Issari's breast. "You are taller and fairer than your sister. She is a worm, but you are a rare flower. You would make a fine bride for my chieftain."

Issari took a step backward, banging her back against the balcony railing. "Stay away, witch! How dare you speak of my sister?"

"Witch? No, I am no witch." Shedah bared her toothless gums in a mockery of a grin. "I am Shaman of the Goldtusk tribe, once the sanctuary of Queen Anai, that diseased reptile, and Laira, the little maggot." She stroked Issari's cheek, her fingernails sharp. "Your mother and sister. I have traveled for long days to this land,

129

moving down the shadowy paths unknown to those of simple minds. I bring news of them, oh princess of distant lands."

Raem snarled and grabbed the old woman's wrist, tugging her away from Issari. "Keep your filthy hands to yourself." He stepped back into the palace, dragging the crone with him. "Guards! Guards, where—"

When they stepped into the chamber, both king and princess gasped. The guards lay on the floor, fast asleep, lips fluttering as they snored.

Shedah cackled and spat upon one. "Weak worms. How did you folk ever build a kingdom of stone and metal? You are guarded by weak boys, their cheeks smoother than my backside." The crone snorted. "Come north across the sea, oh king, and you will see the strength of true warriors."

Raem's face flushed. He slid his khopesh from his belt and raised the curved blade. Issari had to race forward and stop him.

"Father! Wait. She knows Mother. She knows Laira."

Looking back at the shaman, Issari trembled. Could it be? Could this crone be speaking truth? Issari's eyes stung and her knees shook.

My mother . . . my sister . . .

Issari could not remember them, for they had fled too long ago. Father had smashed all paintings, statues, and engravings depicting Queen Anai and Princess Laira, but Issari had always dreamed of seeing them again. If this shaman had news, there was hope.

"What do you know?" she said, turning toward Shedah. "Tell us. Tell us everything."

Shedah licked her lips. "My sweet child, your mother is dead. Burned at the stake. I watched her burn and I spat upon her charred corpse."

Issari stared, unable to breathe, and her eyes stung.

Mother . . . no . . .

Issari had been only a babe when Mother fled this city. She could not remember the woman, but she dreamed about her every night. In her dreams, Mother looked like her—her black hair braided, her eyes green and soft, her face kind. All her life that whisper, that warm vision, had comforted Issari, for she knew that even if Mother was far away, she still lived. She still cared for her daughter.

Dead. Burned.

Tears gathered in Issari's eyes.

"You are lying!" she shouted at the crone.

Shedah reached into her pouch and produced a silver amulet. It bore an engraving of Taal—a man with his head lowered, his arms hanging at his sides, his palms facing outward—a sigil of purity and humility.

"The amulet of Eteer's queen—Anai's last relic of her once royal past." The shaman tossed the talisman toward Issari. "Keep it. And whenever you look at it, remember that your mother screamed like a butchered pig when the flames licked the flesh off her bones."

As Issari clutched the amulet, Raem grabbed the crone's arms and leaned down, glaring at her.

"What of Laira?" the king demanded. "What of my daughter?"

Shedah licked her lips with her long, white tongue. "The maggot fled our tribe. She was heading north when we lost her scent, but I know where she was going." Shedah pressed her withered hand against the king's cheek. "I will reveal all to you, mighty king, in return for but one gift."

Raem clutched the woman's arms so tightly they seemed ready to snap. "What do you desire?"

"The same as you, my lord. The same as all who are wise. *Power.*" She sneered. "For years, I placed leeches upon the flesh of Laira, sucking up her blood for my potions. The blood of a princess is mighty, and my stores run low." The shaman turned toward Issari and gave her a hungry, lustful look. "Give me your one daughter, and I will give you the other."

JEID

He flew.

Sometimes he just needed to fly.

The night stretched around him, moonless, starless, a world without sight, a sea of wind and blackness and cold air. He did not know where he flew. Most nights he no longer cared.

Jeid Blacksmith, men used to call him—a forger of bronze.

Grizzly, his children called him—a shaggy, endearing old beast, lumbering and harmless.

Diseased, said those who lived in wilderness and towns. A creature. Cursed.

Flying here upon the wind, he no longer knew who he was. He no longer knew what to call himself.

"Who am I, Keyla?" he asked, the wind all but drowning his voice.

He saw her face in the night—his wife, her hair golden in the sun, her smile bright. A sad woman—her smile had always seemed sad to him—but one who clung to every sliver of joy, cradling and nourishing it, letting it grow even through pain.

"You are Jeid." She spoke in his mind and touched his cheek. "You are my husband. You are a father to our children."

He lowered his head. He wanted to tell her. He wanted to tell his wife that their youngest daughter was dead, that the people of the plains—perhaps Zerra's wandering tribe, perhaps the people of Oldforge or another town—had poisoned her.

But Keyla already knew. He saw that knowledge in her eyes.

"You're together now," Jeid whispered. "And I want to join you."

The pain constricted his throat. How easy it would be—to shift into human form, to plummet down through this darkness, to hit the ground and feel no pain, only a relief from pain, only the rise of his soul to the stars. And he would be with Keyla and Requiem again. He could hold his wife, kiss his daughter, nevermore feel hurt, nevermore feel alone and afraid and torn.

"You must be strong," Keyla said, and he barely saw her now. His wife was but a wisp, a fading memory, a voice of starlight. "For the others."

Rage filled Jeid. The fire crackled through his body. He released it with a great, showering blaze, a beacon that any roc for marks could see. But Jeid no longer cared.

"Why must this be my task?" His wings shook, and his claws dug into his soles. "Why must I lead this new tribe? I am tired. I want to sleep. I want to be with you again."

He looked up to the sky. The clouds parted and he saw three stars—the tail of the dragon, the new constellation that shone in the skies. And there he saw a silver countenance, no longer his wife but his daughter. Young Requiem shone above, wise and sad like her mother had been.

And Jeid knew the answer.

"Because I vowed to you, Requiem." His eyes stung. "I vowed to build a home in your name—so no others would die like you died." He shook, scales rattling. "But I wish you were here with me. I wish you could live in this home too, my daughter."

The clouds gathered again, the light faded, and she was gone.

Jeid blasted out more fire. He sucked in air, ground his teeth, and kept flying.

He flew in blackness.

He flew throughout the night—to remember and to forget.

Requiem's Song

A hint of dawn gilded the east, and landforms emerged below, charcoal beneath the black sky—the whisper of hills, valleys, and fields of grass. Jeid turned and flew back north until he saw it, a great shelf of stone that split the world. The escarpment spread across the horizon, the cliffs gleaming bronze as the sun rose. He flew across the river, rose above the mountainside, and saw the canyon there—a den, a hideaway, a seed of a home. He opened his wings wide, catching air, and glided down into the gorge.

As soon as he touched the ground, he saw it.

Blood on the stones.

His nostrils flared. The place stank of injury. Jeid moved his head from side to side, clinging to his dragon form.

"Father!" he called out.

His heart pounded. Had the rocs finally dared attack the escarpment, overcoming their fear of the place? Had the townsfolk invaded?

"Father!" he shouted.

Finally the old man's voice rose in answer. "I'm here. It's all right, Jeid. Come into the cave."

Exhaling in relief, Jeid released his magic. He hopped between boulders in human form, entered the eastern cave, and crawled through a short tunnel and into a chamber.

He straightened and lost his breath.

"Stars above."

His father sat on the floor, clad in his blue druid robes, blood staining his long white beard. Before him, a shivering young man lay upon a rug. The stranger's foot was missing. The stump was raw and red, still gushing blood, the shattered bones exposed.

"Hold him down, Jeid," Eranor said calmly. "Quickly. I need you to hold him down."

"Who—" Jeid began.

"Now."

Jeid nodded, stepped forward, and knelt behind the injured man. The stranger was shivering, his skin gray, his eyes sunken. Jeid held onto his arms.

When Eranor reached into the wound, the man bucked and screamed.

"Hold him firmly!" Eranor said.

Jeid nodded and tightened his grip, pinning the young man down. Eyes grim, Eranor fished out the sputtering vein. Fingers red, he tied the vein shut.

"Keep him still." Eranor swiped his beard across his shoulder. "This will hurt him."

"Who is he?" Jeid asked. The young man relaxed in his grip; he shivered upon the rug, his skin the color of the cave walls.

Eranor replied calmly. "A Vir Requis."

Jeid lost his breath. He stared down at the injured man. "You are . . . you can become a dragon."

The young man looked up at him. He managed to nod wanly. "I've heard of you." His voice was weak and hoarse. "You are Jeid Blacksmith of Oldforge. The whole north is speaking of you." He coughed, licked his lips, and managed to keep talking, his voice barely more than a whisper. "I'm from the Redbone tribe. When they discovered my curse, they chained my ankle to our totem. I shifted into a dragon. When my body grew, the chain dug through me. I rose as a dragon." He managed a wry smile. "My human foot remained behind. I—" Coughs overcame his words, and it was a moment before he could speak again. "I heard of the escarpment. I had to find you. I had to . . ."

His eyes rolled back, his body became limp, and he fell silent.

"Keep him down," Eranor said. He reached for a bronze saw and a bowl of boiling water. "He's unconscious, not dead, and he might wake. It's best if he sleeps through this part."

When Eranor raised the saw, Jeid felt himself pale. "By the stars, what..."

"It's not a clean cut." Eranor squinted at the wound. "The bone is jagged. If I sew shut the stump, the bone would only cut through it. I must file it down."

Jeid grimaced as his father worked, sawing through bone, filing the edges down, and cutting out infected flesh. The young man woke once and screamed, and Jeid held him pinned down. When the man fainted again, Eranor pulled skin over the wound and stitched it shut.

"Will he live?" Jeid asked, kneeling above the stranger.

Eranor wiped his hands on a rug. "I pray to our stars that he does."

Jeid's fingers trembled. He stared down at the pale young man, and strangely, despite the blood and horror, joy kindled in him. His eyes stung.

We are not alone.

He was about to speak again when he felt warm wetness against his knee. He looked down to see blood seeping from under the young man's back. When he raised the man to a sitting position, he saw it there—a broken arrow beneath his shoulder blade, sunken deep into his torso.

Dawn spilled into the cave when the young man died.

Jeid held him in his arms, remembering the night Requiem had died in his embrace, and here he was a father again; all these cursed, lost souls were his children now.

"Rise, friend," he whispered and kissed the man's forehead. "Rise to the Draco stars. Their light will guide you home."

That evening, Jeid buried the young man in the valley beside his daughter, and he placed a boulder above his grave. Eranor stood beside him, his beard flowing in the wind, and prayed the old prayers of druids.

Two fallen Vir Requis, Jeid thought, staring at the twin graves. *Two more burdens to bear.* He looked up at the sunset. The first stars emerged, and the dragon constellation glowed above. *Two more souls to guide me.*

"Who am I, Father?" he asked softly.

Eranor placed a hand on his shoulder. "You are a son. You are a father. And you are not alone." The old man stared south across the plains of swaying grass. "Others are blessed. Others need you. You will build them the tribe that you dream of. They will find you, or we will find them, and we—the Vir Requis—will gather here. We will have a home."

That night Jeid did not fly again. He sat in the cave by his father, and he stared at the embers in their brazier, and he thought of Tanin and Maev who were flying south, and he thought of those who had died.

I will fly on, he thought. *But I will no longer fly lost in darkness. Our lights shine across the world. I will be a beacon to them until we shine together.*

LAIRA

"So this is how I end my first hunt," Laira muttered to herself as she crawled through the forest. "Bruised, bound, and covered in mammoth shite."

She sighed, then winced with pain; even sighing hurt now. She supposed it could have been worse. If those rocs caught her, it *would* be worse.

Laira could still hear the birds above. It had been a full day and night since she had escaped the pyre, and the sun was rising again, yet still they hunted her, scanning the skies in pairs. Every few moments, she heard the fetid vultures fly above the canopy, and the oil they secreted fell like foul rain. Thankfully the trees were thick and autumn leaves still covered the branches, shielding her from view. Even in areas where the canopy broke, Laira—covered in mud, dung, and dry leaves—appeared like nothing but a clump of dirt.

Zerra always said I was nothing but filth, she thought, a wry smile twisting her lips.

The latest roc vanished overhead, leaving his stench—like moldy meat—to waft down upon her, mingling with her own smell, which was no more appealing. Laira crawled under a tilted oak, rummaged in a pile of fallen leaves, and finally found a stone the right size. She smashed it against another stone, chipping it into a blade. She sat upright, her head dizzy, and worked for a while, rubbing the sharp stone against her bonds. Finally the rope tore, and she brought her arms back forward and examined her wrists.

They were a bloody, muddy mess, and her hands blazed as fresh blood pumped into them. She cut the ropes around her ankles next and winced. Her feet were in even worse shape. Not only had the ropes chafed her ankles, the fire had burned her soles; ugly welts now rose there. She didn't know what was worse: her burns, bruises, cuts, or the foul paste coating her, but she thought it was the burns. She needed speed now more than anything, and with burnt feet, how could she walk or run? Even with her ropes cut, was she still bound to crawl to whatever safety she could find?

Laira sighed. Was there even safety in this world for her? Even if she did escape the Goldtusk tribe—the only home she'd ever known—would she starve in the wilderness or freeze once the snows began to fall? As a babe, she had lived in a distant land, a sunny kingdom named Eteer, but they had banished her. Eteer too hated and hunted weredragons. Even if she could find her way back, no home awaited her across the sea.

A roc's cry sounded above, and Laira flattened herself down. When it had passed, she winced and bit her lip, spat out the foul taste, and attempted to stand.

Her soles blazed as if new fires burned them. She fell into the dry leaves, moaning and dizzy.

"Maybe I'll just crawl for a while longer."

She crawled until she reached a stream, the shallow water gurgling over smooth, mossy stones. She ached to wash off the dung, which had dried into a flaky paste, but dared not; the rocs could return anytime, and without the stench to mask her scent, they could sniff her out. She couldn't resist washing her feet, however. Dipping them into the stream shot a bolt through her, but soon the cold water soothed her. They had tied her barefooted to the pyre, and so she ripped off squares from her fur cloak, washed them in the stream, then tied them around her feet with vines.

Requiem's Song

When she stood up gingerly on the riverbank, she did not fall. She took one step, wobbled, and then another. She held a tree for support and limped a few more steps. It hurt and her head still swam, but she could walk.

Probably looking like some evil spirit from a fireside tale, covered in filth and leaves, she wobbled onward. There was only one place she could go now.

"The escarpment," she whispered.

For years, she had dreamed of traveling there. Her mother had claimed it was just a legend, yet it had to be true. The rocs dared not fly near the cliffs. Even Zerra never dared hunt in its shadow. Why else would they fear the place if not because . . .

"Dragons live there," Laira whispered, and tears stung her eyes. "Others with my disease. Other banished, cursed souls. I can find a home there."

Her head felt full of fog, and she struggled to remember the last movements of her tribe. Goldtusk had been traveling south throughout the fall, planning to spend the winter in the warm, southern coast. That meant the escarpment would be northwest from here—many days away.

"I can walk," she whispered, shivering. "I can survive the journey. I can drink from streams and I can gather berries and mushrooms. I can make it."

A roc dived overhead, and Laira pressed herself against a tree and remained still until it passed. Then she moved again, limping but trudging on. Using the rising sun's location, she could determine north easily enough. The moss grew on only one side of the trees, another marker to guide her.

"Step by step, Laira," she told herself. "Just keep going and you'll find the others."

A small voice inside her whispered that she was mad, that she could never find a humble escarpment in the endless world. In the vastness of the wilderness, even creatures as large as dragons were small. But walking—even limping—was better than curling up and dying, and so she kept going.

"I will always keep going," she promised herself. "If I die, I die moving."

She kept walking until the sun reached its zenith, its heat dispersing the mist. Dapples of light revealed mushrooms, berries, and fallen pine cones. Laira spent a while collecting a meal upon a flat rock. She had not eaten since . . . she couldn't even remember the last time; it had been at least two days, maybe twice that long. She dared wash her hands and face in a nearby stream, sit down, and eat. The food tasted like the dung. She had hoped the meal would invigorate her, but it only made her belly swirl, and she gagged.

For long moments, she lay on her back, struggling to breathe. She wasn't sure how many scrapes and cuts covered her. It felt like dozens, some mild—mere scratches from brambles—others deeper, like the cuts along her wrists and ankles. She didn't mind the pain, but as she lay watching the rustling leaves, she began to worry about infection. The tribe warriors sometimes rubbed their arrowheads with mammoth dung; they claimed that it would spread rot through a wound. After her splash in the mammoth's waste to conceal her scent, had she doomed herself to slow death by disease? Had she fought, fled, and gone through this pain simply for a lingering demise in the wilderness?

If no more rocs arrive by afternoon, I'll wash myself in the nearest stream, she decided.

For now she had to keep moving. The farther she walked from the tribe, the safer she'd be. She knew Zerra. Sooner or later, he would spit, curse her name, and give up the chase. He would claim she had died in the wilderness, then keep traveling south with his tribe, not willing to abandon his journey for a mere maggot like her.

"But I won't die in the wilderness," she whispered, rising to her feet. "I will find others like me. I will live through this."

She kept walking, every part of her aching, until the sun dipped into the afternoon. Only three times did she hear rocs, and they were farther away, still hunting her but confused, not sure where to look. Slowly Laira's fear of them eased, but her fear of infection kept growing, and her dizziness would not leave her. She needed healing herbs but didn't know the craft. Back at Goldtusk, only the crone Shedah knew healing, and she would share the art with none.

Goldtusk. The very thought of the word made her eyes sting and iciness wash her belly. The tribe had been her only home since she'd been a toddler. Laira had often dreamed of fleeing, of finding others like her, other cursed ones, able to become dragons. Yet now that she had truly fled, the fear would not leave her.

She sucked in breath and tightened her lips.

You can do this, Laira. You are ready. You are strong. You have dreamed of this all your life, and now the day is here.

"Freedom," she whispered. "A chance for a new, better life. All I must do is *live.*"

When evening fell, she came upon another stream. She had not heard pursuit since the afternoon, and she deemed the filth covering her a greater danger than rocs. She had been coated in the mammoth dung for two days now; if the rocs didn't kill her, this poison would.

Wincing, she undressed and stepped into the water. It was so cold it hurt like fire, and Laira cried out in pain. Shivering, she submerged herself and bathed as best she could. Teeth chattering, she then scrubbed her filthy furs between smooth stones to clean out the dried flakes.

She climbed onto the riverbank—trembling, naked, her skin pale blue. After hanging her wet cloak upon a branch, she examined her wounds and grimaced. Brambles had painted her with a network of raw, red scratches. The fall through the canopy had covered her with bruises; some were as large as apples, their blue centers fading into black rings. Cuts surrounded her wrists and ankles, carved by the ropes. The worst wounds were on her feet; the heat had raised welts on her soles and toes, white and swollen.

The sun was sinking rapidly and Laira yawned. It was an action so mundane, so comforting, that it filled her with a little bit of warmth even as she still shivered. Yawning was good. Yawning was healthy. Yawning was *normal*. Her furs wouldn't dry until tomorrow, not in this cold weather, but she could curl up under dry leaves. She could sleep, regain some strength, wake up and search for more food, then walk some more.

Tomorrow she would hum a little tune as she walked, she told herself. She would remember all the old jokes her mother had told her. It would be a happy day—a day free from all the old pain. Zerra wouldn't be around to beat her. Shedah wouldn't scratch her, spit upon her, or leech her for potions. Laira would *live*—perhaps for the first time in her life. She would find a new home and this nightmare would be over. She wiped tears from her eyes, allowing herself a shaky smile.

"I will be all r—"

A roc cried above. Laira froze.

Stars, oh stars, I had just washed off the stench, and they're back.

She clenched her fists.

There is only one above, she told herself. *I can fight one. I can shift into a dragon and burn it. I—*

More shrieks answered. Three rocs, maybe four—no more than a dozen. Laira's head throbbed. She was too weary, too hurt to fight that many, even in dragon form.

The shrieks sounded again, and she took a shuddering breath. The rocs were still far—a mark away, maybe farther. They could not smell her from that distance. She only had to remain silent, to remain hidden, to—

A growl sounded in the shadows behind her.

Laira spun around.

Yellow eyes gleamed in the brush.

The growl rose again in the darkness.

Behind her, the sun vanished behind the trees.

A shadow slunk forward, and in the dying light, Laira saw the creature, and she felt the blood drain from her face.

The saber-toothed cat bristled, muscular and hulking, several times Laira's size. Its fangs shone, large and sharp as swords. The beast took another step toward her and growled again.

Laira gasped and took a step back.

In the distance, the rocs cried; they were moving closer.

Shift into a dragon! Laira told herself. *Become a dragon and burn it!*

Yet how could she? If she flew or blew fire, the rocs would see her. Even just shifting would rattle the trees like a mammoth stampede, raise a ruckus of clattering scales, and reveal her location.

The saber-toothed cat growled louder and crouched, ready to pounce.

Never removing her eyes from its gaze, Laira knelt and grabbed a stone.

With a roar, the great cat leaped.

Laira tossed her stone, hurtling it forward with all her might. The projectile crashed into the cat's forehead, and Laira leaped aside.

The cat stumbled backward into a tree trunk, shook its head wildly, and faced her again. It padded forward, a bleeding gash on its forehead.

Couched in the dry leaves, Laira grabbed a fallen branch. She snapped it across her knee, then waved the sharp end at the cat.

"Be gone!" She bared her own teeth—pathetically small compared to its fangs. "Go! Go!"

If she ran, it would chase. If she showed weakness, it would pounce again. She waved the stick and hopped around, trying to seem as menacing as possible. Naked, scrawny, and wounded, she doubted she appeared like much of a threat.

Her suspicions were confirmed when the cat leaped again.

Laira thrust her stick.

The cat brushed it aside with its paw and slammed into her, knocking her down.

Laira grimaced. The saber teeth shone and drove down.

I have no choice.

With a hiss, Laira summoned her magic.

Scales rose across her. The cat's fangs slammed against them and bounced back.

As her body began to grow, Laira shoved the beast off. She swiped her own paw, lashing her sprouting claws against the animal. The saber-toothed cat whimpered and fell.

The rocs shrieked above, and her body was still growing. A tail sprouted behind her, her neck kept lengthening, and the trees shook as she banged against them. Laira growled, baring her fangs, still only half-dragon.

The saber-toothed cat growled back, then whimpered, turned tail, and fled into the shadows.

An instant before cracking the trunks around her in a ruckus, Laira released her magic.

She shrank back into human form and lay shivering.

The cries of rocs moved farther away, and the last light faded.

Laira lay, enveloped in blackness, shivering in the cold, naked and wounded. Around her in the forest, she heard things stir and move, and a growl rose somewhere to her left, and paws padded to her right.

She hugged herself, unable to stop shaking.

"Please, stars of the dragon, please," she prayed. "Look after me. Don't let me die this night."

She dared not light a fire, not in case the rocs returned. So weak she could barely move, she felt around for her stick and used it to dig a little burrow. She curled up inside and pulled dry leaves over her, hugging her knees for warmth. She had never felt so cold, lost, and afraid.

"I won't die this night, Mother," she whispered between chattering teeth. "I will live. I will live."

She lay trembling and awake, staring into the darkness as growls, snorts, and glowing eyes filled the forest around her.

ANGEL

The voices screamed inside her, shrill, deep, twisting, hoarse, rising and shattering like glass.

We don't want to die!

Feed us entrails!

Attack, fight, bite, eat, feed, tear, rip!

Pain. Pain. Pain! This must end. Stop! Mercy!

Angel sneered, smoke rising from between her teeth, and clutched her head. The voices would forever fill her, she knew. Even here. Even risen from the Abyss. Even upon the soil of Eteer, this kingdom aboveground, the cries echoed.

They hurt.

They hurt us!

Hate! Bite! Tear! Punish!

A thousand voices, all her own. A child in shadows. A child chained, whipped, broken, deformed. A creature risen to domination, to rule upon a land of darkness, to govern minions of flayed skin, of rotted flesh, creatures twisting and begging and laughing.

"I have suffered, King Raem," she said, staring at the mortal. "I have suffered like you cannot imagine. A thousand times I died and rose from death. A thousand hurts coil inside me. A thousand voices of my own scream inside my skull of stone." She unfurled her wings until they banged against the walls of his bedchamber. Her flaming hair crackled, and her saliva dripped from her maw to burn holes into the rug. "Let me grow. Let me become the queen I am destined to be."

Requiem's Song

Raem stood by the window, staring out upon the city. The towers, domes, and walls of Eteer spread below the azure sky. All over the city, the cackle of demons and screams of mortals rose in a song.

"I know what you would ask of me," the king said. "And I refuse."

Angel hissed, leaped toward him, and grabbed his shoulders. She spun him around until he faced her. She bared her fangs, blasting smoke against his face.

"Feed us." She tossed back her head and roared. She dug her claws into his shoulders, and his blood seeped. "Feed us the flesh of mortals. Not weredragons." She spat. "Weredragons taste like the piss of gods. We crave the sweeter meat." She licked her chops, already imagining it. "Feed us the pure mortals of your kingdom, the blessed forms of Taal, untainted with the reptile disease. The silver god of purity is vain. For ten thousand years, he laughed as I screamed in my prison. I would feast upon his sons and daughters."

Raem stared at her, and only the slightest sneer found his lips. "No. You will not feed upon my kingdom. You may eat weredragons, and you may eat the flesh of animals. But the people of Eteer are blessed with Taal's form. I will not allow a horde of diseased, impure creatures to consume my pure people."

Angel sneered, the hunger for human flesh twisting in her belly. She needed his blessing. She was still bound to him, still his prisoner, even here in the sunlight. Even here the ancient laws bound her.

"Feed us!" she screamed. She lashed her arm, knocked over a stone vase, and shattered it. Sparks flew from her flaming hair. "Feed us the flesh of Eteer. Feed us and we will grow. Your demons are still small, King of Mortals. We have shrunk in our prison. We have grown weak. Feed us pure man-flesh and we will become larger than dragons. How can we fight dragons unless we grow to their size?"

Raem snorted. "The weredragons cower. They hide in cellars and sewers. You are more than capable of flushing them out, even with your smaller forms. You will obey me, Angel. If I discover one drop of pure human blood consumed, I will hold you accountable."

Angel snickered. Fast as a striking asp, she thrust a claw, scratching Raem's cheek. Blood spilled. Angel brought the claw to her lips. She licked Raem's blood and a shiver ran through her. The cracks on her body of stone widened, spewing droplets of lava.

"You taste of reptile." She spat. "The weredragon disease flows in your blood. Did you think I could not smell it? I knew of your shame my first day here. You—"

He slammed his sword against her cheek.

Her stone face cracked, spilling smoke, and she laughed.

"You forget your boundaries," Raem said, glaring at her.

Lava dripped from her shattered cheek as Angel cackled. "You do not like me speaking of your secret, do you? Perhaps I will trumpet the news from the city walls. Perhaps all shall know that Raem, King of Eteer, is a filthy were—"

"By the light of Taal!" he shouted, interrupting her. "Angel, Queen of Demons, harken to me. As King of Eteer, I hereby banish you back to the Aby—"

She shrieked.

She lashed all four arms, cracking his armor, shattering the room around her. A clay urn shattered, spilling wine across the floor. She leaped, swiped her claws, and knocked down a limestone statue of an ancient, bearded king. Her arms spun, tearing down the room, digging ruts into the walls and floor. Clay tablets bearing cuneiform writings—epic tales of ancient heroes—

fell off shelves, shattering into a heap of shards. Her flames blasted out, and tapestries burned.

Raem stood as she raged, calm, staring.

"Speak your treasonous words again," the king said, "and I will complete the banishment."

"Then send me hunting outside your borders." Angel panted, tongue lolling. "Send me to the deserts of Tiranor in the west. Send me to the barbarous lands north of the sea. Send me to the city-states in the south, your old enemies. I will find mortal flesh elsewhere."

Raem shook his head. "You are not to leave this city, Angel. The walls of Eteer are your boundaries. I have given you more freedom than you've known in ten thousand years, but you are still my slave. You will remain here until you've captured all the weredragons."

She howled. "Your weredragons do not satisfy the hunger in our bellies. Your flesh stinks of starlight."

"Once they are all dead, I will send you hunting beyond my borders. Not until then." Raem leaned down and lifted a small, obsidian statuette of a winged bull. He placed it back on a shelf. "More remain in this city. Still your demons unearth one every day. Your servitude will continue." He turned back toward the window. "I have errands in the north. I seek a particular weredragon across the sea—a weredragon that betrayed me, a weredragon I will hurt. A weredragon named Laira." He turned back toward Angel, and his fists clenched, and his eyes hardened. "While I am away, you are not to leave this city, nor are you to touch my people. My daughter Issari will sit upon the throne until I return. You are to obey her, even as the hunger eats through your belly."

You will break!
You are broken!
You will never rise!

Help, mercy, stop, take it back!

Yes, Angel hungered. Forever hunger lived inside her. Hunger for an end to those voices. Hunger for blood, for flesh, for power, for freedom. Hunger for a child.

She placed her hand against her belly, aching for spawn, for the rustle of unholy life within her. The ravenous lust blazed through her loins with dark fire.

She grabbed Raem's shoulders again.

"I hunger for you. Take me."

He grabbed onto her hard, stone body that leaked smoke and flame. She sneered, turned her back to him, and dropped to her hands and knees. She howled as he took her, head tossed back, her flames blasting out from her eyes, her claws digging into the floor.

The fire consumed her.

For a precious few moments, the voices fell silent.

For now her craving was sated, but as he took her, Angel swore: *I will slay all his weredragons, and I will feast upon the flesh of his people, and when he has placed a child within my womb, I will feast upon Raem too.*

She welcomed his seed into her, and she smiled.

TANIN

Whenever Tanin slept, he remembered.

Even here in the forest, his sister sleeping beside him, he thrashed, half-awake, the memories clawing at him, dragging him down to that dark place eleven years ago.

"We have to run," Jeid had said, bursting into the smithy with wild hair and flushed cheeks. "We have to fly."

Tanin had stood at the forge that day, fourteen years old, an apprentice to his father. The brick walls of the smithy rose around him. Upon hooks hung hammers, tongs, pokers, and all the other tools of the trade. A cauldron of bronze bubbled beside Tanin, drenching him with heat, and sweat dampened his hair. He had the mold ready—a sickle for Farmer Gam who grew rye outside the town—and was just about the pour the liquid metal.

"What do you mean?" he asked his father.

He had never seen the old man look like this. Jeid Blacksmith—Grizzly to his children—was always a little disheveled, what with his shaggy hair, wild beard, and rough cloak of fur and leather. But today, for the first time, Tanin saw his father look scared. Tanin had seen Grizzly knock out malevolent drunkards, fight an invasion of a roaming tribe, and even battle a saber-toothed cat with only a simple dagger. But Jeid had never looked *scared*, and that fear now seeped into Tanin.

"They saw me fly," Jeid said, voice low. "They know. We have to run."

Tanin froze, unable to breathe. He grabbed his hammer.

They know.

From outside rose the townsfolk's cries. "Weredragons! The curse has come to Oldforge. Burn the Blacksmiths!"

Tanin could remember little of what happened next, only the heat of flames, the bite of an arrow in his thigh, the mad faces dancing around him, hundreds of men come to slay him. Maev flew above, a green dragon roaring fire, pelted with arrows. Mother tried to stop the mob; Zerra clubbed her, knocking her down, and the villagers stomped her, dragged her body through the village behind a horse. And blood. Everywhere the blood of men and dragons. A burning child ran between the huts, screaming as the flames engulfed him.

"Fly, Tanin!" Jeid called.

"Tanin, where are you going?" Maev shouted. "Fly!"

But he would not fly. He ran through the village. The arrow protruded from his thigh, and behind him, he heard his own uncle—Zerra, twin to his father—shouting to kill the creatures. But Tanin kept running, limping now, until he reached her home.

"Ciana!" he cried, barging into the hut. "Ciana, where are you?"

She emerged from shadows, dressed in her white gown. A girl of fourteen, she had long, dark hair and large gray eyes that he thought very beautiful.

"Tanin," she whispered. A haunted sound. The sound of old ghosts. A sound of old pain. Even then, Tanin knew that the sound—that soft utterance, that whisper of his name—would forever echo through his mind.

"Flee with me." He panted and reached out to her. "I must leave now. Flee with me to the mountains. We can marry in the wilderness. We can live together far from this place." The cries of the mob rose from the fields; they would be here soon. "I love you."

Ciana—his beloved, the girl he had kissed upon the hill just last night, the girl he had vowed to marry someday—stared at him silently, and something filled her eyes. Not love. Not fear. Slowly Tanin recognized it.

Disgust.

"You are a weredragon." She took a step back, and her father approached and placed an arm around her. "You . . . you are diseased." She shuddered. "I kissed you. I let you hold me." Tears streamed down her cheeks, and her voice rose to a hoarse cry. "Kill him, Father! Kill the creature!"

As her father reached for a knife, Tanin fled. He too wept. They waited outside—the mob of townsfolk, waving torches, firing arrows. Beyond them he saw his family: his wise grandfather, Eranor, a white dragon; his father, Jeid, a copper dragon blowing fire; his younger sister, Maev, a slim green dragon. They flew above the fields, arrows whistling around them, calling for him.

Tanin shifted.

He too became a dragon.

Arrows slammed into his scales, and one pierced his wing, and he flew.

They fled over the forest. They raced across the wilderness until they found a hidden cave and cowered, wounded, afraid, banished. And still Ciana's words echoed in his mind.

Tanin.

You are diseased.

Kill him, Father!

"I love you," he whispered, reaching out to her, seeking her through shadows and light. "I'm not a creature. I love you. I—"

"Stars above, Tanin! I love you too, but stop grabbing at me like a drunkard."

He opened his eyes.

He blinked.

His sister sat beside him, wrapped in furs—no longer the young girl from that day but a grown woman, her face a mask of fading bruises, her arms strong and her bottom lip thrust out in her permanent gesture of disdain.

Tanin looked around him, for a moment confused, but then remembered his location. Of course. They had been flying for three nights since leaving the escarpment, heading south toward the coast. Birches grew around him, their trunks dark in the sunset, their leaves deep red. The sun was only an orange sliver between the boles; soon it would be gone.

"I was dreaming." He sat up in his bed of leaves and fur pelts.

Maev snorted. "I could tell. You kept talking about loving this and loving that." She rolled her eyes. "What were you dreaming about—being some hero? Saving a damsel in distress?" She shoved him back down. "Quit dreaming and get ready to fly! We're flying to save a prince, dear brother, not a damsel for you to bed." She tapped her chin. "Unless you prefer princes. But in that case, you'll have to fight me for him, because I'm claiming him for myself."

He groaned and rose to his feet. The evening was cold, and he shivered and stuffed his hands under his armpits. Since leaving the escarpment, they'd been spending the days sleeping, hiding under leaf and fur, and flying only under cover of darkness. As Tanin hopped around for warmth, he watched the sun disappear below the horizon, and shadows—the best friends of a Vir Requis—fell across the forest.

"I hope you fly faster tonight," Maev said; he could just make out her frown. "You fly slower than a dove against the wind."

"I'm eating breakfast first. Or dinner. Or whatever meal it is now." He reached into his pack, rummaged around, and found a salted sausage. The meat was cold and damp—the rain had wet his pack overnight—but better than an empty belly.

It was Maev's turn to groan. She mimicked him, speaking in a deep whine. "I want breakfast. I want to sleep longer. I want to love." She rolled her eyes. "Bloody stars, brother! I swear you're a princess yourself." She shoved him. "Toughen up and let's fly."

She snatched the rest of the sausage from him, stuffed it into her mouth, and shifted. A green dragon, she crashed through the forest canopy and rose into the sky. Already mourning the loss of his sausage, Tanin grabbed a handful of nuts from his pack.

"Tanin!" rose the dragon's cry above. "Shift or I'm going to burn down the damn forest."

Grumbling under his breath, Tanin stuffed the nuts into his mouth and shifted too. A red dragon, he rose through the shattered canopy to hover beside Maev.

"Try to keep up this time." She slapped him with her tail, then darted off, wings beating. With a sigh, Tanin followed.

They flew through the night. Clouds hid the stars, and the moon was only a pale wisp behind the veil. It began to rain again, the drops pattering against Tanin's scales, pooling atop his wings, and entering his nostrils. He could barely see Maev ahead, only brief lights when sparks fled her mouth.

In the darkness, like in sleep, it was easy to remember.

"Ciana," he whispered.

He had not loved a woman since. He had barely *seen* women since, aside from his sister, whom Tanin was convinced was half warthog. That had been the day everything had changed: the day Mother died, the day they fled into exile, and the day Tanin made his vow.

I vowed to find others, he thought as the rain fell. *To find people like us—exiled, afraid, alone. I vowed that they will have a home, a place to belong, a place to feel not diseased but blessed.*

Jeid called that home Requiem, naming it after Tanin's youngest sister whom the villagers had poisoned. Tanin didn't care what their tribe was called. He only cared for that person out there—a person like him, rejected and scared.

"If you're out there, Sena," he said into the rain, "we'll find you, my friend. We'll bring you home."

They flew for a long time in the darkness. Maev—damn her hide!—kept flying so far ahead that Tanin nearly lost sight of her. The old wound in his wing—a hole from a hunter's arrow—ached in the cold, and air whistled through it. His breath was wheezing with a similar sound. Every time he caught up with Maev, she only flashed him a toothy grin, blasted a little fire his way, and darted off again, faster than ever.

"Maev, in the name of sanity, this isn't a race."

She grinned over her shoulder at him. The flames between her teeth lit her green scales. "Everything is a race, brother. We're racing to save a prince. We're racing to forge a tribe. We're racing to finally find you a female companion, because I swear you've been looking funny at sheep this past year."

"Very funny, Maev. Now I'm a heavier dragon than you, and you know I have a hole in my left wing, so please slow dow—"

She cut him off with a blast of smoke, turned back forward, and raced ahead again.

Tanin was grumbling and pounding his wings, trying to catch up, when the shrieks rose ahead.

His heart seemed to freeze.

He knew those sounds. He had heard them before when hunting upon the plains.

"Uncle's rocs," he muttered.

Tanin winced. That day he had fled into exile, his uncle too had left Oldforge. Zerra—disgusted with his twin's disease—had since dedicate his life to hunting those he called weredragons. Wandering the wilderness with a bronze sword—a sword Jeid himself had forged for him—Zerra had finally joined a wandering tribe of roc riders. The Goldtusk tribe had been but a ragged, near-starved group of barbarians, and Zerra had slain their aging chieftain with a single blow from his blade—a blade such as these ramblers, with their stone-tipped spears, had never seen. Since then, Zerra had swelled their numbers, breeding the rocs from a humble dozen to a hundred beasts, starving and tormenting the great vultures and teaching them hatred of reptiles.

And now those rocs flew ahead—invisible in the darkness but cawing louder than thunder.

The rain intensified.

Lightning flashed and Tanin saw them: dozens of the rotted vultures, not even a mark away, hunters upon their backs.

He beat his wings, reached Maev, and tapped her with his wing. "They might not have seen us," he whispered. "Swallow your fire. We descend. We land in the forest and hide."

But Maev—damn warthog of a sister!—howled in rage. Instead of swallowing her fire, she blasted out a great pillar.

"Uncle!" she roared, eyes red, wings beating. "Uncle, come face me. I will burn you!"

The rocs shrieked. The hunters upon them shouted battle cries. Maev tried to fly toward them, to challenge them all, but Tanin grabbed her tail, holding her back.

"Maev, no! We can't fight them all."

Panting, her wings beating, she turned toward him in the sky. Her face was a mask of rage. "He killed Mother, Tanin." Smoke blasted out of her nostrils. "He's probably the one who poisoned Requiem. Now I kill him."

She wrenched free from his grasp and shot toward the hundred rocs. Her fire blazed across the sky. The rocs flew nearer, eyes bright yellow, their oily wings blazing white with every bolt of lightning.

Tanin cursed as he followed his sister. He sucked in air, filled his belly with crackling fire, and blasted out a flaming jet.

The stream spun, crackling, and crashed into a roc. The beast burst into flames, stinking and blasting out smoke, but still it flew toward him. The rider upon its back screamed, a living torch, skin peeling and flesh melting. Feathers tore free and glided through the sky, still burning. The flaming bird kept flapping its wings. It crashed into Tanin, biting and clawing.

Tanin screamed as the beak drove into his shoulder, chipping his scales. Claws slashed at his belly, tearing through skin. The fire engulfed him, so hot he closed his eyes for fear of them melting. Blindly, he clawed and bit. His teeth sank into flesh, and he was horrified to find that it tasted like delicious, savory fowl. He spat out a chunk, whipped his tail, and clubbed the beast. The flaming roc tumbled down like a comet, leaving a trail of fire.

"Maev!" Tanin shouted, mouth full of the animal's blood. His own blood dripped from his belly. "Get out of here!"

He spotted her fighting ahead, blowing fire in a ring around her. A dozen rocs surrounded her, daring not approach. Their riders shot arrows. Most shattered against her scales, but one drove into her back, and she bucked and roared.

"Hello, nephew and niece!" The cry rose above, high-pitched and raspy and thick with mirth, a banshee cry. "Fly to me. Fly to your favorite uncle."

Tanin looked up and growled.

Zerra.

His uncle flew there upon a massive roc larger than any dragon. The chieftain wore a cloak of buffalo hide and bore a long, scrimshawed bow. Yet he no longer looked like Jeid, his twin. Years in the wilderness had weathered the chieftain, turning him into a lanky strip of a man. Half his head looked like melted wax, hairless and grooved and sagging. His left ear was gone and his eye drooped, peering out of the scars, blazing with hatred.

Dragonfire did that, Tanin thought, and hope sprang through his fear. *There are other dragons.*

"You die now, traitor!" Maev shouted. She blasted fire and soared, knocking past two rocs. She seemed to barely feel their talons, even as those talons tore into her legs. "You betrayed your own family. Now I will burn the rest of you."

She blasted out a jet of flame.

Zerra kneed his roc and the bird banked, dodging the inferno. He soared and aimed his bow. His arrow flew, capped with metal, and sank into Maev's back.

She cried out.

Suddenly she sounded very young—no longer the gruff warrior but the frightened girl fleeing her town.

"Maev!" Tanin cried out.

He flew toward her through a rain of arrows. He howled as one scraped along his head. He blasted fire, aiming at Zerra, but his uncle banked again. Tanin swung his tail, driving its spikes into Zerra's roc. The oily bird screeched, its stench overwhelming, and fell back.

Tanin grabbed his sister. "Fly, damn you! Show me your speed."

She panted and growled. "I will kill him."

"Not tonight! Not like this. Tonight we flee." More rocs flew toward them, and more arrows whistled. "I have a plan. A plan to trap him. See if you can fly faster!"

He turned and darted forward, motioning her to follow. She blasted flame, scattering rocs, and dashed after him.

A dozen of the rank birds flew toward them, eyes blazing and talons gleaming. Twin blasts of flame sent them scattering. Tanin and Maev shot forward, claws lashing, teeth biting, tails clubbing the vultures aside. Talons drove into Tanin's flank, and he howled as his scales cracked. He torched a roc, cursed as an arrow hit his left horn, and kept flying.

They broke past the last defenders and entered open sky. They beat their wings madly, flying faster than ever. Tanin's wounds ached and sticky, black roc blood still filled his mouth. When he looked over his shoulders, he saw the horde following. Zerra led them, sneering as he drew another arrow. Tanin ducked and the projectile whistled over his head. He answered with a blaze of fire, turned back forward, and kept fleeing.

"What is your damn plan?" Maev shouted at his side. Her fangs were bared, her eyes narrowed. Blood seeped from the wound on her back; the arrow still thrust out of her flesh.

"Save your breath and keep flying!" he shouted.

In truth, he had no plan—that is, other than hoping they were faster than rocs. Fighting these creatures meant death. Running through the forest would offer no sanctuary; the beasts' sense of smell could pick out a hare in its burrow a mark away. All Tanin could hope for was to outfly them.

He rose higher, so high his ears ached and he could barely breathe. He entered the cover of clouds. Maev joined him and they flew through the vapor, blind. Behind him, Tanin heard shrieks and knew the rocs were following. The wind gusted and he spun, nearly lost his balance, but managed to right himself and keep flying. Lightning pierced the clouds. Behind him a roc screeched, and Tanin glanced over his shoulder to see the animal burning. It tumbled down and vanished.

Another lightning bolt flared. The stench of seared meat rose. The wind gusted again, and Maev spun and knocked into him. Tanin tried to keep flying forward, but he could barely tell left from right, up from down. He could see only several feet ahead, and more lightning blasted. Rain slammed into him, and the wind beat his wings like a man beating dusty rugs.

"Damn it!"

A roc rose ahead of him, then another, their eyes yellow, their beaks opened wide. Tanin blasted fire. He burned one, and

Requiem's Song

another barreled into him, talons scratching. Lightning flashed again, searing the bird, and Tanin screamed; the energy passed through the roc into him. His scales crackled, his teeth rattled, and his ears buzzed.

He dropped from the sky.

He tried to beat his wings but they were too stiff, too hurt. He tumbled.

"Damn you Tanin!" Maev shouted above. "Fly!"

He could not. He fell. He managed to stretch out his wings, to catch an air current, to glide, but the rocs surrounded him again, and arrows flew, and somewhere his sister screamed.

Is this the end? Tanin thought. *Do we die here, far from home, two more weredragons for them to hunt?*

He tried to summon fire, but only sparks left his maw. He was too weak, too weary. He dipped again in the sky.

And then he saw it.

"There!" Tanin shouted, pointing his claws. "On the mountain below!"

A cave. It looked too small for rocs. Summoning the last of his strength, he narrowed his eyes and swooped.

The wind roared around him. He pulled his wings close to his body, his head pounding at the descent. Maev dived at his side, blasting out a wake of smoke. The mountain rose below, a shard of stone piercing the night sky. Tanin clenched his jaw as the wind shrieked and the plunge hammered at his skull. He leveled off and shot toward the cave. The entrance was no larger than a doorway.

An instant before he would slam into the mountainside, Tanin released his magic.

He tumbled into the cave in human form. His knees banged against the craggy stone floor, and his teeth knocked together. Behind him, Maev shouted as she shifted back into a human. She too entered the cave, slamming against his back with a curse.

"Run deeper!" Tanin said. He pushed himself up and raced down the tunnel.

He could see nothing. Somewhere in his pack he had a tinderbox and an oil lamp, but he had no time to rummage for them. He moved as fast as he could, holding the walls for support. The tunnel was just wide enough for him to walk.

Maev moved behind him, holding his shoulder. "You're leading us to a dead end!"

Behind them, Tanin heard the rocs shriek. When he spun around, a flash of lightning illuminated the cave entrance. The great vultures were clawing at the stone, trying to enter, but were too large. A second bolt revealed the riders dismounting and climbing into the darkness.

Maev growled and drew her sword. The broad, leaf-shaped blade gleamed when lightning flashed again. "I'll kill them one by one."

He grabbed her arm and tugged her deeper. "Keep moving! I told you I had an idea. Come on!"

The shouts rose behind him, echoing in the chamber. An arrow whistled and slammed against the cave wall by Tanin's head. Another sliced his hair. He winced but kept running. Torches blazed behind, filling the cave with red light. Dragging Maev with him, Tanin rounded a bend an instant before arrows clattered into the wall where he'd just stood.

The cave became so narrow he had to stoop, then crawl on hands and knees. Icy water trickled beneath him. Maev crawled before him, cursing as she went.

"I'm not a damn worm," she said. "Let's fight them, Tanin."

He shoved her onward. "Keep crawling unless you want an arrow in your backside."

The shouts rose behind them. "The weredragons are trapped. Find them. Burn them. Slay the diseased creatures!" Men cursed, grunted, and spat. One burst into a rude song about buggering dragons with his spear. His companions laughed, and another shouted that he'd grab the female and thrust into her with the spear between his legs. That incurred more laughter from the men—and a fresh stream of curses from Maev.

"That's it!" she said, stopped crawling, and tried to turn around. "Get out of my way, Tanin, or I'll kill you before I kill them."

Tanin growled. "Keep moving!"

He gave her a mighty shove forward . . . and she vanished. He blinked.

"Tanin, you sheep's wormy bladder!" she cried, voice distant and echoing.

The torchlight grew nearer behind him. When Tanin leaned forward, he saw that the tunnel opened up into a great, round cavern. Maev slid down the smooth, bowl-like slope until she toppled over in its center. She looked no larger than a bean dropped into a goblet. A single hole, roughly the size of a heart, pierced the ceiling, letting in rain and a blast of light when lightning blazed.

"Slay them!" rose a shriek behind him—Zerra's voice. "Slay the reptiles!"

Arrows whistled. One scratched along Tanin's shoulder. He grunted and leaped into the sloping chamber.

"Skin them!"

"Shatter their bones!"

Arrows flew.

Tanin slid down the clammy stone slope, summoned his magic, and shifted.

He beat his wings.

He spun around, rose back toward the tunnel, and stuck his head into the opening. The corridor was so narrow his horns banged against the ceiling; he felt like a man trapped in stocks. His wings flapped behind him, keeping him afloat.

The hunters were close now, crawling forward with their torches. Another bow fired, and the arrow slammed into Tanin's cheek, shattering against his scales. He sucked in air. He blew his fire.

The jet blazed through the tunnel, a shrieking inferno of heat and light, white-hot, spinning like a typhoon of sunfire.

The hunters screamed. A few tried to crawl back, withering, dying in the blaze. Others farther back rolled as they screamed, trying in vain to extinguish the fire, only for new waves of the inferno to crash over them.

Tanin pulled his head back long enough to look over his shoulder.

"Maev, see the opening in the ceiling?" he shouted down to her. "Claw a way out!"

She leaped, shifted into a green dragon, and flew up toward him. "Move! Let me into the tunnel. Let me kill them."

"You claw us an exit, I'll hold them back. Go! Widen that hole!"

She growled. "I'm not escaping. Let me through!"

She grabbed his tail, but he shoved her away. More hunters were racing down the tunnel, crawling over the remains of their burnt brethren. Tanin returned his head into the tunnel and blew more flames.

When his fire died, he heard Maev shout behind him. "All right, I carved your damn escape route. Come on!" She tugged his tail. "Hurry."

He pulled his head free, leaving the tunnel full of corpses, and saw that Maev had widened the hole in the ceiling—it was now just wide enough for his human form. He beat his wings, scattering smoke, and flew toward the hole. He grabbed the rim with his left claw, released his magic, and dangled as a human.

"Maev!" he shouted.

The green dragon still flew by the wall below. She was now blowing her own fire into the tunnel. Smoke blasted out and heat and light bathed the chamber.

"Burn, you bastards!" Maev shouted, and her eyes were red when she pulled her head back. "Burn in the Abyss, you goat-shagging clumps of shite." Tears gleamed on her scaly cheeks, and she blasted more fire. "I will burn you all."

Tanin pulled himself through the makeshift opening, emerging onto the mountainside. Rain fell and wind beat his hair and tunic. When lightning struck, he saw the rocs farther below upon the mountain. Riderless, they did not yet see him.

"Maev!" he shouted down into the hole.

She sent another blast into the tunnel, beat her wings, and rose toward the opening. She too grabbed the rim, shifted back into her human form, and crawled out onto the mountainside. They stood side by side in the rain.

"There are more in the caves." Maev balled her fists and her legs trembled. "We'll get them from the other side. We'll burn them all. We'll—"

He placed a hand on her shoulder, hushing her. He spoke softly. "They still have rocs down there. We can't fight them all tonight. We hurt them. We killed many. Now it's time to fly south." When she opened her mouth to object, he hushed her again. "Prince Sena needs us. Another Vir Requis. We can't save him if we die here."

Maev spat and cursed, and her tears mingled with the rain. "They killed Mother. They poisoned Requiem. I hate them. I hate all of them."

Tanin closed his eyes, seeing that old memory.

Kill the creature!

Father, kill him!

Forever would his old beloved fill his mind, he knew. Forever would Ciana's words wound him.

He spoke in a soft voice, more to himself than to his sister. "The best revenge isn't killing your enemy. The best revenge is living well. We must live. We must build our tribe. And tonight we must fly south."

She nodded, finally silent. They shifted together and flew into the storm. By the time they heard the rocs pursuing again, they were deep into the clouds and rain, flying south in darkness, flying to that hint of light, that shred of hope, that dream of another—another like them, hunted and hurt, needing that revenge, needing that new life.

They flew through the night, silent, leaving the Goldtusk tribe to lick its wounds far behind them. They flew until they saw it in the dawn, gleaming white and gold—the southern coast.

"The sea," Tanin said. He glided upon the wind, his wounds still aching.

"Beyond it lies Eteer." Maev flew with him, blood still staining her scales.

They were both hurt, weary, consumed with pain and memory. They wobbled as they descended. They landed in the sand, shifted back into human forms, and huddled together, watching the waves.

ISSARI

Issari walked through the city of demons.

Once this had been a city called Eteer, the thriving, bright heart the world's greatest civilization. Once this had been a beacon of light, of hope, of order in a world of chaos. Once this had been her home. Now as Issari walked down the cobbled street, she moved through a hive of rot, blood, pus, and evil from the depths.

The demons swarmed everywhere. They scuttled up walls like monkeys. They perched upon domed roofs. They swung from palm trees, raced through gutters, and clattered and crawled and slithered along the streets. Their stench wafted, and their leaking sores coated leaves and stones. No two were alike. Some towered on stilt-like legs, withered beings like mummified corpses, their eyes glowing blue. Others dragged themselves forward, obese balls of fat, eyes peering between folds of skin, tongues licking their warty lips. Some flew as bats, scaled and horned, cackling as their heads spun. Others lurked in shadows, conjoined twins stitched together, four or five in each clump, writhing things of many legs, eyes, and tufts of hair.

"Creatures of nightmares," Issari whispered, clutching her robes as she walked down the street. "Terrors of the Abyss."

She had grown up hearing tales of the Abyss, that forbidden land that festered underground. For many generations, the kings of Eteer had guarded that unholy kingdom's doors; by ancient right, they governed the lands above and below the ground. Now her father had opened the seal. Now this terror swept across the city, and Issari—heir to the throne—did not know how this kingdom could ever light the world again.

"Weredragons, weredragons!" the demons cried. "We seek weredragons to kill. Brides, brides! We seek brides to fill with our spawn."

Ahead, several creatures—they looked like men turned inside out, their organs dripping—moved down the street, sniffing and snorting.

"We smell for dragons, brothers! Do you smell dragons? We smell for brides too."

The creatures approached a brick house and pounded on the door, shattering the wood. Screams rose inside. One demon raced through the doorway, then emerged dragging a woman. A few years older than Issari, her hair disheveled and her eyes wide with terror, the woman screamed and kicked.

"Dragon? Dragon?" The demons tossed the woman onto the ground and sniffed, their snouts quivering. "We smell no dragon blood. Bride! A bride!"

Issari stared in horror. Her fear froze her; she could barely even breathe. The glistening creatures, blood seeping from their skinless bodies, tore at the woman's clothes, ripping her tunic, revealing her nakedness.

"She will be my bride!" cried one of the demons, the largest among them. His heart thudded outside his chest, and his entrails bustled with worms. He leaned down and licked the struggling woman's cheek. "You will spawn my offspring."

The woman screamed, pleading for aid, trying to free herself, but the other demons held her down.

As the demon began lowering himself over the woman, Issari finally snapped out of her paralysis.

"Stop!"

She marched forward, reached into her robe, and pulled out her mother's amulet. Shedah the crone had brought the silver charm home from the north, proof of Queen Anai's death. Upon its round surface appeared an engraving of Taal, the god of purity—a slender man, his arms held at his sides, his palms open. It was a symbol of goodness, of light and hope. To Issari, it was also a symbol of her mother. She shook in the presence of this evil, but she held the amulet out before her.

"Stand back, demons!" she cried.

In her hand, the amulet burst into light.

The demons squealed. The inverted creatures stumbled back, covering their bulging, bloodshot eyes. One's liver burst, showering blood.

"The light burns!" they cried, shattering, organs ripping. "How can she burn us? Who is the seraph?"

Issari took a step forward, the amulet thrumming in her hand, casting its light.

"This was the amulet of Queen Anai of Eteer!" she cried out. "She ruled the throne that rises above your underground lair. From this relic shines the light of Taal, a god greater than your mistress." She took another step, and the light intensified, bleaching the world. "By this light and blood, I banish you!"

The demons screamed. Their bones snapped. Whimpering, they fled behind several brick houses, leaving a trail of gore and a lingering stench.

Issari breathed out in relief. She lowered the amulet, and its light dimmed. Her legs trembled and sweat dripped down her back.

Her father had traveled north a few days ago, following the crone's map, seeking Laira in the cold hinterlands. Issari had only this amulet for protection—a guard against the demons he had freed, a shard of holiness, a gift from her mother.

"I was only a babe when you left, Mother," she whispered. "And you're gone now. But still you watch over me."

Fingers shaking, she tucked the amulet back under her tunic.

"All flesh is theirs to claim," King Raem had said before leaving. He had stroked her hair. "All but yours. Stay in your chambers. Do not tempt them. They are forbidden to enter your room."

Yet Issari had left her sanctuary. She could not remain in her palace as her city bled. The people of Eteer needed her. How could she stay in safety while they suffered?

Still trembling, she approached the fallen woman.

"Rise, friend," Issari said, reaching down a hand to the woman. "You are safe."

The woman rose, clutching her tattered tunic to her nakedness. Issari wore a veil of tasseled silk and a hood hid her hair; only her eyes were visible. To all, she looked like a simple priestess, not the Princess of Eteer.

"Thank you." The woman wiped away tears. "Bless you, daughter. Bless you."

As the woman stepped back into her home, Issari pulled her hood lower, praying the woman did not recognize her. If Raem returned and heard of Issari's doings, he would beat her. She took a shuddering breath, raised her chin, and kept walking.

Down a street strewn with smashed pottery, the bones of an eaten dog, and puddles of blood, she saw it. The pottery shop. The safe haven.

A demon lingered on the street. It had the body of a massive centipede—as large as a python—covered in metallic plates and lined with many clawed legs. Its torso, arms, and head were those of a human child, pale and warty, its mouth full of hooked teeth and its belly swollen and bulging with kicking, living innards. When Issari pulled out her amulet, the creature fled from the light, its many feet pattering.

Requiem's Song

Issari approached the shop. Its bricks were pale white, splotched with demon drool, and a winged bull was engraved on the door—the god Kur-Paz, a sigil to ward off evil. When Issari stepped inside, she found that the sigil—unlike her amulet—had failed at its task. Three small red demons, no larger than cats, were hopping upon the shelves, smashing clay plates, bowls, and vases. The potter, a graying man with a wide mustache, was fighting them off with a broom. His daughter was flailing, trying to rip off a demon that tugged her hair. When Issari raised her amulet, the light blazed, and the scaled creatures fled out the window, leaving trails of smoke.

"I think they smelled something this time," said the white-haired potter, visibly shaken. "We can't keep them here any longer."

Issari nodded. "The ship sails out today." She handed the old man a few coins. "For your trouble."

He shook his head, gently pushing her hand back. "I don't do this for reward."

"I know, kind sir." She kissed his bristly cheek. "But keep these coins. They're pure gold. Rebuild your shop."

Tears dampened his eyes as he pocketed the money. "Taal bless you, Princess Iss—"

"Hush." She placed a finger against his lips, her heart leaping. "I'm but a nameless priestess, that is all.

She tightened her shawl around her face, knelt, and pulled back the rug, scattering pieces of broken pottery. She revealed a trapdoor. Issari gave her braid a nervous tug, squared her jaw, and climbed down a ladder into the darkness.

A dark, dusty chamber awaited her. Packs of clay wrapped in cloth lay upon a dozen shelves. The only light came from a small sliding window near the ceiling. A sunbeam fell into the chamber, gleaming with dust. They huddled behind the last shelf, wrapped in cloaks, their hair dusty and their faces pale—the weredragon family.

Issari knelt by them. She spoke softly. "It is time. A ship awaits."

They peered up at her, lost souls, thin and pale. A mason and his wife. Their five children, their eyes huge in their gaunt faces. Cursed. Diseased. Or maybe blessed.

Weredragons, we call them, Issari thought. *The name of monsters. But if they are monsters, so is my family. So are my exiled sister and my dead mother. So is my brother, imprisoned in the tower.* She reached down a hand to help the family rise. *To me they are simply souls to save.*

"We will walk quickly," she said. "We will head straight to the port. The ship will take you north to the cold, barbarian lands. I don't know what awaits you there. I don't know how or where you will live. But you will be free. You will start a new life." Her eyes stung. "Nobody will hunt you there."

The family stood up, shivering.

"But there are demons outside!" said the youngest child, a girl with tangled brown hair. "They can smell us. They smelled my grandmother's magic." Tears welled up in her eyes. "They ate her."

Issari knelt and embraced the girl. "My amulet will protect you. I will protect you." She kissed the girl's forehead. "You will be brave."

The girl nodded. Issari smiled but trembled on the inside. What if the demons spared her but slew the family? What if the amulet's power could not overcome their lust for weredragon blood? She tightened her lips and began to climb out of the cellar. She had no choice. She had to risk this. The demons had already invaded the pottery shop's ground floor; during the next raid they might find the cellar.

I must lead these people to the sea, and they must sail north. This kingdom is death.

As they stepped outside the pottery shop, the family blinked in the sunlight, momentarily blinded after long days in the dark. The youngest child whimpered and clung to Issari.

"I will be brave," the girl whispered. "I will be brave like you."

They walked down the street, moving slowly, barely daring to breathe. White columns rose around them, and a palm tree grew from a ring of stones, swaying in the wind. The sun was bright, the sky azure. Trails of demon drool gleamed upon the street. Drawings covered houses' walls—some depicted the sigils of the gods, wards against evil drawn by the city folk, while others were demon creations painted in blood, depicting demons devouring the heads of men, tearing off children's limbs, and mating with women. Issari held the child's hand, and the rest of the family walked behind her, their footfalls soft.

When they rounded the corner, Issari grimaced. Several beasts clustered ahead around a well. One demon, a lanky being like a strip of dried meat, was chewing on a dying dog. Two other demons, blobby creatures like dripping tallow, blinked and groaned as they copulated in the dust. A few more demons danced atop the well's rim, skeletons draped in bits of flesh. All turned toward Issari and the family. All sniffed. All let out shrieks and leaped forward.

The family gasped. Issari winced, pulled out her amulet, and cried out, "Let me pass! Stand back, demons of the Abyss. I bear the mark of Taal. Stand back!"

They screamed. The sunlight reflected off the amulet, beaming forward in blinding rays, and the demons covered their eyes.

"Quickly!" Issari said, looking over her shoulder. "Hurry by them. Do not look at them. Stay near me."

They walked, crossing the square. One creature tried to leap at them; the amulet's light slammed into it, knocking it back and tearing off its legs. The other creatures cowered. Issari walked briskly, leaving the square and entering an alleyway between shops.

They kept moving through the city. They passed by a marketplace where once vendors had hawked figs, olives, dates, and freshly cooked meat from tin plates. Today demons rooted through the supplies, guzzling wine and stuffing food down their gullets. Issari and the family kept walking, passing by the old Temple of Taal, a towering building of white columns capped with gold. Priests stood outside the temple's bronze doors, blowing ram horns and swinging incense, holding back the foul creatures who tried to leap, crawl, and slither up the stairs. Street by street, the amulet held out before them, Issari and the family made their way to the port.

The thriving boardwalk Issari had known was gone. No more jugglers, puppeteers, or buskers performed here. No more peddlers hawked dried fruits, salted nuts, or their own bodies. The booths of seers, healers, and games of chance were gone. What sailors remained moved methodically and wordlessly, loading and unloading their wares from the ships that lined the piers. Issari had once found the smell of salt, fish, and sailors unsavory. Today the place reeked of rot, and she missed the old aroma.

At every pier stood a guardian of the Abyss—some taller than three men and lanky as poles, others squat, some dripping, some dry, some hooked and bladed, some wet and soft, some hooded in rags, others naked and glistening. As every sailor walked the planks, stepping on and off the ships, the demons sniffed, groped, drooled, seeking weredragon blood.

"I will be brave," whispered the potter's girl, clutching Issari's hand.

I will be brave, Issari thought, chin raised, as she walked along the wet cobblestones.

The boardwalk took them along the canal that thrust into the city. Without the usual chants of sailors, cries of peddlers, and bustle of merchants, the place seemed eerily silent. Even the gulls had fled. Issari and the family walked by a towering, tree-like creature, its many eyeballs blinking upon fleshy branches. Each of its fingers sprouted its own hand, twitching and sporting rotten claws. Issari forced herself to keep walking calmly, ignoring every demon they passed.

Finally, at the edge of the canal, the scent of open sea filled her nostrils, some relief from the stench of the Abyss. There she waited: the *Silver Porpoise*, a long ship of many oars, her canvas sails wide. She was a ship of traders; she had brought Eteer many fur pelts, barrels of tin ore, and salted meats from the lands across the sea. Now the *Silver Porpoise* sailed north again—with bronze tools, soft cotton, southern Eteerian spices . . . and hidden life.

"This ship will take you into the sea," Issari whispered to the family around her. "She will take you to the cold north. She will take you to hope, to new life."

A towering, demonic spider guarded the ship, human heads speared upon each of its legs, their eyes still moving, their mouths sucking in air. The creature tried to clatter toward Issari, and the severed heads opened their mouths wide, revealing metal teeth. At the sight of the amulet, the spider hissed and darted back, cowering against the ship's hull.

"These are sailors," Issari said. She forced herself to glare at the spiderlike demon, though her insides trembled. "You will let them pass, and you will not speak of them, or this amulet will burn you."

The demon squirmed and hissed, and the family members began to board, walking up the plank one by one. Issari hugged the young child.

"You will be brave," she whispered.

The girl nodded and touched Issari's cheek. "You will be brave too. You need bravery more than I do."

With that, the child ran onto the ship.

Issari climbed the city wall, and she stood between the battlements for a long time, watching the ship sail away. The family stood at the stern, looking at her, and the little girl raised a hand in farewell. The distance swallowed them until the ship was just a speck . . . and then was gone.

Issari lowered her head. The stench and laughter of demons wafted from below, and she wished that she too could sail away, she too could leave this kingdom behind. But she must stay. She had more to save. She must save whatever weredragons she could, whatever brides the demons wanted to claim, and whatever remained of her kingdom's light.

She turned around and faced the city again. Across hills of homes and shops and winding streets, Issari saw it rising—Aerhein Tower. In that cell he languished—her brother.

"And I must save you too."

Wind blew, scented of rot and blood. A distant scream rose—the demons claiming another bride or perhaps slaying another weredragon. So much death, so much pain; how could she stop this?

"My father is in the north now, hunting Laira," she whispered to herself. "Taal . . . please. Please let Laira kill him." She found herself clenching her fists. "Let my father, King Raem Seran, die in dragonfire."

The thought horrified her, and she gasped and covered her mouth. She was his daughter! She was Princess Issari Seran, heiress to the throne!

She tightened her jaw. Her knees shook. She reached into her robes and clutched the hilt of her dagger. She pulled her hood low, climbed off the wall, and walked home in silence.

LAIRA

When dawn broke, Laira felt so cold, hurt, and weak that she wasn't sure she could rise.

She lay under the pile of leaves, her breath frosted. When she touched her hair—short, ragged strands Zerra had cut himself—she found it frosted into hard spikes. Fingers numb, she parted the blanket of dry leaves covering her and gazed up at the forest. Mist floated, and the boles of maples and birches seemed black in the dawn, rising to an orange canopy. A murder of crows sat upon the branches, staring down at her with beady eyes.

They're waiting for me to die, she thought. *But I won't.*

She rose. Naked and trembling, she approached the branch where she had hung her patchwork fur cloak to dry. It was still wet. Laira hugged herself, shivering, teeth chattering. She should never have washed the garments in the river; she should have let the dung dry, then shaken off the flecks. Now the cold would kill her just as readily as the rocs or her wounds. She examined those wounds and winced. The welts on her feet were swollen, and one seemed full of pus.

"It's infected," she whispered, every word sending out puffs of frost. "I need healing herbs or the rot will crawl up my leg."

She wondered if she could find another tribe; others wandered the plains and forests, hunting and gathering and sometimes battling one another, and they had shamans of their own, perhaps less cruel than Shedah who would only scorn, strike, and spit upon Laira whenever she asked for a poultice. Yet Laira remembered the few times she had seen the other tribes, nomadic groups bearing their own totems—bronzed skulls of beasts, gilded buffalo horns, and even one tribe that bore the mummified body of a goddess child. Whenever Goldtusk would come across another tribe, arrows flew, spears thrust, and often lives were lost.

"If they find me, they'll know I'm a stranger," Laira said through chattering teeth. "They'll kill me or worse—capture me to be their slave. They will not heal me."

But . . . *they* could heal her.

The thought filled her with both hope and fear—hope for finding others like her, fear that others were only a myth. Perhaps in all the world, Mother had been the only other weredragon. Perhaps Laira was the last.

"But if that's true, let me die in the wilderness."

She shoved her frozen hands under her armpits and hopped around for warmth. She considered donning her wet cloak but decided it would only chill her further. After a moment's hesitation, she lay down and rolled around in the mud along the riverbank, then in piles of dry leaves. When she rose again, she wore a garment of the forest. It was an ugly thing, but it would keep her warm and provide some camouflage. She lifted a fallen branch, slung her wet fur upon it, and carried the bundle over her shoulder. She kept limping through the forest, heading north, her burnt feet aching with every step. Despite the pain, she dared not fly. Here under the canopy she was hidden; in the open air, she would be seen for marks around.

Today she heard no rocs; perhaps they had abandoned the search or were searching too far away. As she walked and the sun rose, some of her chill left her, and a new discomfort arose— hunger.

"If it's not the rocs, my wounds, or the cold, hunger can still kill me," she said to herself and looked around, determined to find a meal.

She saw no more mushrooms, no pine cones, no berries. The canopy was thicker here than farther south, letting in less light; less grass, brambles, and reeds grew from the forest floor. That floor was a crunching carpet of dry leaves, fallen boles, and mossy boulders. Mist floated between the trunks and birds called above, too far to grab. If she still had her bow, Laira could have tried to hunt them, but now they were morsels beyond her reach.

She lifted a fallen branch and spent a while sharpening it against a shard of flint, forming a crude spear. It was noon when she finally saw a rabbit, tossed her spear, and missed. The animal fled into the distance. Her belly growled, and she thought it would soon stick to her back. Thirst dried her mouth. She had left the stream behind, for it traveled west while she moved north, seeking the fabled escarpment.

When it began to rain, she was thankful for the water—she drank some off flat leaves—but it made her colder. The downpour washed off her garment of mud and leaves, and strands of her hair hung over her eyes. At least the rain brought out some worms. She managed to catch three. She stuffed them into her mouth, chewed, and swallowed before her disgust could overwhelm her.

Resigned to being wet, she dressed in her drenched tunic and cloak. The rat fur clung to her, clammy and still foul; she doubted the smell would ever leave it. The rain kept pouring, and her spirits dampened with it. She could not stop shivering, but still she walked on.

It was afternoon and her belly was rumbling when she finally saw the bush of blueberries. Her mouth watered. The rain was finally easing up and a real meal waited ahead.

"A little gift of hope," she whispered.

Swaying with weakness, she walked toward the berries, already tasting the healing sweetness.

A growl rose.

Laira was only steps away when the bear emerged from behind the trees.

Shaggy and black, the beast placed itself between her and the berries, rose upon its back feet, and roared.

Laira froze.

She held only her pointed stick as a weapon. She was a small, scrawny thing, barely larger than a child. Before her bellowed an animal that could slay her with a single swipe of its claws.

Stand still, Laira, she thought. *If you flee, he'll see you as prey. He'll chase. Stand your ground.*

The bear fell back to all four paws, snorted, and turned toward the berries. It began to eat.

Laira found herself growling. Hunger and weakness gave her the courage she'd normally lack. That was her meal. Three worms were not enough. Without these berries, she could die.

Pointed stick raised, she took a step closer to the berries. Maw stained blue, the bear turned back toward her and growled.

"Away!" Laira waved her stick and bared her teeth. "Go, go! My berries!"

It reared again, several times her size, and lashed its claws. Laira leaped back, waving her stick.

"Go! Go!"

It swiped at her again, and she stepped backward, tripped over a root, and fell into the dry leaves.

The bear drove down to bite.

Laira winced, reached down deep inside her, and grabbed her magic.

The bear's fangs slammed against her scales.

Wings grew from her back, pushing her up. Her own fangs sprouted. Her tail whipped, cracking a tree, and her face lengthened into a snout. With hunger and fear, she lashed her hand—only it was no longer a hand but a dragon's foot, clawed and scaled. It slammed into the bear, knocking the small animal down; the beast now seemed smaller than a cub. Laira leaned down and bit deep, tearing through fur, ripping off flesh, tasting hot blood and sweet meat, and she knew nothing but her hunger and craving and the heat of the meal. She feasted.

She ate the bear down to the bones.

When her meal was done, she lay on her scaly back, smoke pluming from her nostrils. She was no longer hungry. She was no longer cold. Her wounds—agonizing to her human form—seemed like mere scratches now.

"I can lie like this for a while," she said softly. She was surprised to hear that her voice, even in dragon form, was the same. "I haven't heard rocs since this morning. I will lie a while and digest."

She wouldn't even consider returning to her human form with an entire bear in her belly. That could not end well.

Her furs were gone. She had taken them inside her when shifting, and yet her pointed stick lay beside her. She wondered why clothes could shift with her—they had reappeared last time she had returned to human form—and not the stick.

"If I ever do find others, maybe they'll know how the magic works."

She tilted her head, scales clanking. Magic? For so long, she had thought this a curse, a reptilian disease. Yet lying here, her belly full and warm, it was hard to think of shifting as a curse.

"Maybe it's a gift," she said to the rustling autumn leaves above. "And maybe others like me are out there, alone and afraid. I have to find them."

As she lay digesting, she thought she heard a roc once, but it was distant, possibly only a crow. When the sun set, Laira rose to her clawed feet. Her body pressed against the trees, and fire sparked in her maw, raising smoke.

Tonight she would not sleep in a hole, small and afraid and hurt. Tonight she would fly.

She crashed through the canopy, showering autumn leaves, and into the sky. The stars spread above her, an endless carpet. The Draco constellation shone above, brightest among them, cold and distant but warming her soul. She beat her wings, bending trees and scattering leaves below. For so many years, she had felt weak, miserable, and worthless.

"But now, in this night, I am a dragon."

She clawed the air and flew north, gliding on the wind.

ISSARI

When Issari returned to her bedchamber, she found the witch waiting inside with a bucket of leeches.

"Hello, princess," said the crone, hissing out that last word like a taunt. She smiled, revealing toothless black gums, and sniffed loudly. Her bulbous nose quivered, the hairs on its moles twitching. "Yes, yes, I can smell it. Smells like ripe fruit." She smacked her lips. "The blood of a princess—a more powerful elixir than the ichor of gods."

Issari stood at the doorway. Instinctively, she pulled out her amulet and held it before her. "Leave this place!" Her heart pounded, and cold sweat trickled down her back. "You are not to enter my chambers again, old woman."

The crone cackled—Shedah was her name, Issari remembered. "Your amulet cannot work on me, sweetling. I have no demon blood. Old I am, and ugly I must appear to you. Yes, you are young and fresh and delectable." She licked her lips, reached into her bucket, and plucked out a squirming leech. "Yet I am no barbarous brute. I crave not your high breasts, your soft skin, or the warmth between your thighs. I seek a greater prize— the blood of a princess for my potions."

Issari entered the room, shoulders squared, trying to ignore the pounding of her heart. She grabbed the old woman's arm. "I will escort you downstairs to the chamber my father gave you."

"Oh, feisty, are we, young thing?" Shedah would not budge. Her squat form seemed as immovable as Issari's canopy bed of carved olive wood. "Your sister was feisty too, but we broke her spirit soon enough. I am over two hundred years old, did you know? The blood of princesses feeds me, keeps me alive, keeps me fresh. Your sister fed me for years. She came to love the leech, for when she bled, I did not beat her. It was a relief for her pain." Shedah's eyes narrowed. "You too can choose—pain or blood."

Though Issari trembled, she managed to raise her chin and speak clearly. "If you try to leech me, it will be your blood that spills."

Across her bedchamber, Issari could see signs of the crone's presence. A glob of spit bubbled on the floor. The chamber pot was full and foul. Drool covered some of Issari's stone figurines, mostly the ones representing Nahar, the shapely goddess of fertility. The witch seemed to have slept in Issari's bed; the sheets—soft silk embroidered with birds—were unkempt and damp. Issari had promised her father to remain in her chamber, safe from the demons that even now shrieked outside the windows. How long had the witch lingered here, and would she report Issari's absence to the king?

Shedah stepped closer, raising the leech in one hand. Her other hand reached toward Issari, her fingernails like claws about to strike.

"Your father himself promised me your blood," Shedah said. "That was the price of my tidings. He flies now to bring Laira home. Once the harlot is here, she can bleed too. For now . . . you will have to feed me alone." She spat. "Your sister is a small, weak little maggot, her blood thin; I have perhaps drained her too often. But you are ripe. You are strong and fresh."

Issari paled to think of Shedah beating her sister, draining her blood, and mixing it in her potions. She turned to leave. She would summon her guards. They were perhaps her father's men, but they were loyal to her too.

"I will have you tossed into the dungeon for your impudence!" she said and headed toward the doorway.

Before Issari could step outside, Shedah snapped her fingers and the door slammed shut. The walls rattled. Several clay tablets engraved with letters—poems Issari had written in her childhood—fell from alcoves and shattered. Issari grabbed the knob and twisted. The door was locked.

"You cannot flee me, child." Shedah drew closer and placed a leech on the back of Issari's neck.

The clammy creature latched on. Issari gasped and spun back toward the witch, one hand trying to pluck off the leach. It clung hard, and she could not remove it.

"Guards!" Issari shouted.

Shedah only laughed. "They cannot hear you. I have blocked this chamber from sound. Hush. Listen. Do you hear?"

When the crone fell silent, Issari listened. She heard nothing. The trees no longer rustled below in the gardens. Though she could see demons flying outside her windows—winged, oozing creatures—she could no longer hear their shrieks.

"Guards!" she cried again, and she knew they could not hear. She reached into her cloak, drew her dagger, and held the blade before her. "Stand back."

Ignoring the blade, Shedah drew another leech from her bucket. She tossed the squirming worm, and Issari winced and leaped back. The bloodsucker landed on her cheek, attached itself, and began to feed.

Issari cried out. Before she could reorient herself, pain flared on her wrist. Through wincing eyelids, she saw Shedah twisting her arm.

"I must whet my appetite . . ." The crone leaned in, and her rotted gums cut into Issari's wrist.

"Release me!" Issari shouted, but Shedah kept biting, and blood gushed, and the crone's throat bobbed.

She's drinking my blood.

Issari's fingers uncurled.

187

Her dagger fell to the floor.

Issari had never fought anyone before. All her life, she had been sheltered from the scraps so many children fought on the streets of Eteer. But today she balled her free hand into a fist. Today she was no mere princess; she was a savior of weredragons, an heiress to a crown, and she would not let this filthy creature defile her.

She drove her fist forward.

Her knuckles connected with Shedah's head with a *crack*.

Shedah released her wrist and hissed, opening her mouth to reveal bloodied gums. Her moles twitched and her brittle, white hair thrust out like a halo. The crone leaped forward, claws outstretched, and barreled into Issari. The two crashed onto the floor.

"Feisty, yes indeed." Shedah grinned above. Her gnarled knee drove into Issari's belly. "Your blood is as hot as your temper. It is delicious." A long, white tongue unfurled from the crone's mouth to lick Issari's cheek, smearing her with bloody saliva. "I will eat all of you."

Shuddering with disgust, Issari struggled, trying to kick off the witch. But the small, frail woman seemed stronger than a warrior. Issari could barely breathe. The crone's knee drove deeper into her belly, and Issari thought she would split in two, that her every internal organ would shatter. She reached across the floor, pawing for her dagger, but could not feel it.

Shedah raised a third leech and dropped it. It attached itself to Issari's neck. She felt it pulse as it sucked her blood.

"With your blood, I will brew potent potions, yes." Shedah spat. The glob landed on Issari's cheek, sizzling like acid. "They will make me live for many years."

Issari could barely breathe. The crone's hand wrapped around her throat, constricting her. The second wizened hand tore at Issari's tunic, and Shedah placed a new leech upon her; it sucked at the top of her breast. Weakness flowed through Issari, and her head spun. She felt blindly for the dagger, desperate to find it.

I have to stop her. I have to. Or she'll do this to Laira again. Tears budded in Issari's eyes. *She did this to my sister so many times. I must stop her.*

Her hand connected with something wet and soft—the toppled bucket of leeches, she surmised. Blindly, she grabbed one of the worms.

"Perhaps your father will let me keep you, princess." Shedah grinned her bloody grin. "You will be mine—my giver of life, my toy to torment, my—"

With a choked gasp, Issari thrust up the leech she held.

She slapped it against Shedah's eye.

The worm squirmed, latched onto the eyeball, and began to suck.

The crone screamed.

It was an inhuman sound, the buzz of a thousand insects, the cry of shattering bones and ripping souls, the cry of steam, of cracking wood in fire, or burning men. The witch stumbled back, and Issari gasped for breath and pushed herself to her elbows.

Shedah stood, grabbed the leech with her knobby fingers, and ripped it off. The leech came free with the eyeball still attached, leaving an empty socket.

No. Don't faint. Issari sucked in breath. *Fight her.*

She spotted her fallen dagger near the bed; it lay among several smashed statuettes. Issari grabbed the hilt, leaped up, and pointed the blade. "Stand back!"

But Shedah, enraged, leaped forward. She rose into the air and hovered for a moment, a creature of blood and rage and drool, more demon than human. Then she plunged down, claws extended, blackened gums bared.

Issari grimaced, blade held before her.

Claws slashed her shoulder.

Issari screamed.

Her blade thrust into the crone, tearing through leathery skin and into crackling, dry flesh.

For a moment Shedah hung upon the blade, suspended in the air like some deformed, bloated sack. Then she crashed down, twisting, writhing, screaming. Smoke rose from her and worms escaped her wound.

"I . . . I'm sorry." Horror pulsed through Issari. "I didn't mean to stab you. I just . . ." Her heart thumped and she knelt by the witch. "I can heal you. I know some healing. I—"

She gasped when Shedah clutched her arm. The witch stared with her one good eye. Ooze dripped from where the second eye had once peered.

"I curse you, child." The witch spat. "I curse you with the pain of a thousand deaths in fire. I curse you to become a creature like your sister. I curse you with the heat of demons and the blood of reptiles. You will forever be unclean."

With a last spasm, Shedah retched, clawed ruts into the tiled floor, and lay still.

Issari stood, trembling, the bloody dagger still in her hand.

I killed.

She took a shuddering breath and her head spun.

I sinned. I promised to save lives. Now I've taken a life.

To be sure, she had taken a foul life. She had ended a creature that had tortured and betrayed and hurt many. But it was a life nonetheless. Issari had sinned. Murder was an abomination unto Taal, and when she touched her amulet, it felt so cold it hurt.

"I have to hide this."

She looked around the room. It was a mess of blood, ooze, and spilled leeches. Some of the worms were still attached to Issari, and she winced.

First I must take them off.

Requiem's Song

Knees shaking, she rummaged around for her tinderbox and lit a candle. Eyes narrowed, she held the flame to the bloodsuckers. With hisses, they burned and fell off her skin, bloated with her blood.

Next she stared down at the dead crone.

Do I burn her too?

If anyone discovered Shedah's corpse here, Raem would hear of it. Shedah had served the king, delivered Laira's location to him.

He will beat me bloody if he knows I slew her.

Issari did not know what to do. A princess, she had no friends to call upon, only guards and servants—men who would report to her father. Her only friend was her brother, and he languished in his cell. She bit her lip. She could not burn the body, not without raising a pillar of smoke for all to see. She considered dragging the corpse through the streets and out the city, but how? Even if Issari wrapped up the body, the city folk would smell it; Shedah had smelled bad enough when living, and her corpse already stank of rot and human waste.

The demons can get rid of her.

The thought chilled Issari. She remembered seeing the demon by the well chewing upon a dog. She remembered hearing Angel, the fiery queen of the creatures, begging her father for human flesh.

Issari tightened her lips, swallowing down her fear. She grabbed hold of Shedah's corpse. She tugged. The body was surprisingly heavy, and Issari grimaced as she pulled it inch by inch; it felt like dragging a sack of iron ore. She opened her sliding doors, grunted, and dragged the corpse out onto the balcony.

At once, as if attracted by the stench, three demons came flying toward her.

One of the creatures looked like a strip of dried flesh, its insect wings buzzing. Another could barely keep airborne; its bloated belly swung beneath it like a sack, and its red eyes burned in its pasty face. The third creature looked like flying entrails, warty and red and squirming as it flew, wingless. They were as large as horses, festering and reeking.

Issari took a deep breath, squared her shoulders, and pointed at the dead crone. "Eat." She clenched her teeth and stepped back. "Eat until nothing is left."

One of the demons—the bloated creature with the swinging belly—gazed at her and hissed. "King Raem has forbidden the Children of the Abyss to feast upon the flesh of mortals."

Issari forced down the urge to gag; the stench of the creatures was overwhelming, even worse than the corpse. "King Raem has flown across the sea! I am his daughter, Princess Issari. I sit upon the throne in his absence. I give you leave to eat one mortal—this body alone! Feast upon it, then demand no further flesh."

The demons descended like buzzards and tore into the meal. Gobbets of meat flew. Bones crunched. The thin demon tore off the crone's jaw and gnawed.

Issari stepped back into her chamber, grimacing. As she watched one demon tear into Shedah's entrails, she couldn't help it. She doubled over and gagged. Her body trembled and it was a long moment before she could straighten again. Covered in blood, she stumbled back toward the balcony and gripped the doorpost for support.

All that remained of Shedah was a red stain.

The demons stood upon the balcony, necks bobbing as they swallowed their last bites. They gazed at Issari, eyes red, saliva dripping down their chins.

As she watched, they began to grow.

The living strip of meat lengthened, widened, sprouting higher and higher upon the balcony until it wavered like some malformed tree of rot. The pale creature with the swinging belly ballooned in size. Its abdomen extended so widely Issari thought it might burst, and through its translucent skin, she saw snakes coiling between its organs. The last creature, tube-like, bulged and lengthened into an obscene tapeworm the length of a boat. They could no longer fit upon the balcony but flew to hover before it.

They are as large as dragons, Issari thought, reaching under her tunic for her amulet. *That's why they craved human flesh. It makes them grow.*

They hissed at her, smacked their lips, licked their teeth, and reached out their tongues.

"We want more." Their voices were dry as old bones. "We want your flesh too."

She pulled out her amulet and held it before her.

"Leave!" She took a step closer, letting the sun gleam against the talisman. "You may never eat more human flesh. Nor will others of your kind. Leave!"

They flew closer, almost reaching her. One's claw caressed her cheek. Another demon's tongue licked her neck. She refused to cower or flee.

"We want more."

"You will have no more!" She raised her amulet as high as she could. "Here is the sigil of Taal, the god who banished your queen five thousand years ago. I banish you too! Leave this city. Fly to the sea and nevermore return to this land. Leave now or feel Taal's light."

The amulet shot out a beam, blinding, crackling, searing. The demons screamed, beating their wings madly, slamming against the balcony railings, ripping into stone, clawing at their faces. One demon ripped out its own eye, a horrible mimicry of Shedah's mutilation.

"Leave!" Issari shouted.

They're too strong, she thought. *They've grown too large. They will not be cowed.* Yet she snarled, stepped closer, and placed the amulet against one's flesh.

"Feel this burn and flee this place."

The demon skin sizzled, raising foul smoke. The amulet blazed red, and Issari cried out, for it burned her hand. She would not release it. She pulled the amulet back—it tore free with ripping skin—and placed it against another demon.

The creatures howled.

They wept blood.

They turned and fled the balcony.

Issari panted, her hand burning. She stared at the bloated demons; they were the size of the ships in the canal. They flew across the city, wobbling, crying out in anguish. The smaller demons watched from below, cawing up at their swollen friends. Only once did the three turn back, and when Issari held out her amulet again, they turned and kept fleeing. She stood watching from the balcony, shining her light, until they fled across the shore and vanished over the sea.

She dropped the amulet. It clanged against the floor, red-hot. When she looked at her palm, she saw the sigil of Taal branded upon her.

She stumbled back into her chamber, fell to her knees, and trembled for a long time.

Requiem's Song

TANIN

Tanin woke up upon a dragon's back, saw only sea around him, and yawned.

"Still no sign of land?" he asked, tapping his sister's scales.

He rubbed his eyes, yawned again, and sat up. He was in human form, but his sister flew as a dragon, her scales green, her horns white, her mouth full of fire. She looked over her shoulder at him, and her eyes narrowed.

"Are you blind? No land. No damn land. Not a sign for three days now." Maev blasted flame over his head, nearly searing his hair. "And we're running low on food. We turn back."

Tanin cracked his neck and rose to his feet upon the dragon's back. He wobbled and held out his arms for balance. Since leaving the southern coast, they had seen only water. Their packs—which rested behind him—held enough fresh water, ale, and food for perhaps another three days.

"We'll find land." He shielded his eyes with his palm and stared south. "According to my map, Eteer is near."

Maev growled. "A charcoal drawing on tattered old buffalo hide isn't a map." She sighed. "Maybe Grizzly was right. Maybe Eteer is only a myth. Maybe—"

"Oh, be quiet and get some sleep," Tanin said, interrupting her. With another yawn, he leaped off her back.

He fell through the sky, the wind whipping his hair and clothes. He smiled, enjoying the freedom of it. Somehow falling felt even better than flying. He was only a small seed floating in the air, trapped in a world of blue—the water below, the sky above, and his sister a mere little annoyance. Sometimes Tanin wished he could fall forever.

Yet the sea grew near, and his sister waited. Tanin sucked in his magic and shifted. Beating his wings and blasting smoke, he soared as a red dragon. The green dragon dived from above, positioned herself above him, and aligned her wings with his. She descended slowly, finally landing on his back, her limbs draped across him. The weight nearly shoved Tanin back down toward the sea.

When Maev shifted into human form, the weight vanished. As a woman, she seemed to weigh almost nothing. When Tanin looked over his shoulder, he saw her on his back, a human again.

"One more day!" she said, her hair streaming in the wind. "If evening falls and we still see no land, we turn back home. Agreed?"

He grumbled and spat out fire, knowing they had no choice. Failure was better than death.

And yet I don't want to turn back, he thought, and a sigh rattled his scales. What did he have to return to? Life in a cave? Juggling in town squares as people booed and tossed refuse his way? Flying south was dangerous. He had already battled rocs, and who knew what other dangers awaited. Yet Tanin was willing to keep flying, to keep fighting, to drown his fear under hope.

Maybe I have no home, he thought. *Not unless I find others. Not unless we build a tribe.*

He looked back toward the southern horizon. "Agreed. But I still say the map was accurate. I—" Tanin blinked. "Maev . . . what is that?"

Three creatures were flying toward them across the sea. Tanin gasped. Rocs? Other dragons? When he squinted, bringing them into focus, his breath died.

"Stars above," he whispered.

Wings beat and scales clanked above him—Maev shifting back into a dragon. She moved to fly at his side, the sunlight bright against her green scales. She wrinkled her snout. "The stench of them. What are they?"

"They're . . ." Tanin grimaced. "Stars, I don't know."

The creatures were large as dragons, maybe larger. One was a bloated thing, its belly swinging like a sack, gray and bristly with hairy moles. It wings seemed impossibly small upon its ridged back, and a dozen red eyes blinked upon its swollen, warty head. A second creature was slimmer, cadaverous, barely more than a skeleton. Black, wrinkled skin clung to its knobby bones, and it beat insect-like wings. The third creature looked like a clump of flying entrails, red and wet, coiling forward, a parasite the size of a whale.

Maev hissed, filled her maw with fire, and flew toward them. "Whatever they are, they're in my way. They will burn."

Tanin growled, beat his wings madly, and flew alongside his sister. He let the fire rise in his belly and crackle in his throat.

The three creatures were close now. Their stench wafted, smelling like rotted meat and mold. Their mouths opened and they shrieked, a cry like shattering metal, like snapping bones, like a world collapsing. One of them—the bloated, sagging thing with the swinging belly—emitted a gagging sound and spewed out yellow liquid. The jet flew toward the two dragons.

Maev and Tanin scattered, and the jet blasted between them. Heat and stench like vomit assailed Tanin. Droplets landed against him, and he screamed. Each drop felt like an arrow, and smoke rose upon his scales. A hole spread open in his wing.

Acid.

With a roar, Tanin soared toward the sun and swooped, blowing fire. At his side, a second flaming jet pierced the sky—Maev raining her heat.

The inferno cascaded onto the demons.

They screeched, the sound so loud Tanin thought his eardrums would shatter. Two of the demons ignited, but they kept flying, balls of flame. The cadaverous creature, mere bones and skin covered in black hooks, shook off the fire. It swooped toward Tanin, its mouth opening wider and wider, splitting the creature in two, peeling it open. Its jaw seemed to extend across its entire body, down to the tailbone, until it formed a great mouth full of teeth. Human limbs filled the obscene maw, half-chewed.

For an instant, Tanin could only stare in horror. He had faced rocs in battle, great hunters of the north. Yet here was no earthly terror; this was a creature of nightmares.

"Tanin!" Maev cried somewhere above.

He snapped out of his paralysis. As the demon charged toward him, Tanin soared and blasted flames.

The jet crashed against the creature, filling its mouth, roasting the meal within. The demon spun and soared after him, covered in smoke. Its flesh was too dry to burn, Tanin realized with a grimace.

He tried to see Maev, but smoke and fire filled the sky, and the demon jaws charged again. Tanin growled, swooped toward the creature, and lashed his claws.

He screamed as his claws banged against the creature's flesh. He might as well have attacked a boulder. Sparks rose and the creature seemed unharmed; Tanin felt like his claws had almost torn off. The creature snapped its great jaws, and Tanin fluttered backward. The jaws managed to close around his wing.

He howled. Tears of pain filled his eyes. The jaws chomped down, grinding his wing, and Tanin screamed and leaned in to bite. His own jaws were large enough to swallow lambs whole; they seemed puny by this beast. Yet still he bit, and his teeth drove through mummified flesh and scraped against bone.

Requiem's Song

The creature released him. Tanin fell through the sky, his left wing pierced with holes; wind whistled through them.

"Maev, some help!" he shouted.

He glimpsed her battling two creatures above. Both were still smoking and crackling with fire. Blood covered Maev's leg.

"I'm battling two already!" she shouted down to him. He could swear he saw her roll her eyes. "Grow up and fight your own battles."

Before he could reply, the gaunt demon swooped again, mouth opening wide, splitting the beast down to the tailbone like a halved fruit.

Tanin gritted his teeth, growled, and soared.

He flattened himself into a spear, driving upward. The creature dived down, cackling, raining drool and bits of rotted flesh.

Heartbeats away from a collision, Tanin grimaced.

He roared as he soared, driving into the creature's mouth, shoving himself into the beast.

The jaws began to close around him. Tanin kept soaring, horns pointing upward.

The force of his onslaught split the creature at the tailbone, tearing the great jaws apart.

The demon's two halves tumbled through the sky. Each wing beat independently. The broken pieces spun wildly, shrieking their own cries, until they crashed into the sea and vanished.

Tanin spat. "Stars damn it."

Wincing, his wounded wing a blaze of agony, he rose higher.

He found Maev spinning in a circle, scattering flames, holding the remaining two demons at bay. Cuts ran along her leg, and a gash bled upon her forehead. Still she managed to glare at him.

"Are you done playing your games, brother?" She swiped her tail, clubbing one of the beasts. "Go on, choose one and kill it, damn you!"

The two demons hissed, their flesh charred, fires still burning upon them. Their skin had peeled back and their muscles blazed; through the flames peeked black, jagged bones. Yet still they flew, cackling. The slimmer one, a creature like discarded entrails, thrust toward Maev, snapping its teeth. The obese demon, his charred belly swinging like a tumor, turned to fly toward Tanin.

The demon's many eyes blazed like cauldrons of molten metal. Its mouth opened, lined with sword-like teeth. Its wings—so small they were almost comical—flapped mightily, propelling the creature toward Tanin like some obscene bumblebee toward a flower. It pulsed as it gagged, spewing another stream of acid.

Tanin grunted and swerved.

The jet blasted above him, its raining droplets searing his scales.

The creature dived, snapping its teeth.

In midair, Tanin flipped upside down, dipped several feet, and raised his claws. The demon shot above him, unable to stop. As it flew, Tanin's claws drove along its swinging belly, gutting the beast.

Snakes, worms, and maggots with human heads spilled from the wound, smacking their lips and biting at Tanin like ticks. He screamed and shook himself, knocking them off, and blew his fire again.

He caught the demon as it was turning back toward him. The flames entered the gutted creature through its wound, filled its innards, and blasted outward like a collapsing pyre. With a final shriek, the creature tumbled from the sky. It crashed into the sea with hissing smoke.

Tanin looked over his shoulder, panting, to see his sister bite into the last demon's rotted flesh. The green dragon tugged her head back, ripping out a chunk of flesh, and spat. Gurgling, the creature tumbled. It gave a pathetic whimper before crashing into the water. It vanished into the depths.

"Well, well," Tanin said, tongue still lolling as he panted. "Looks like your older brother can still teach you a few things. I believe my count is . . ." He feigned counting on his claws. "Two demons. And you . . . well, technically one demon, though he was the smallest."

Maev roared, flew toward him, and barreled into him. Blood dripped down her chin, and her eyes flashed.

"The smallest—" She blustered, for a moment unable to form more words. "You only killed two because I burned them! They were already wounded."

He nodded. "Sure, Maev. It was only because you helped." He patted her with his wing. "You're a real warrior."

Suddenly he winced. Pain drove through his wing where the creatures had cut it. Maev was wounded too, several of her scales chipped.

"What were they, Tanin?" she whispered, fear replacing the anger in her eyes. "They . . . they were even worse than rocs, I think. Evil spirits. *Demons*." She winced. "What kind of land are we flying to?"

Tanin looked south. There upon the horizon he saw it—a faded tan smudge.

The southern coast.

The kingdom of Eteer.

"We're about to find out," he said.

They flew toward that distant coast, silent. Even as they left the smoke and stench behind, the demon shrieks echoed in Tanin's ears and he shuddered.

LAIRA

She flew until the dawn, letting no fire fill her maw. She was weary. Her cuts still hurt. Her forehead burned even in the cold air, the infection blazing through her. She felt lost and afraid; she had never been alone before escaping her tribe, and she did not know if she'd live much longer. It was the longest, coldest night of her life.

It was also the best night of her life.

"I am strong," she said into the wind, and her laughter clanked her scales. "I am fast and high and I am free."

Tears flowed down her scaly cheeks. Zerra would nevermore slap her, shove her into the mud, or spit upon her. He would nevermore shear her hair, clothe her in rags, and give her only scraps to eat. For ten years, he had mistreated her, turning her into a short, scrawny girl covered in mud and tatters, a creature he made, a pet to torment.

And he will nevermore bed me, she thought. Scales clattered as she shivered. That night returned to her—the night she had stepped into his tent, selling her body for a chance to hunt. She remembered the burnt half of him pressing against her, his tongue licking her cheek, his manhood thrusting into her.

"Nevermore," she swore. "You will nevermore use me, hurt me, torture me. You kept me hungry for years, and perhaps I will never grow taller, and I will always be the size of a child. But I can be a dragon too. That you cannot take away."

Her eyes stung, her wings felt stiff, and she bared her fangs. As she flew in the night, she made another vow.

Requiem's Song

"I will have revenge." Fire filled her mouth. "You killed my mother. You hurt me. Someday we will meet again, Zerra . . . and you will feel my fire. I will finish what my mother began."

Dawn rose in the east like dragonfire, a painting all in orange, yellow, and red. The autumn forest below blazed with the same fiery majesty, rolling into the horizon. Laira looked around, seeking pursuit. Up here in the air, she would be visible for many marks. She saw only a distant flock of birds, but she felt it safest to descend.

A silver stream cut through the forest, and she dived down toward it, the wind whistling around her. She landed on the bank, dunked her head into the icy water, then pulled back with a mouthful of salmon. She gulped down the fish for breakfast, then drank deeply. Back in the Goldtusk tribe, as the lowest ranking member, she would always eat last, and always only scraps. She could not recall the last time she had eaten a whole fish. Since her mother had died, fish had meant nibbling on bones and chewing rubbery skin. She dipped her head underwater again, caught another salmon, and swallowed it down, relishing the oily goodness.

She could not walk through the forest in dragon form, not without toppling trees, and she was not ready to become a human yet. She yawned, releasing a puff of smoke, and shook her body to hear her golden scales rattle. She squeezed between a few oaks, curled up on a bed of dry leaves, and laid her head upon her paws.

"Maybe I'm the only one left," she whispered to herself. "If I am, I will live like this, wild and free and solitary like a saber-toothed cat. But I will never stop searching. I will seek the fabled escarpment in the north, and if more dragons fly there, I will find them."

She yawned again, closed her eyes, and slept.

When night fell again, she flew.

For three days and nights she traveled, sleeping in the sunlight, flying the darkness, until at dawn on the fourth day she saw it ahead.

The escarpment.

It rose across the land, stretching into the horizon, a great shelf of rock and soil thick with birches, oaks, and maples. Waterfalls—thin white slivers from here—cascaded down its cliffs, disappearing into the forest before emerging as streams to feed a rushing river. It was as if half the world had sunk, dropping the height of a mountain, leaving the northern landscapes to roll on to a misty horizon, unscathed. Countless birds filled the sky, fleeing from the sight of her—a golden dragon large enough to swallow them whole. Mist floated in valleys, and boulders rose gray and thin from the forest like the fingers of dead stone giants.

"It's real," Laira whispered upon the wind, not even caring that she flew in daylight. Tears filled her eyes. "The place where rocs dare not fly, the place even Zerra fears. A place of dragons."

Geese and doves fleeing before her, the golden dragon glided on the wind. Soon she flew along the escarpment. The highlands rose to her left, the cliffs plunged down beneath her, and the landscape rolled low to her right. Every movement in the sky sent her heart racing, but it was always a hawk, seagull, or other bird. The escarpment stretched into the horizon. If others lived here, others like her, did they hide as humans?

She flew for a long time.

"Dragons!" she called out and blasted fire, a beacon for her kind. "Answer my call! I seek dragons."

Only birds answered, calling in fright and fleeing the trees.

Laira flew as the afternoon cast long shadows, as clouds gathered, and as rain fell. A few marks ahead, the escarpment sloped down into the land. She had traversed it all and found nothing.

Requiem's Song

A lump in her throat, Laira turned around and retraced her flight, moving back west, surveying the escarpment a second time.

"Dragons!" she cried out. Maybe she had missed them. Maybe they had been out hunting and were now returning home. "I seek dragons!"

The sun dipped into the forest, and orange and indigo spread across the sky. The rain intensified and soon hail pattered against Laira's scales and wings. A gust of wind nearly knocked her into a spin. Yet still she flew, calling out, hoping, dreaming.

There.

Warmth leaped inside her. Her eyes moistened. She blasted fire.

"Another dragon."

She trembled and smoke rose between her teeth. She could barely keep her wings steady. It was hard to see in the shadows, but when she narrowed her eyes, she saw it again—the dark form of a dragon perched upon the escarpment, all but hidden under the trees.

Smiling shakily, Laira dived.

She had still not mastered landings. The past few attempts, she had smashed through trees, shattering half their branches and often their trunks. This evening she billowed her wings, letting them capture as much air as they'd hold, slowing her descent. With a few more flaps, she steadied into a hover, pulled her legs close together, and gently lowered herself between the boles. At least it was gentle compared to her earlier landings; she still shattered a dozen branches and sent down a rain of wood and leaves, but at least the trees remained standing.

The dark dragon rose ahead, perched upon the escarpment's ledge, staring south across the cliff. A waterfall crashed below the shadowy figure, vanishing into darkness. If the dragon noticed her—and how could it have not?—it gave no sign, only kept staring into the distance.

Laira sniffed, and her scales chinked as she trembled. *Another dragon. I'm not alone.*

Panting, fire sparking between her teeth, she hobbled toward the hulking shadow.

"Fellow dragon!" Joy leaped inside her, emerging from her eyes with tears. "I knew there were others. I knew it. You're not alone, my friend. You—"

She drew closer . . . and froze.

A statue.

Her tears of joy became tears of frustration.

She reached the statue, placed her claws against it, and yowled.

"Just a statue. Just . . . just a totem long forgotten."

Her spirits sank so low she lost control of her magic. She became a human again, slid down onto her bottom, and lowered her head.

"There are no dragons here." She balled her hands into fists and pounded her lap. "Just a legend. Travelers saw this statue and told stories of dragons. But there are no other dragons. Only me."

Tears streamed down her cheeks—all her unshed tears from all her troubles. They were tears for Zerra burning her mother—the tears she could not shed as the woman had burned. They were tears for years of pain, of suffering under Zerra's heel. They were tears for her wounds, her weariness, her loss of hope—a diseased girl, lost, alone in a world that had no place for her.

"Because it *is* a curse." Her voice shook. "It *is* a disease. This curse had me banished from Eteer. This curse had me fleeing Goldtusk. This curse dooms me to forever be an outcast." She turned back toward the statue and pounded her fist against it, bloodying her knuckles. "A curse!"

She was panting, her head lowered and her chest shaking with sobs, when the voice rose behind her.

"Easy on the statue, stranger! I'm still working on it. Don't scratch it."

Laira froze.

She spun around.

Night had fallen but firelight blazed between fangs, reflecting in large dark eyes, copper scales, and white horns. Among the pines and oaks, staring down upon her, stood a living dragon.

RAEM

Flying upon his demonic mount, King Raem stared down at the barbarian tribe, grimaced, and brought a handkerchief to his nose. Truly this was a benighted land.

It was the tribe he sought, had been seeking for days. A wooden totem pole rose upon a hill, and upon its crest hung a gilded mammoth tusk. Tents sprawled around the pillar, dotting the hills and valleys like warts, crude things of buffalo skins stretched over cedar poles. Raem came from a land of stone towers, lush gardens that grew atop palaces, and a canal that drove into a city in a wonder of architecture. Below him festered a hive of worms.

The tribesmen themselves were no more impressive than their tents. Back home in Eteer, soldiers wore breastplates and bore bronze khopeshes, yet these northern warriors wore only animal pelts, and they bore humble spears and arrows tipped with flint. Their beards were long, and tattoos and piercings marred their forms, abominations unto Taal's teachings. Perhaps this distant land was beyond Taal's reach.

"Disgusting," Raem said.

His mount—a gift from Angel, Queen of Demons—grunted beneath him. Raem stroked the creature. The beast had been a woman once, perhaps a girl, a soul who had fallen into the Abyss centuries ago, lost or exiled or snatched. The demons had broken her, reformed her, stretched her over a new frame. Her arms now extended, long as dragon wings, the skin pulled back like obscene sails. Her head stared forward, twisting in anguish, mute, her eyes leaking tears. Three spine ridges now rose down her back, for the demons had added to her, sewing and augmenting, stitching in new victims until they had created this thing—a slave of flight, a demonic bat cobbled together from shattered souls.

"For long centuries, you flew in the dark caverns of the Abyss, feeding upon the corpses of buried mortals," Raem said, sitting in a saddle of bones. He stroked the creature's wispy blond hair. "Now you fly for the glory of a king."

The beast was ugly, deformed, an abomination. But she was the fastest creature to have risen from the underground, and she had brought Raem all the way here without rest.

"The creatures I seek are just as fast and many times stronger," Raem said. He looked down, saw them between the tents, and smiled. "There they are."

A hundred rocs stood outside the camp, tethered to pegs. Larger even than dragons, the birds clawed the earth, snapped their beaks, and cawed. Their feathers were black and oily, their necks scraggly, and even from up here, Raem could smell their stench. The birds saw him now, and they alerted the tribesmen. The hairy barbarians hopped about, pointing and nocking arrows.

Raem smiled grimly. "They are fools . . . but useful fools."

He tugged his mount's reins, spiraling down.

Below, the tribesmen shouted and fired arrows.

The deformed bat shrieked and banked, dodging the assault.

"Warriors of Goldtusk!" Raem shouted. He had studied their language as a child, for all children of the Seran royal family spoke the tongues of surrounding lands. "I am Raem. I come from Eteer, a distant land of plenty. I come with gifts."

Circling above the camp, he opened the sack at his side and spilled its contents. Copper, tin, and bronze coins rained onto the tribe. The warriors below lowered their weapons and knelt. They crawled in the mud like worms, grabbing the coins, baser than hens pecking for seeds.

The deformed bat landed with a hiss, her bones creaking, her eyes weeping. When Raem dismounted, the pathetic creature—perhaps still clinging to some memories of her old, human self—curled up into a ball of skin and jutting bones.

Raem stood upon the hill below the totem pole. As pitiful as his mount was, he was glorious. He wore armor of polished bronze, and a jeweled helm covered his head. A shield bright as the sun hung upon his arm.

The tribesmen—clad in muddy furs, their jewelry mere beads of clay—gasped at Raem's splendor. A few covered their eyes and whispered prayers. Many knelt and began to chant.

"Raem! Raem! A god of metal!"

Several rocs gathered around, still tethered to posts, and hissed and clacked their beaks. Their talons tore up soil, and their yellow eyes blazed, and wind shrieked into their nostrils. The beasts were larger than his human bat—they dwarfed any one of his demons. The malformed creature, sensing the danger, shrieked and bared her teeth. Her human face—bloated and pale—twisted in a mix of fear and hatred.

My demons are small, Raem thought, stroking the creature. Only human flesh could make demons grow as large as dragons, a price Raem was not willing to pay. He would not feed healthy humans to his demons, for all human life was a gift of Taal—even these barbarians. With his unholy swarm, Raem could perhaps root out the weredragons hiding in Eteer—frightened, weak creatures who lurked in shadows, daring not shift. But to find Laira . . . to find the escarpment where the wild, northern dragons flew . . .

Looking upon the rocs, Raem allowed himself a thin smile.

These ones will kill dragons for me.

"Who leads you?" Raem shouted, an idol of metal, standing above the kneeling tribesmen. "Bring your leader to me."

Requiem's Song

The tribesmen below parted. A tall man came limping up the hill, clad in buffalo hides. Here was the chieftain. He wore necklaces of true gold, and a bronze sword hung at his side—not a curved sword like those in Eteer, but a wide, leaf-shaped blade the length of asuch metal man's forearm. Half the chieftain's head was burnt away—the ear gone, the eye peering from scars. The wound stretched down his arm and leg.

Dragonfire, Raem knew. *Good.*

"Are you the one they speak of?" Raem called down to him. "Zerra of Goldtusk?"

The chieftain reached him. The two leaders stared at each other, only a foot apart. While Raem was clean-shaven and bald, a meticulous man, his armor priceless and gleaming, the other—Zerra—was a brute of hair, fur, and grime.

He is a barbarian, Raem thought, *but he will serve me well.*

"Who are you, man of metal?" Zerra said. Half his mouth faded into scars, and his teeth were yellow.

"A king," said Raem. "A soldier. A bringer of gifts."

He pulled the second sack, the larger one, off his demonic bat. It clanked onto the hill, opening up to spill its treasures. Helmets, shields, and bronze daggers clattered into the grass.

The tribesmen gasped. Raem smiled thinly. He saw but a single bronze weapon here; a cache of this much metal would be priceless to this tribe.

Zerra looked down at the treasure, then back at Raem. His eyes narrowed. "Do you style yourself a god?"

Raem smiled thinly. "To you I am. And I will bring you more metal. Spearheads. Arrowheads. Swords. Vases and chalices and a throne to sit on. I will make you a king in the north."

The chieftain lifted a bronze helmet, sniffed at it, and tossed it aside. He spat. "I am Zerra, Son of Thagar, Chieftain of Goldtusk. I take no gifts from gods or men. I am no beggar." He drew the bronze sword from his belt. "I take my metal with blood. I slew the warrior who wielded this sword. I did not take it as a gift."

Raem raised an eyebrow. "That's not what I hear. They say along the river that Zerra, Son of Thagar, Chieftain of Goldtusk, was once a humble villager living in a clay hut. They say his brother, a blacksmith, forged this sword for him—a gift of love, not a trophy of battle. They say this brother is a weredragon, that he leads a clan of weredragons, and they say, Zerra . . . they say you fear him."

Half of Zerra's face, leathery and stubbly, flushed a deep crimson. The other half, a ruin of scars, twitched. He raised his sword and his fist trembled.

"I do not ask you to accept these gifts without a fight, chieftain," Raem said calmly. "But I am not your enemy. It is not me you should fight."

Zerra stared into Raem's eyes, his gaze judging, dangerous, seeking. Finally he grunted.

"Follow," the chieftain said and began walking downhill.

They approached his tent. The buffalo hides were painted with scenes of hunters and bison. When they stepped inside, Raem found lion pelts upon the ground, a crackling fire in the center, and statuettes of voluptuous women—their hips wide, their breasts hanging low—carved of stone. A living woman lay upon a rug, not as luscious but attractive enough, her breasts painted with blue rings, her thighs red with bite marks. Zerra sent her fleeing the tent with a kick.

"You speak dangerous words, stranger," said Zerra. He limped toward the campfire, pulled out a burning stick, and extinguished it inside his burnt hand, perhaps an attempt to impress his guest. He waved the smoking branch. "Why are you here?"

Raem lifted one of the female figurines. He caressed the stone form, remembering his wife. It had been years since he'd seen Anai, since he had caressed her body like this. He had caught his wife shifting, and she had fled him to these northern lands, to this very tribe, her reptile spawn Laira with her.

"Two weredragons traveled with you," Raem said. "A woman named Anai. A child named Laira. The woman was my wife, the child my daughter."

Zerra barked a laugh, a horrible sound. "I bedded them both. Here in this tent. The child was particularly willing. Thrust right into her, nearly broke her. The poor thing screamed."

Raem placed down the statuette and frowned. The chieftain stared at him, mocking, caressing his sword.

He's goading me, Raem thought, refusing to take the bait.

"If you catch Laira again," Raem said, "you may bed her as much as you please, so long as you give her to me once she's worn out. Then she would be mine to torment."

The chieftain smirked and tossed another branch into the fire. "Your wife is dead. I killed her myself. The maggot child escaped."

Raem raised an eyebrow. "And you are such a mighty warrior that you cannot capture her? The whole north is speaking of this . . . *escarpment*. Of this canyon in the stone, a network of caves of some sort. They say it's a fortress." Raem snorted. "And they say you fear to fly there."

Zerra spun toward him, enraged. He drew another flaming branch and waved it. "I fear nothing! Nothing, metal man. The rocs refuse to fly there; the birds are cowardly. You claim to be some king? Fly there yourself. Fly upon that malformed demon of yours. The escarpment is swarming with the reptiles."

"My bat is swift but small, barely larger than a mule. Your rocs are larger than dragons. Do you want more treasures of bronze? Then you will get your rocs to fly." Raem clutched the man's shoulder and sneered. "I will make you a king in the north, but first you will slay dragons for me."

Zerra stood very still, staring, the burning branch still clutched in his hand. The flames were licking his wrist, but he would not drop the stick.

"Two hundred spears tipped with bronze," the chieftain said. "Two hundred swords and ten thousand arrows. A breastplate and helm for every warrior in my army, chalices for them all to drink from, and plates inlaid with jewels. And you will send me three smiths and a hundred miners, so that we may forge the metal on our own. That is my price to you. Promise me these things, and I will slay the dragons for you, all but Laira. She will be mine to break, then yours to keep."

The man is greedy, Raem thought. *The man is cruel. This is exactly the man I need.*

He nodded. "They will be yours." He turned to leave, walked toward the tent door, then froze and looked over his shoulder. "Is it true, then? That your brother is a weredragon?"

The chieftain grinned horribly, displaying his rotting teeth. "Twin brother. I will kill him last . . . and slowest."

Raem turned to leave again. This time Zerra's words stopped him.

"And is what I hear true as well?" the chieftain called out. "That your own son, your heir and prince, is one of the diseased creatures?"

Raem's throat tightened. He clenched his jaw. He looked back at the chieftain and found the man smirking.

"Concern yourself with my daughter, not my son, barbarian. He is mine to deal with; she will be yours."

With that, Raem stepped outside the tent, stood in the wind and mist, and felt the old rage, fear, and sickness rise inside him. He craved. He needed the release.

He needed to become the reptile.

The urge nearly blinding him, he approached his demon. He mounted the creature, spurred her flanks, and soared into the sky.

As he left the tribe far below, he realized he was digging his fingernails into his palms. The blood dripped down his arms and Raem narrowed his eyes and prayed to his god.

TANIN

Tanin walked through the city of stone, seeing demons everywhere.

"By the stars, Tanin," Maev whispered, walking beside him. His gruff, golden-haired sister clutched her bronze sword under her fur cloak. "This place is as haunted as your undergarments." She sniffed and wrinkled her nose. "Smells as bad too."

Tanin scowled. "This is no time for your jokes. Keep both eyes wide open. We're looking for Vir Requis."

She thrust out her bottom lip, looking around her. "So are about a thousand demons."

The creatures flew above, cackling and beating insect wings. They laughed upon palm trees and domed roofs. They ran through the streets, chasing women, pawing and groping and tearing off garments. Some creatures were small, no larger than cats, scuttling little things on crab legs. Others were as large as horses—some scaled, some bloated, some creatures of bones and horns, others balls of slime.

"Dragons, we seek dragons!" they chanted.

The city must have once been beautiful, Tanin thought—a place of marvel such as he'd never seen. Cobbled roads stretched between houses—real houses of stone, several stories tall and topped with domes, not simple clay huts like men built across the sea. Palm trees, fig trees, and flowers grew along the streets, and bronze statues stood in city squares, shaped as winged bulls. Far ahead, past a hundred streets and countless homes, rose a palace, a building that Tanin knew nobody in the north would believe

Requiem's Song

could exist. Columns lined its walls, blue and gold, and lush gardens grew on its roof.

Whoever had built this city had created a wonder, but today this was a place of rot. Demon drool covered the cobblestones and blood stained the walls. Several corpses lay strewn across the street, torn apart. Demons were feasting upon the entrails.

"Dragons, we seek dragons!" they chanted, sniffing, moving from street to street. They spoke in many tongues; Tanin could understand his own language and make out several others.

"I guess flying is out of the question," Tanin muttered.

Maev grabbed his arm and pointed. "Look, past that dome! A tower. The stories say the prince is kept in a tower. Let's grab the boy and get out of this place." She walked by a dead monkey—demon teeth marks could be seen upon it—and shivered. "I want to go home."

Tanin grinned bitterly. "What happened to Maev the Brave, the girl who spent years boasting of being an explorer, an adventurer, a heroine?"

She gave him a withering glare. "Say another word and that girl will plant her foot so deep up your backside, you'll be able to bite her toes." She tugged him along. "Now come on, you stupid lump of a brother."

They kept walking, moving down a cobbled road lined with wineshops. Soon they reached a palisade of columns, each rising taller than oaks. Their capitals were shaped as silver men, their heads lowered, their arms hanging at their sides, the palms facing outward. Beyond the columns spread a wide boulevard, its flagstones smooth and polished. A procession was moving down the road. Priests walked at its lead, clad in white, swinging pots of incense. One priest held a clay tablet engraved with cuneiform writing; he sang out the words. Behind them moved seven bulls, tugging a great chariot of wood and metal. Upon the chariot rose a great statue of the same slender, silver man, his palms open, his head lowered.

"Taal!" chanted city folk, kneeling on the roadside as the procession passed by. "Taal!"

The demons swarmed above, hissing with hatred, sneering, spitting. Yet they dared not approach the procession, and when the smoke of the incense wafted near them, they fled with shrieks.

"This city's in the middle of a bloody war," Maev said, peering from behind a column. "Taal must be their god, the slender silver man."

"And the demons aren't too fond of him." Tanin winced to see one of the creatures scuttle by, dripping rot. The procession was moving directly ahead now; the demons fled like water from the prow of an advancing ship.

Maev seemed unusually subdued. She spoke softly. "These demons are hunting dragons. You heard them. There might be many more Vir Requis in this city, not just the prince. I think these demons are Eteer's bloodhounds; hunters." She shook her head. "By the stars, Tanin. What have we found here?"

He squared his jaw, watching the last priest move by, his cloud of incense lingering like a wake. "A place I want to leave. Now let's race to that tower, free your paramour, and go home."

Gripping his sword, he was about to step out onto the boulevard when several voices rose in the alley behind him.

"Weredragons . . ."

Tanin spun around and felt himself pale.

"Bloody stars," Maev muttered and drew her sword. The doubled-edged blade—as wide and long as her forearm—gleamed in the sunlight.

A demon lurked in the alleyway, a creature of many human heads strung together like a string of beads. The unholy strand rose like a cobra about to strike, taller than Tanin. Each of the heads leered, full of sharp teeth. They all spoke together.

Requiem's Song

"We smell weredragons. Comrades! Comrades, come to feast!"

A dozen demons appeared upon the surrounding roofs—great winged insects, hooks and blades growing from their bodies. When Tanin heard a wet *slush* behind him, he turned to see a towering blob, dripping and sprouting hair, crawl forward to block the alley's exit. Tanin could see mice, two cats, and a dog trapped within the translucent jelly, still alive and writhing.

"Weredragons!" the creatures cried.

Tanin sliced the air with his dagger. "Don't shift," he told his sister. "We'll fight them off with blades. If we blow fire, the entire city will see."

She snarled and raised her own blade. "I don't need to shift to kill these buggers." She spat toward the string of heads. "Come to me, darling, and taste my blade."

The ring of demons tightened around them. They leaped from the roofs, landing before them. Trapped in a circle of rot, the siblings swung their blades, prepared to kill or die.

A high voice rose, piercing the alleyway, pure and strong.

Light flowed.

The demons hissed and cowered.

The voice rose higher. Tanin could not see its source, nor could he understand the words. The voice spoke in the tongue of Eteer; Tanin understood only the word "Taal" repeated twice.

The demons wailed. The creature with many heads retreated, coiling into a doorway. The winged beasts fluttered off, vanishing over the roofs. The blob slithered away, leaving a trail of slime. The pure, white light filled the alleyway, blinding them. Tanin and Maev shielded their eyes with their palms, blinking and trying to see.

Through the glare, Tanin could discern a figure walking forth, clad in white. It looked like a ghost or goddess of starlight.

219

The light slowly faded, revealing the figure. She was a young woman, a few years younger than him, clad in a white tunic hemmed in gold. Her eyes were large and green, and a black braid hung across her shoulder, tied with a golden ribbon. A headdress of golden olive leaves and topaz gemstones crowned her head. The light seemed to come from an amulet that hung around her neck. When she tucked the talisman under her tunic, the last rays faded, leaving only sunlight to fall into the alleyway. The noon sun blazed overhead, yet its light seemed dull after the splendor Tanin had seen.

The young woman stared at them, eyes widening. When she spoke again, she spoke in their tongue, her accent thick.

"You are northerners?" She looked down at their fur cloaks, then back up at their faces. "From across the sea?"

Maev growled. "How dare you banish those demons? I was going to slice them all. I was going to pummel them into mush. I was—"

"Maev, for pity's sake!" Tanin interjected. He shoved down his sister's blade and turned back toward the young woman.

By the stars, he thought. *She's . . . she's . . . well, she's beautiful.*

A strange tingling filled his blood. For many years of hiding in the canyon, dreaming of Ciana's face over and over, Tanin rarely talked to women—aside from his sister, whom he often wished to bury under a boulder. At the sight of this stranger, he suddenly felt awkward, too tall and gangly. His eyes strayed down to her body, which was slim and pressed against her tunic, and he quickly looked away, feeling even more self-conscious.

"I . . . I mean we . . ." He cleared his throat. "Yes, we're from the northerners. I mean—the north. We are. From there."

Maev rolled her eyes. "Oh in the name of sanity. Does your brain *have* to turn to mush every time a pretty girl is around?" She shoved him back. "Yes, we're northerners. Who are you?"

Requiem's Song

The young woman gazed at the two, eyes wide, as if she wasn't sure whether they were warriors or jesters.

"You're not traders, are you?" Her voice dropped. "You . . . you came for him. For Prince Sena."

Tanin puffed out his chest, seeing a chance to reclaim some dignity. "All's in a day's work, really. We're used to saving people. I—"

His breath left him and his cheeks burned when the young woman leaped forward and embraced him. His heart thumped, and he patted her head, more joy and fear than ever coursing through him.

"Thank you," the young woman whispered. She pulled away, leaving Tanin feeling incredibly cold and tingly, and embraced Maev next. "Thank you for coming."

Maev's eyebrows rose so high Tanin thought they might fall off. The gruff wrestler squirmed, trying to free herself from the embrace. When the young woman stepped back, tears filled her eyes. "I am Princess Issari Seran. The prince is my brother."

* * * * *

Not long after, the three sat in a winehouse, a little place with a domed ceiling, pale brick walls, and several tables crowded with patrons. Figurines of gods, animals, and even phalli stood in alcoves; Tanin and Maev raised their eyebrows at the latter statuettes until Issari explained that they were fertility symbols. The three companions sat at the back, in shadows, beneath a bronze engraving of a winged bull. Issari had pulled a hood over her head and hid her mouth and nose behind a shawl.

"I am not to be seen," she whispered, leaning across the table toward Tanin and Maev. "Many here would recognize the face of Issari Seran, Princess of Eteer." She glanced around, but the remaining patrons were busy imbibing wine, squabbling over games of mancala, and admiring a scantily clad dancer who swayed upon a stage. "In the underbelly of this city, I am merely the Priestess in White, a savior of weredragons."

Maev thrust out her bottom lip, raised her chin, and clenched her fists. "We are *Vir Requis*."

Issari blinked. "What does it mean? I thought 'weredragons' was your name."

With a growl, Maev leaped to her feet, knocking back her chair, and looked ready to brawl. A few patrons glanced over. Tanin pulled his sister back down, shoved a mug of wine toward her, and told her, "You drink. I'll talk."

Maev snorted. "Fine with me." She brought the mug to her lips and began to gulp it down.

Tanin turned back toward Issari. "It means 'people of Requiem.' We're building a tribe of our own in the north. There aren't many of us now—just me, the warthog here, and my father and grandfather. We've come seeking others to join us. We weren't sure others even existed."

"Many did live here." Issari lowered her eyes. "Many died. My father, King Raem, summoned the demons to hunt them. His wife was a were— I mean, a Vir Requis. So is my sister Laira, but she fled our kingdom many years ago. Many others lived here, but he killed most. Some I saved and sent north in ships, though I fear for them too; my father has flown north to hunt Vir Requis in the wilderness as well. I don't know if others still live in this city—aside from my brother." She clutched her mug of wine but did not drink. She looked up Tanin with those huge green eyes, and her lips quivered. "Can you save him?"

At that moment, looking into those endless green eyes, Tanin would have promised her to save the sun from the sky, rescue sunken cities from the depths of the sea, and free every last chained man and animal across the world.

Maev had to ruin the moment, slamming down her mug of wine. "My brother can barely free his manhood from his pants fast enough to piss." She slammed her fist against the tabletop and shouted, "More wine!" She returned her eyes to Issari. "But I'll free the boy. I'll fly right into that tower. I'll burn every last demon around it, and I'll burn every last guard. Sounds like fun."

Their conversation halted as a serving girl poured more wine. When they were alone again, Issari shook her head.

"You cannot burn the guards," the princess said. "They are innocents."

Maev raised her eyebrows again. She spat right on the floor. "Bloody stars! They're guarding your jailed brother!" She scrunched her lips and looked at Tanin. "Then again . . . in some cases, that might not be a bad thing."

Issari shook her head wildly, her braid swaying. "They are following my father's orders. I know those guards. I grew up with them. They guarded my chambers in my childhood. They guard the tower entrance, and they guard the cell's door. But they do not guard the window." She raised her chin, and deep fire filled her eyes. "You can fly. You can reach that window. You can tear open the bars."

Tanin sighed, his earlier feelings of heroism fading. He spoke wearily. "I saw the tower. A hundred demons fly around it. Demons are smaller than dragons, but they outnumber us greatly. If we fly up there, they'd take us down like wolves taking down a buffalo."

Issari pulled out her amulet from under her tunic. With no demons nearby, it no longer emitted light. "That is why I will ride you." She reached across the table and touched Tanin's hand. "The light of my god will clear your path."

Her hand was soft and warm, her eyes earnest. Tanin would have agreed to fly into the Abyss itself.

223

LAIRA

Laira stood upon the escarpment, staring at the dragon.

For so long—so many years of exile, pain, and tears—she had dreamed of others like her, of people with the dragon disease. Hiding in tents, shivering in the cold among the dogs, crawling through the forest, bruised and bleeding, she had yearned for this, prayed for this, never knew if others even did exist. Now she stood—a frail girl clad in rags, her hair sheared, her body lacerated, her jaw shoved to the side, a wreck of a thing barely alive—no longer alone.

When dreaming of this moment, she had imagined crying in joy, running toward the others, hugging them, laughing with them, feeling safe, feeling whole.

Instead she felt fear.

The dragon regarded her, a large copper beast, larger than her mother had been, larger than she was; the dragon was almost as large as a roc. His scales triggered an ancient memory; they looked like scales of burnished armor from her old forbidden home across the sea. His horns were long, his fangs like swords, his flicking tail bristly with spikes.

And Laira was afraid.

She had thought her father, King Raem, had loved her, but he had tried to kill her and her mother, forcing them into exile. She had thought Goldtusk could be a home to her, but its chieftain had brutalized her. Laira's eyes burned. Was here another enemy, another one to hurt her?

"Hello there," the dragon said, his voice a deep rumble, and wisps of smoke seeped between his teeth. "And who might you be?"

Facing him, she shifted into a dragon.

She was a smaller dragon, barely half his size. Her golden scales were softer, supple, more like fish scales than plates of armor. Her horns were only two little buds, and her claws were more like daggers than swords. And yet she filled her mouth with crackling flames, and she stretched her wings wide.

"I am one of you," she said, and now she could not curb her tears. "I am sick like you. Please help me."

Suddenly all those old emotions flooded her—shame of her curse, fear of being different, relief and shock and confusion at finding another. The feelings were so powerful that her magic fizzled away, and she found herself on her knees, a human again, trembling, her cheeks wet.

I am not alone.

The copper dragon released his magic too. He stepped closer and knelt before her.

When Laira gazed upon him, she gasped and scampered back.

"Zerra!" She grabbed a stone, pushed herself away from him, and prepared to fight. "Zerra, you . . . How . . . ?"

He had found her! Somehow the cruel chieftain had—

She narrowed her eyes.

She tilted her head.

"You're his twin," she whispered.

The man before her was tall, broad, and shaggy like Zerra, but he was not burnt. No dragonfire scars marred his face and hand. His hair was wild and brown, his beard thick, his arms wide. His eyes, which stared from under bushy brows, were his most distinguishing feature. Whereas Zerra's eyes were cruel and hard, digging into her like blades, this man had large, compassionate eyes—eyes that had seen much pain, that had watched the skies for years, and Laira knew: *He has been seeking me for as long as I've been seeking him.*

"My name is Jeid." His voice was soft, lacking the cruelty of his brother. It was the voice of a healer, of a friend. "You're hurt."

She smiled shakily am him. "I . . . I . . ."

She wanted to say more, but she was too weak, too hurt; she had suffered too much. Her eyes rolled back and she tilted. He caught her before she could hit the ground.

Barely clinging to consciousness, she felt him lift her. His arms seemed nearly the size of her entire body, and his chest was warm. He carried her down a rocky path, heading into a canyon that cracked the escarpment. Though wide and burly, he was surefooted, easily hopping from one mossy stone to another. Finally they reached the canyon floor. The walls rose at their sides, green with vines and moss. Trees grew upon the canyon ledges above, barely clinging on. Caves gaped open in the walls, leading to shadows.

"My father knows the art of healing," Jeid said as he walked. "The old man's out collecting herbs. I'll do what I can for your wounds until he gets back." When they reached a cave's entrance, he placed her down gently. "You'll have to crawl in. Can you do that?"

She smiled wanly. "I made my way halfway across the world to here. I can crawl."

She climbed up a pile of stones—they creaked beneath her—and wriggled into the cave. It was dark and a tight fit. She wondered how Jeid, twice her size, would enter. After crawling down a tunnel, she emerged into a wide chamber and gasped.

This was no mere cave.

It's a home, she thought, her eyes dampening. *It's the most beautiful home I've ever seen.*

Murals covered the craggy walls, depicting bison, deer, and dragons flying under the stars. Fur rugs covered the floor, strings of beads curtained passageways into other chambers, and clay pottery stood on a flat boulder. A tin brazier crackled with embers, its smoke rising to waft out a hole in the ceiling.

"It's not much," Jeid said, "but it's—"

"Home," she whispered.

She wobbled and nearly fell again, her weariness catching up with her. She sat upon a bearskin rug and hugged her knees.

Jeid—himself much like a bear—rummaged around, pulled herbs from pouches, and tossed them into a pot with water. A sweet scent filled the cave, a scent of spring, bringing vigor to Laira.

"It smells nice," she whispered. "Nicer than I do."

He muttered something under his breath, looking uncomfortable. He brought her a bowl of the steaming water. "Drink."

She held the bowl, blew upon it until it was cool, and drank. The tea flowed down her throat, sweet and healing, filling her with warmth. Jeid clattered about and returned with bowls of mushrooms, nuts, and wild berries. Laira's stomach felt so weak. She could only nibble on a mushroom, feeling too sick for more.

"Thank you," she whispered. "I traveled for so long. For so many years, I didn't know if others were real. I . . . I lived in a kingdom, and then a tribe, and . . . " Her eyes stung and her tongue stumbled over the words.

"Hush now," Jeid said, but his voice was kind. "There will be time for tales. First we must do something about your wounds."

She looked down at herself. Her ragged cloak—a patchwork of rat furs—barely hid her body, revealing many scratches and bruises. Her wrists and ankles were still a raw mess. Her feet were the worst; the welts from the blazing pyre were infected and turning green.

What must I look like to him? Laira thought, feeling ashamed. A scrawny thing barely larger than a child, clad in filthy rags, her jaw crooked, her hair sheared short, infected and foul—hardly the kind of weredragon he had dreamed of someday meeting, she reckoned. She half-expected him to toss her out into the cold.

And yet he didn't, and his eyes remained kind, and he brought forth clay bowls of ointments. When he smiled at her, it filled her with as much warmth as the tea, for it was a smile of relief, of goodness.

He likes me here.

"This should help the infection," he said, dipping the cloth into the bowl. "It might sting a bit, but—"

A loud voice boomed from the cave entrance.

"Jeid Blacksmith! What in the name of sanity do you think you're doing?"

Laira leaped up and the bowl clattered down. She sucked in her magic, prepared to shift, to blow fire, to attack any enemy who approached. Had Zerra found her? Had her father's soldiers tracked her down?

When she saw the figure at the entrance, however, she tilted her head, keeping her magic at bay, not yet shifting.

An elderly man stood there, glaring at Jeid. He wore blue robes and a woolen cloak and hood. His beard was long and white, his eyes glittering blue, his eyebrows snowy and bushy. He held a staff formed of an oak's root; the root split at the top into wooden fingers, clutching a blue crystal.

"I am healing her—" Jeid began.

"You were about to burn her feet off." The elderly man scowled. "Root of blackthorn? That's used to heal frostbite, you fool. The lass is clearly suffering from infected burns. She needs greenroot, for stars' sake."

Requiem's Song

The old man stepped forward and smacked Jeid on the shoulder. The big, burly bear of a man scowled and stepped back with a grunt.

Laira gazed at the pair with wide eyes.

"Ignore my dolt of a son," said the old man. As he approached Laira, his scowl faded, and the kindliest, warmest smile she had ever seen creased his face and twinkled in his eyes. "Grizzly means well—that's what we call him, you can imagine why—but he has the brains of a pebble. All muscle and no wit, that one. Call me Eranor, my dear, or Grandpapa if you like. I am a grandfather to any who enter my home." He pulled a packet from his cloak and unrolled it, revealing green paste. "This will do the job much better."

Laira sat back down and stretched out her feet. Eranor gazed at her wounds, clucked his tongue, and began ordering his son about. Jeid—Grizzly, that was—though large as a great warrior, rushed about at every command. He fetched a bowl of steaming water, a cloth, and several needles and brushes.

"Now get outside!" Eranor said to his son. "Go on. You know the rules. Somebody always stands on the watchtower and guards. Go!"

Grumbling under his breath, the shaggy man shuffled outside.

Eranor watched his son leave and sighed. "I remember when he was a bundle I could hold in one hand. Now look at the boy."

"He does look like a bear," Laira said, remembering the bear she had fought in the forest.

Smiling, Eranor got to work—washing Laira's feet, applying ointment, and stitching up the open wounds.

"I hope Grizzly didn't frighten you. My son tends to do that. I've seen saber-toothed cats flee at the sight of him. I urge him to cut his hair and beard, wear wool instead of fur, and start to look like a proper person, but he won't listen. Children rarely listen to their fathers."

"It's true," Laira whispered, thinking of her own father, a cruel king who had banished her. She wished she had a father like Eranor instead. "Thank you, Grandpapa."

A thought struck her, and she sucked in breath. *But he's Zerra's father.* A chill flooded her as the realization sank in. This kindly old man who was healing her . . . was father not only to Jeid, but also the cruel chieftain, the brute who had abused her for so many years. Would Eranor attack her now, tie her up, hand her over to the chieftain?

But the man only smiled up at her, seemingly unaware of her distress. "Good! Call me Grandpapa from now on. I like the sound of that." He moved to her ankles, applying more ointment to the cuts. "So, my dear, you are Vir Requis too? I saw you flying outside in the forest. I came back here as soon as I could. A beautiful golden dragon! Now there's a new color."

At the talk of dragons, her fear eased, and she was able to push Zerra to the back of her mind.

"Vir—what?" she asked. "Are you . . . a weredragon too?"

Eranor paused for an instant, and his eyes seemed to darken. Then he smiled again and resumed his work. "I do not like that word, my sweetness. It's a crude word, a word those who don't understand us use. We call this canyon Requiem, a name my son gave it. It was my granddaughter's name. We call ourselves Vir Requis—people of Requiem." He smiled. "And yes, I too am proud to count myself among our number."

He produced soft, cotton strands and began to bandage up her cleaned wounds. Laira lifted her bowl of tea and sipped, letting the warmth flow through her. For the first time in many days, she didn't hurt.

"But . . . proud? Grandpapa, it's a disease. Like the one infecting in my feet."

"Nonsense!" Eranor tossed his beard across his shoulder. "Utter rubbish. Our enemies say such things, and perhaps you believed them. Sweetness . . ." He held her hands, kneeling before her, and gazed into her eyes. "You are not cursed. You are not diseased. You are blessed with a great gift from the stars. You are magic. You are wonderful."

More than the tea, the coziness of this cave, or the healing ointments, those words changed something in Laira. As Eranor had drawn the pus from her wounds, those words seemed to draw out all the pain, fear, and shame from inside her. She found herself trembling, and tears streamed down her cheeks.

"Oh, dear child," said Eranor, his expression softening. He pulled her into his arms, and she embraced him, weeping against his chest.

"Thank you," she whispered as he smoothed her hair. "Thank you, Grandpapa."

When the sun set, and only the light of the brazier filled the cave, Eranor stepped outside into the night for his guard shift. Laira asked to guard too, but father and son raised their eyebrows and told her to stop being so silly.

Jeid cooked a stew of hares, mushrooms, and wild tubers. It was the best meal Laira had ever eaten. She sat wrapped in a great, warm cloak of bear fur, her body washed and rubbed with sweet-scented creams. For the first time since her mother had died, she was clean, well fed, and clad in warmth. Her eyes would not stop stinging.

I am magic. I am wonderful.

She wanted to tell Jeid about all her pain—about how her father had exiled her, how Zerra had burned her mother, how the chieftain had shattered her jaw and starved her, how she had crawled through the forest for so long, nearly dying. But she could bring none of it to her lips, and Jeid did not probe her, only fetched her clear water to drink, more food to eat, and even sang an old song to soothe her.

That night they lay upon soft fur rugs. Laira watched the embers for a while, feeling warm and safe. She had not slept in a shelter since her mother had died, only in the dog pen, huddling and cold.

This is safety. This is warmth. This is home.

Soon Jeid was snoring softly, and the sound comforted Laira. She wriggled a little closer to him, feeling the warmth of his body, and lay beside him.

Your twin hurt me, she thought, *but you won't. You protect me.*

Her true father was cruel. Perhaps, she thought, Jeid and Eranor could be like the father and grandfather she needed. She closed her eyes, smiled softly, and slept.

In her dreams, yellow eyes opened and black wings spread wide. Hundreds of the rocs flew, slamming against the canyon, clattering at the caves, screeching for her blood, and Laira screamed and cowered as their talons ripped into her flesh.

TANIN

They flew across the city at sundown, two dragons beating their wings and roaring fire, driving into a cloud of demonic fury.

Aerhein Tower rose before them from a hive of devilry, a bone rising from a wound. Hundreds of creatures bustled around the old structure, rising like flies from a disturbed carcass, hissing and shrieking and buzzing and flapping their wings. The demons of the Abyss saw the dragons, and they howled, and they drove forward with clouds of rot and fire and smoke.

"Shine your light, Issari!" Tanin shouted, diving upon the wind, the air whistling around him. "Scatter them!"

At his side, Maev pumped her wings. Her green scales gleamed in the sunset, and she roared and blasted out fire. The flaming pillar spun, crackling, and crashed into a cloud of demons. The creatures—rotting winged horses with hollow eye sockets—burst into flames. Tanin added his fire, torching a cackling green creature with bat wings. Yet countless more demons flew beyond those they slew; they covered the sky, a tapestry of horns and scales and boils.

"Issari!" Tanin cried to the princess who rode upon his back.

He heard her chanting above in her tongue, speaking the name of her god. A soft light grew, pale as a moonbeam, subdued amid so much darkness. Several demons shrieked and scattered, but the others jeered and spat, mocking the light of Taal. A lumbering creature dived down, a rotting bull with leathern wings, a mockery of the city sigil. It opened its mouth and spewed down acid.

Tanin dodged the rancid jet and blew more fire, torching the creature. The bull shrieked, blazing, and tumbled from the sky, only making room for a cloud of flayed women with feathered wings, their fangs long, their eyes flaming. Maev fought beside him, whipping her tail at swarming horseflies the size of wolves.

"Issari, what's wrong?" Tanin shouted. "The amulet's light is dim!"

"There are too many!" she shouted from his back.

Tanin cursed, spat out a jet of flame, and torched a rising cluster of eyeballs and fingers.

"Keep praying and shining what light you can!" he shouted back at her. "Maev!" The green dragon slew a festering cluster of rot, spat in disgust, and flew up toward him. Tanin pointed at the tower. "Maev, you break into that tower! Tear open the bars in the window. Issari and I will cover you."

She growled. "I'm a fighter. I'm going to kill them all. I—"

"Do it!" Tanin shouted. "Go!"

With a grunt, Maev turned and drove forward, barreling into a cloud of cackling creatures—they looked like old men with canine faces—knocking them back with tail and claw. Aerhein Tower rose ahead from the smoke and flame of the creatures, its window peering like an eye. Tanin flew at his sister's side, blowing fire, clawing, biting, slaying demons of every size and shape.

A flying, flaming snake wrapped around his neck, and Tanin screamed in pain. A desiccated, winged giant of a man—ten feet tall and flapping bat wings—grabbed Tanin's wing and tugged off the claw at its tip. Tanin howled as the claw came free, showering blood. A rotting glob of boils drove into his belly, its skin acidic, sticky and burnt, and Tanin bucked as he clawed it off.

"Taal! Shine your light!" Issari shouted upon his back. Her amulet's beam drove forward, gaining some strength. The flaming snake hissed, loosened its grip on Tanin's neck, and fell. The lanky, winged giant covered its eyes, and Tanin sent it tumbling down with a swipe of his tail.

"Issari, clear a path for Maev!" Tanin shouted. "Shine your light around her. I'm fine. I—"

Before he could complete his sentence, more creatures slammed into him, great flying jaws with no bodies, and he roared as their teeth dented his scales. He kept flying, the creatures clinging to him. Balls of claws landed upon his wings, digging, cutting, and he roared and flapped madly, scattering them, flying on, blowing fire. Atop his back, Issari kept chanting, shining her light, a single beam nearly drowning in the clouds of darkness. The sun faded. Night fell and countless red eyes burned.

Pain flooded Tanin. Blood coated him. But he had to keep flying. This was the flight of his life, the battle he'd been waging since that day years ago. Jaws clamped around him, and acid rained against his scales, and as the pain flooded him, he was flying there again in the darkness, flying away from Oldforge, away from his beloved, away from the only home he'd known. And still he sought a home. Still he fought for his family, for his people—for Requiem.

"For you, Requiem," he whispered. "For my fallen sister and for the nation we will build in your name."

He blew his fire. He burned them down. He cut and bit and roared with fury, and finally he drove through the horde, and Aerhein Tower rose before him. He landed upon its crest, tossed back his head, and howled to the night sky. The city of Eteer rolled below him, two hundred thousand souls, countless lights, and beyond it the sea—beyond it Requiem, that distant tribe, the heartbeat of his lost, cursed, forsaken people, the people he would raise to greatness. He blasted his fire in a ring, beating his wings, burning down the forces of the Abyss that still clawed and swarmed toward him.

"Tanin, hold them off!" Maev shouted below, her maw full of blood, her wings pierced with holes. "I'll tear the damn bars open."

His sister, a green dragon with chipped scales, clung to the tower. As she began to bite at the bars in the window, demons swarmed and landed upon her back, biting and clawing.

"In the name of Taal, you are banished!" Issari shouted. Clinging to Tanin's back, she shone her light down onto Maev. As the beam hit the green dragon, the demons hissed and fell, tumbling down to the courtyard. Yet hundreds more were flying toward the tower now, rising from every roof and alley in the city. Tanin leaped off the tower top and hovered by Maev, protecting her with his body, blowing his fire.

Arrows slammed into him.

He roared in pain.

Soldiers of the city stood below, nocking more arrows into their bows. Tanin sucked in breath, prepared to burn the men.

"Tanin, no!" Issari cried. "We cannot kill humans. We—"

Tanin growled. He spewed down his flames. The jet crashed into the courtyard ahead of the soldiers, sending them scurrying back. One man caught fire, fell, and rolled. The others leaped behind columns. Another blast of flame sent them scurrying away from the courtyard.

"Maev, damn it, hurry up!" he shouted. Glancing behind him, he saw her still gnawing at the bars. She had tugged only one out from the window. A prisoner stood inside—it must have been Prince Sena, for he looked like his sister Issari, his hair dark and his eyes green. Maev began tugging the second bar.

"Maev, for goodness sake, can you do this a little faster? I—"

Before Tanin could complete his sentence, demons swooped from above, shaped like hairless, eyeless moles the size of bears. Their tongues lashed out, as long as their bodies, slamming into Tanin. Their drool burned, and the tongues wrapped around his neck and limbs, tugging him away from Maev.

Tanin roared. He tried to blow more fire, but only sparks left his mouth; one creature's tongue was constricting him, keeping his fire at bay like a tourniquet. He could barely breathe, let alone blow flame. He clawed and lashed his tail, but more demons landed upon his wings, tugging him down, laughing. One creature landed on his back, tore off a scale, and tossed it aside with a cackle.

Issari screamed and shone her light, but the eyeless moles seemed unaffected. Their tongues tightened around Tanin, tugging him away from the tower. Behind him, he heard Maev shout as demons landed upon her too.

"They're blind—the light won't work!" Tanin whispered hoarsely, unable to speak any louder, struggling to blow more flame.

Issari cried out wordlessly. He heard a hiss—a blade being drawn from a sheath. A weight lifted off his back. A flash of white flew before him. Tanin gasped—it was Issari! She leaped through the air, a dagger in her hand, and landed upon one of the blind moles. She drove her blade down, severing the creature's tongue which wrapped around Tanin's neck.

He gasped for breath.

Issari leaped again. She landed on his wing, thumping down upon the leathery surface. Tanin looked over his shoulder to see her lash her blade again, cutting down a demon. With a third leap, she landed upon a remaining mole, severed another tongue, and hissed like a wild animal. When first meeting the princess, Tanin had seen an angelic figure, a goddess of piety. Now, covered in blood, her eyes narrowed and full of rage, Issari seemed as fierce as any demon.

The princess leaped again, legs kicking in the air, and caught his neck. She swung around and landed on Tanin's back. The demons, bloodied and squealing, hovered before them.

"Burn them, Tanin!" she shouted.

He sucked in air. He blasted his fire. Demons burned and fell. Tanin kept blowing his flames, lighting the night, spewing sparks and smoke like a gushing volcano.

"Got him!" Maev cried behind.

Tanin turned and saw his sister spit out another window bar. Prince Sena—thin and pale, his lips tight—climbed onto the windowsill. Chains bound his wrists and ankles.

"Maev, lift him in your claws!" Tanin shouted. "He can't shift with chains."

Maev grunted. "Oh, I'm not carrying him. He'll fly." As Tanin blew more fire, holding off a new swarm, Maev grabbed his chains between her claws. She grunted as she snapped the bronze links—first around the prince's ankles, then his wrists, and finally the chains that wrapped around his torso.

"I've never flown before!" the prince shouted, standing on the windowsill. "I've only shifted in my room."

Maev grunted. "Now's your time to learn!" She flicked her tail, knocking him down from the window.

"Maev, damn it!" Tanin shouted.

Issari screamed.

As the prince tumbled down, Tanin made to dive, to try to catch the boy, already knowing he had no time. All he could do was watch.

An instant before Sena could hit the courtyard, the prince shifted.

A blue dragon rose, wreathed in smoke, blowing flame.

The demons, perhaps in awe of a third dragon joining the fight, screamed and cowered. Tanin found himself grinning,

Requiem's Song

found tears in his eyes. It was true. All the stories had been true. There were other Vir Requis. There was hope.

Requiem lives.

The dragons soared. They blew their fire together. The three flaming jets crashed into the army of demons, scattering them, and the creatures fled. The dragons of Requiem flew into the night, ringed in fire.

ISSARI

As she rode upon the dragon, holding the amulet before her, Issari felt something new, something that dampened her eyes and lit her heart. For the first time, she felt pride. She felt power. She knew then that dragons were not weak, cursed creatures for some to hunt, for others to pity and save. She knew that Vir Requis, the children of Requiem, were mighty and strong.

I am proud to fight with you.

As they flew across the city, casting back the demons with fire and holy light, sadness too dwelled inside her, for she knew that she would never see her brother again.

You will fly north with them, Sena, she thought. *You will be proud and free.*

She looked at him—a blue dragon, the beast that had shifted in their chamber in secret, that now flew and blew fire and roared. Issari had often pitied him, thinking his magic a handicap, but now she envied him. Now she wished she too could shift, could fly, could fight with fang and fire.

She looked down at the city—a city of evil, of fear. And she knew that her task was different than his. Her burden, heiress of a kingdom, was to rule.

Ahead she saw it—the coast of Eteer and the black sea. It would take him home. It would leave her here, empty, missing him, a single light in a dark city.

"Fly north with us!" Tanin said between blasts of fire. The red dragon looked over his shoulder at her, his tongue lolling, his face scratched but his eyes bright. "Join us in Requiem."

Riding on his back, Issari lowered her head. She looked down at her city, and she saw it there, rising from smoke and shadow—the palace. Her father was in the north now, enlisting his allies, hunting Laira. This was Issari's kingdom to rule, to inherit, to save from damnation.

"I cannot," Issari said. "Place me down upon my palace, my friend, I—"

Fire blazed ahead.

Issari stared, gasped, and her heart seemed to stop.

The demons across the sky shrieked and fled like birds from a running dog.

Below in the palace courtyard—the place where Raem had beheaded so many Vir Requis—the ground shattered. Cobblestones flew. A rent tore open, and a creature burst from underground, wreathed in fire, beating bat wings. The figure soared, leaving a trail of smoke and cinder. Her body was carved of stone, curved and cracked, seeping flames and smoke. Fire girded her loins, and her fangs shone. Her eyes blazed like cauldrons of molten metal, and a ring of fire haloed around her head. She stretched out her arms as she rose, a pillar of sulfur and heat and light, laughing, shrieking, painting the city with red light.

"Angel," Issari whispered. "Queen of the Abyss."

The three dragons halted, reared, and clawed the sky. Their wings beat, scattering smoke and fire. Sparks flew off Angel, showering the city, igniting trees and gardens. The Demon Queen wasn't much larger than Issari—small compared to the bulky dragons—yet she did not cower. She let out a shriek like shattering glass, so loud that Issari covered her ears, and the dragons shook as the sound waves blasted them. The demon laughed, and rings of fire blazed into life around her, unholy halos that spun around her body, sending out heat and light. Smoke pounded and her wings beat, the wind tearing down trees, scattering stones, and sending the dragons into a spin. At that moment, Angel seemed larger than any dragon.

"Greetings, reptiles!" she cried. "Greetings, stinking, cursed creatures of disease." As she laughed, the cracks on her body of stone widened, seeping lava like blood. "Do you see this kingdom? Do you see this hive the humans call Eteer? Look upon it! Here is your graveyard. Come to die."

Sena winced; the blue dragon turned away from the flames. Tanin growled, but the red dragon dared not approach, and sparks sizzled against his scales. Sitting upon Tanin, Issari raised her amulet, but the chain caught fire, and she cried out and tore it off her neck. The amulet seared her palm when she held it, and she could barely see through the pain.

Maev—her green scales chipped, her face bloodied, her wings tattered—seemed the only one undaunted. She reared, roared, and shot forward.

"Enough talk!" Maev roared. "Taste some fire."

With that, she blasted out her flames.

White-hot, the blaze crashed through the rings of smoke and flame, slamming into Angel.

Engulfed in the inferno, the Demon Queen laughed. She tossed back her head and stretched out her arms, basking in the fire.

"I am a creature from the molten rock inside the womb of the earth!" she shrieked, her voice rising like typhoons from the blaze. "Your dragonfire cannot harm me. Now you will taste true heat."

The Demon Queen swung her arm. A fireball flew from her grasp and tumbled forward, leaving a wake of light. The projectile slammed into Maev.

The green dragon let out a cry like a wounded animal. The flaming ball shoved her back in the sky. Scales cracked. Blood spilled and the smell of burnt flesh rose. Maev fell from the sky, wings beating uselessly, and crashed into the palace below. The rooftop gardens ignited and smoke hid Maev, curling upward in a cloud.

"Maev!" Tanin cried. The red dragon looked down toward his sister, then back up at Angel, seemingly torn between flying to Maev and battling his enemy.

Sena seemed to reach a decision more quickly. The blue dragon let out a roar—a sound that shook the city below.

"For long days, I languished in a cell," Sena cried out. "I watched as you and your kind destroyed my city, my kingdom, my home. My father is away, and I am Prince of Eteer, and I banish you back into the Abyss. Leave this place!"

Angel only laughed and tossed another ball of fire. Sena beat his wings, rising above the flaming missile, and blasted his own flame. The jet crashed into Angel and Sena swooped. The blue dragon slammed into the demon, biting and clawing. Smoke and flame enveloped the two.

"Sena!" Issari cried from Tanin's back.

Through strands of smoke, Issari glimpsed the demon spinning, clawing, ripping off scales. Sena's cry rose, torn in pain. Blood rained. The blue dragon and the Demon Queen fought within a sphere of light and heat.

Tanin was flying toward the melee, but it was too late. Sena fell from the inferno, scales cracked, and slammed into a house below. The roof collapsed under him, and the dragon-prince vanished into a pile of rubble and dust. Only his tail rose from the debris, flicking weakly.

Smoke rose from Issari's hand as the amulet seared her. The pain drove up her arm and along her ribs, and the tip of her braid crackled with fire. Clutching the dragon tightly between her thighs, she raised her chin, and she held her amulet high.

"Hear me, Angel!"

The demon looked toward her, eyes white-hot, searing, blinding Issari. All the princess could see was the white light, two unholy suns.

She shouted louder, "Angel, hear me! I am Issari Seran, Princess of Eteer, a priestess of Taal, heiress to the throne. My father flies across the sea. My brother is fallen, maybe dead. I rule Eteer now. You will stand back! You will let us pass!"

She gripped Tanin's horn, and she rose to her feet upon the dragon's nape. She raised the amulet as high as she could, and it blazed to life, humming in her hand. The fire spun all around. Rings of flame burst out, thudding into her dragon, and wind whipped Issari. Burn marks spread across her tunic, and her skin reddened. Yet still she shouted.

"Stand back, Queen of the Abyss! I am Issari Seran, and you are bound to my house. In the name of Taal, god of purity, I banish you. Stand back or my light will burn you!"

The Demon Queen screamed. An inferno of fire and wind, greater than typhoons, burst out from her. The shock waves slammed into Issari, knocking her down. She clung to Tanin's horn, her legs swinging over open air. The dragon rolled in the sky, wings beating, trying to steady himself. The world spun around Issari—a flaming sky, collapsing buildings, and everywhere that horrible light of the underworld, those two white eyes, those great bat wings.

"You will be my whore!" shrieked Angel, lava spraying from her mouth. "I will take you into the Abyss, Princess of Eteer, and I will break you, and I will feast upon your living flesh, and my demons will thrust into you, and you will feed us. Your blood, your pain, you sex, your flesh; they will be ours to feast upon, and you will scream forever in the depths." Angel beat her veined wings, rising from the holocaust, and came flying toward her. Her claws stretched out, and her teeth gleamed white in her red, fiery smile. "You will scream for mercy. You will scream for thousands of years. And I will answer you with more pain—your soul, your sanity, your secrets—all will be mine to shatter."

Overcome by the fiery winds, Tanin howled and began to fly backward, fanning back the smoke.

"Fly to her, Tanin," Issari said softly, straddling his neck. She patted his cracked, hot scales. "Fly to her and be brave."

"We must flee, princess!" he said, panting. Blood filled his mouth.

Issari shook her head. "I will not flee from her. Fly, my friend. For Eteer and for Requiem."

As Angel laughed, spitting out flame, Tanin roared—a roar so great it tore across even that demonic laughter. Cobblestones below shattered. Palm trees cracked and fell. And Tanin, red dragon of Requiem, drove forward into the blaze.

Angel hovered before them, wings churning the smoke.

Issari rose to her feet upon the dragon's head, clinging to his horn, and leaped forward.

She sailed through the air, legs kicking, and slammed into Angel.

It felt like falling into the sun.

Issari screamed.

The heat and light engulfed her. Wings wrapped around her, and claws slashed her, and those eyes peered into her, those white forges tearing through her veins. She closed her eyes, but still that light blazed.

She felt herself fading.

No. No, Issari. A voice spoke within her—perhaps the voice of her lost mother, perhaps of her soul. *You will not die here tonight. For Laira. For our home.*

Issari screamed and opened her eyes.

She dug her fingers into a crack on Angel's body. Clinging on, she drove her amulet forward. The metal slammed into Angel's face, shattering stone, and light flared out in a dozen beams.

Angel screamed again, and this time it was no scream of rage. This time she was hurt.

Stone cracked and melted. The light of Taal flared, washing over the world, and silence fell. Issari heard only the ringing in her ears.

She plummeted.

She smiled as she glided between sky and earth.

Above her Angel writhed, clawing at her face, and shards of stone fell from her. The demon let out a shriek so mighty that buildings shook. In the distance, Aerhein Tower cracked and fell with a shower of dust and bricks. Above, caught in the winds, Tanin beat his wings, spinning.

Issari's back slammed down against a palm tree.

She crashed through the fronds, fell through hanging vines, and thumped down onto a patch of grass.

She lay in the rooftop gardens of her palace, she realized. Plants burned around her. Smoke unfurled and flames spread, drawing closer. When she looked aside, she saw Maev lying beside her. The Vir Requis was in human form again, her hair singed; she coughed and rose to her knees.

"I'm alive," Issari whispered, lying in the grass, the ringing still filling her ears. When she looked at her hand, she found the amulet fused with her flesh, embedded into her palm like a jewel into a crown. "Taal saved me."

Wings beat above. A red dragon and a blue one—Tanin and Sena—landed in the gardens.

"We must leave," Tanin said, panting. "Now. Angel retreated but she still lives. She will summon a new horde of demons." He lowered his wing by Issari like a ramp. "Climb onto my back."

Issari rose to her feet, shaky. Past the flaming gardens, she caught glimpses of her city—pain and terror still filled it. She could not abandon this place.

Requiem's Song

She shook her head. "I stay. You are children of Requiem. Go north, find safety, and build yourself a home. But I don't share your magic. My battle is here. My home is in Eteer."

The blue dragon shifted back into human form. Sena approached her, hair singed and face sooty. He held her hands.

"Are you sure, sister?" the prince whispered. Tears filled his eyes. "You can come with us. Please come with us."

Tears streamed down Issari's face. "I don't know where Father flies upon his demon; perhaps he has found Requiem, and you will meet him in the north, and perhaps he heads back home, and I will face him in the ruins of Eteer. But I know this: Here is my battlefield, and here is the kingdom I must fight for." She embraced her brother. "If you find Laira . . . if you find our sister . . . tell her that I love her. Tell her that I will fight for her."

Scales clanked as Maev shifted and took flight. "Come on, let's fly out of this place!" She growled. "Demons are gathering. Boys, shift and fly for pity's sake! No time for goodbyes."

Sena gave Issari a last look—a look that said everything, that spoke of his love for her, of their loss, of their fear. He kissed her cheek, stepped back, and rose as a dragon.

Coughing in the smoke, Issari made her way to the roof's trapdoor, entered the palace, and walked down corridors and staircases. She stepped onto her old balcony, the same place where the demons had eaten the crone, the same place she would always stand and gaze toward the sea and think of her missing mother and sister. She stood gazing at that sea now, hand raised.

In the darkness, almost invisible in the night, three dragons flew across the water.

"Goodbye, Tanin and Maev," Issari whispered. "Goodbye, my brother. I love you."

The light blazed out from her hand, a beacon of farewell.

LAIRA

Warmth.

    Safety.

    Love.

    For several days now, these strangers—these foreign feelings, these new spirits—surrounded her. And for several days now, Laira had been scared.

    Life in the escarpment felt like a dream, like a strand of gossamer trembling in the wind, ephemeral, vanishing when the light caught it wrong. She spent nights in a cave by a fire, not a muddy pen of dogs. She ate real food—stews of wild game and mushrooms, bowls of berries, apples, wild grains—and not once did she root in the mud for bones or peels. No one beat her here. No one scolded her. Jeid and Eranor told her tales by the fire, wrapped warm blankets around her at night, and tended to her wounds. They treated her not as a creature, but as a friend.

    And Laira had never felt more afraid.

    Love and warmth. These were new feelings for her. She didn't think she was worthy of this love. Whenever Jeid approached with a bowl of stew, she expected him to toss it at her, not serve it to her. Whenever Eranor approached with healing herbs, she flinched, expecting him to strike her, not heal her.

    "I'm not worthy of love," she would whisper every night, curled up in the cave, the fire warming her. "I'm ugly. I'm deformed." She shivered. "Why do they love me so?"

    Every morning she expected it to end—to wake up, to realize it had been a dream, a cruel joke, a trap. She kept waiting for Zerra to step out from a cave, to reveal that he'd been working with Jeid and Eranor all along, to shout, "Maggot, how dare you flee me?"

One night as she lay shivering, thinking these thoughts, she heard Eranor and Jeid whispering above her. They thought she was asleep, but how could Laira sleep? How could she dare sleep when so many nightmares filled her—visions of her mother burning, of Shedah and her leechcraft, of Zerra and his fists? And so she lay still, eyes closed, and listened.

"The poor child," said Eranor, and she could imagine the old druid stroking his white beard. "When will we see her smile?"

Jeid sighed. "My brother shattered her jaw. Maybe she can no longer smile."

"She could smile with her eyes, but still they are sad." Eranor too sighed. "I can heal the wounds of the body. The wounds in her soul run deeper. Those may never heal."

Jeid grunted. "To heal wounds, first the poison must seep out. Healing hurts. Her soul is healing now and it pains her. And I promise to the stars: I will protect her. I will keep her safe until she is healed."

That night, for the first time since arriving in the escarpment—perhaps for the first time in her life—Laira slept the night through, no nightmares haunting her.

The next morning, Jeid and she went into the forest to collect wild apples, berries, nuts, and mushrooms. They walked atop the escarpment's ledge, the trees rustling around them. It was late autumn, and many of the leaves had fallen, but small apples still grew upon the trees, and mushrooms still peeked from the carpet of red and orange leaves. A waterfall cascaded, raising mist, and geese honked above.

Laira wore the new fur cloak Jeid had given her, the best garment she had ever worn, and leather shoes—the only shoes she had ever owned—warmed her feet. As she walked, she gazed upon piles of fallen branches, mossy stones, and leaves that lay within bubbling streams, imagining faces. She had often played this game, seeking eyes, mouths, and noses in the forest, imagining that someday one of these creatures—perhaps with boulders for eyes, a log for a nose—would open its mouth and speak to her, an ancient spirit of the woods.

For a long time, Jeid walked silently. There was sadness in him too, Laira thought—something deep, dull, older than her pain but no less potent. Whatever his pain was, he never spoke of it. And Laira never spoke of hers. And so they walked silently, and that silence comforted her.

Finally, upon a slope thick with brush, he spoke. "Here, look. Wild apples."

Laira smiled to see the apple tree. She began to collect what fruit had fallen. Jeid—burly and tall, his arms almost as wide as Laira's entire body—proved surprisingly agile at climbing the tree. He tossed the fruit down to her, and she collected them in a pouch.

"I didn't know grizzly bears could climb!" she said, and for the first time in many years, she felt something strange, something that tugged at her crooked mouth. For so many years, her slanted mouth had remained closed, stiff, sad. Yet now warmth spread through her, and her lips tingled, and Laira smiled.

Jeid smiled down from above—a huge grin that showed his white teeth. "Grizzlies are excellent climbers. We—"

Suddenly he wobbled. Laira gasped. The branch he stood on creaked, and Jeid fell. He landed hard on his feet, wobbled for a moment, then fell onto his backside. He blinked up at Laira, seeming more confused than hurt.

"I guess not," he said.

Laira sat down beside him, the leaves crunching beneath her. She leaned against him. He was beefy and huge; she was a

Requiem's Song

wisp of a thing. She thought that if anyone passed by, they would mistake them for a gruff old bear and a scrawny little fox.

"I like it here." Her voice was quiet, and she played with a fallen oak leaf. "I like the rustle of the wind in the trees. I like the cold wind. I like . . . I like who I am here."

He held her hand in his—a pale lily in a paw—and something broke inside her. The pain flooded her, gushing out like blood from beneath a scab peeled off too soon.

And she told him.

She needed to talk.

She needed to share this with him or she thought it would never leave her.

She told him of fleeing Eteer when she had been three, almost too young to remember, but old enough for the fear and pain to linger. She told him of Zerra burning her mother at the stake as she watched. She spoke of Shedah leeching her for potions, of Zerra beating her, of years of hunger, cold, neglect, and pain. Of the shattered bones, of the shivering nights in rain, and of her hope—her hope to find others, to find the escarpment, to find him. Her voice remained steady, and her eyes remained dry, and she simply spoke—remembering, sharing, healing.

He listened. Sometimes his eyes widened, and sometimes he gasped, and at other times he seemed both mad and pained. But he did not speak until she was done. And then he simply held her, silent.

They returned to the canyon. Laira had learned that many tunnels and caves ran underground here. There were chambers for sleeping, for cooking, for storing supplies. There were secret rooms for defense; their walls had small openings like arrowslits, outlets for a dragon to blow fire into the canyon. There were secret traps of boulders to topple onto invaders. There were deep caves for hiding when danger came. It was both a secret, magical labyrinth and a fortress of stone and moss.

That night, Jeid and Laira lay down to sleep in one of the caves, a fire burning beside them, its smoke wafting out a hole in the ceiling. Eranor stood outside upon the watchtower—that pillar of stone that rose between the trees, affording a view of the valleys below. Firelight painted the cave, but Laira still felt cold.

She rose, wrapped in her fur blankets, and settled down beside Jeid, and he held her in his arms. They lay together, sharing their warmth. She laid her head against his chest, and his one hand held the small of her back. She felt safe. He would not hurt her. He would not try to lie with her as his twin brother had.

"I will keep you safe," he whispered. "Always."

She believed him. And she loved him. She did not know if she loved him as she loved a foster father, a man, or a friend. It did not matter. She loved him and that was enough.

I'm happy here, she thought. *This is my home.*

She was drifting off to sleep when she heard the shrieks.

She jerked up, sure she was dreaming.

She knew those shrieks. They still filled her nightmares.

When Jeid sat up, eyes wide, she knew it was no dream.

"They're here," she whispered. She leaped to her feet and grabbed a burning stick from the fire.

A shadow darted and Eranor rushed into the cave, gasping.

"Rocs!" the old man said. "Rocs outside!"

Laira ran. She bolted past Eranor, raced out into the canyon, and looked up into the night sky. A hundred of the foul vultures flew above, larger than dragons, their riders bearing torches and bows.

The Goldtusk tribe attacked.

JEID

He allowed himself only an instant of fear.

My brother attacks.

The rocs no longer fear us.

We will die under stone.

The thoughts pounded through Jeid. His fingers shook and his heart thrashed. Then he took a deep breath. He clenched his fists. He turned toward his companions.

"Laira, you stay in this cave. When I give the signal, blow fire through the exit. The rocs won't be able to enter." He unclasped his sword from his belt and handed it to her. "And take this blade. If you must race into the tunnels, you'll only fit in human form; you'll need a sword."

His voice was soft, and he worried that Laira would tremble, that her fear would overcome her. But the young woman nodded firmly.   She took the short, broad sword and held it steadily. She raised her chin and stared back. "They will not enter."

This one has been fighting all her life, Jeid realized. *She is perhaps the strongest among us.*

He nodded and turned toward his father. The old man stared back grimly, eyes dark beneath his white brows.

"Father, hurry down the tunnel to the pantry," Jeid said. "Wait for my signal, then blow your fire too."

Jeid pointed to the two tunnels at the back of the cave. The left one led to the pantry, a hidden chamber full of their nuts, dried meats, fruits, mushrooms, and other foods for winter. The right tunnel gaped open beside it; that one dived underground, twisted under the canyon floor, and emerged into a chamber in the opposite cliff.

Eranor nodded, tossed his beard across his shoulder, and raced into the left tunnel. He vanished in the darkness.

The shrieks rose outside, louder now; the rocs were descending into the canyon. Men shouted too, crying out to find the weredragons, to flay and bugger and disembowel the creatures until they begged for death.

Damn it, Jeid thought. *Stars damn it! I need Tanin and Maev here for this. Just when we need to fight, the two little buggers are away.*

"Where will you go, Grizzly?" Laira asked, voice quiet.

Jeid managed a wry smile. "To cook some birds." He touched her cheek, leaned forward, and kissed her forehead. "Be strong, Laira. We will defeat them."

With that he raced into the second tunnel at the back. The passage was narrow; he had to crawl. As he moved in the darkness, his heart thudded and the sneer would not leave his lips. He was not afraid for his life, he realized. His cared not whether he lived or died. He was scared for his father. For Laira. For Requiem. The tunnel walls shook as the rocs shrieked outside.

Finally the tunnel curved sharply. He climbed a slope, emerging into a chamber that held their tools and weapons—fishing gear, blades, pelts, arrows, and sundry other items. A small opening gaped in the cliff side, looking out into the dark canyon, barely larger than his head.

"I see no weredragons, my chieftain!" rose a deep, hoarse voice outside. A roc cawed.

A second voice answered, high-pitched and twisted with cruelty. "This is the place. The reptiles are hiding here. Down into the canyon! Find them."

Jeid recognized that second voice, and a growl rose in his throat.

Zerra. My twin brother.

Wings beat, men cursed, and he heard talons clatter down against the stones outside. Jeid approached the small opening and peered outside. He could see them below, the great vultures—larger than dragons—barely fitting into the gorge. Their talons scattered stones, and their riders gazed around, hands on their bows. Last time Jeid had seen them, the tribesmen had worn fur and leather and fought with stone-tipped arrows. Tonight they wore bronze breastplates and helms, and metal tipped their arrows.

Somebody armed them, Jeid realized. *That's why they no longer fear us. Somebody gave them armor and weapons . . . and sent them here.*

He pulled back from the opening. An eerie silence fell. Men began to dismount and spread out across the canyon, searching. Their torches crackled.

"I see a cave!" one man cried, pointing toward the chamber where Laira hid.

"There's another cave here," said another man, pointing toward the pantry where Eranor was awaiting the signal.

"It's time," Jeid whispered.

A rope dangled above him. Jeid gripped it with both hands, clenched his jaw, and gave it a mighty tug.

For a moment nothing happened.

Jeid held his breath.

A creak rose, almost inaudible at first, then growing louder. Dust rained across the cave exit.

Then, with the sound of crashing mountains, a hundred boulders crashed down.

The avalanche slammed into the canyon, shaking the cliffs. Cracks raced across the cave walls around Jeid. Dust and shards of stone blasted into the chamber, nearly blinding him. When he peered outside, he saw the boulders rolling—some larger than men, craggy and mossy, others sharp and small.

Blood splattered the canyon.

Boulders slammed into rocs, snapping their spines, burying the birds. Men screamed. Arms reached out from the rubble. More rocs flew above, helpless to rescue their brethren.

"They're here—find them!" Zerra cried above. "Land on the boulders and into the caves."

Jeid shifted. His dragon form, bulky and long, filled the chamber, pressing up against the walls. He shoved his snout out of the exit.

"Fire!" he shouted.

He roared his flames.

The jet blasted out into the canyon, crashed against the fallen boulders, and sprayed up like red waves. Through the blaze, Jeid saw Laira and Eranor breathing their own fire from their holes, adding their jets to his.

The canyon roared, a great oven.

Tribesmen screamed.

Rocs ignited and fell.

A man ran, a living torch, and collapsed.

When Jeid had to pause for breath and their flames lowered, he beheld a ruin. Melted flesh clung to stones. Arms twitched under the rubble. One man still lived, crawling across boulders; his legs were gone, ending with trailing stumps and jutting bones, and the skin on his face had peeled off. But more rocs and riders still lived. Dozens of wings beat above, and dozens of men cried out.

"Get down there!" Zerra was screaming. The voice came from the sky above the canyon; the chieftain had not yet dared enter the gauntlet. "I don't care how much fire they blow. Get down there and dig them out!"

Jeid found himself trembling again, his scales chinking. He ground his teeth. He dug his claws into the stone beneath him. That day returned to him, the day he still dreamed of: fleeing Oldforge with fire and blood, leaving his dead wife behind.

"Turn back, Zerra!" he shouted into the gorge. "Turn back and I will spare your life. This place is forbidden to you. Enter this canyon and it will be your tomb."

He heard his twin laughing outside. "It is you, my dear brother, who is buried now. It is you who lurks in your grave. Emerge to fight me or die like a coward. I care not." Zerra emitted a horrible laugh that sounded like snapping bones. "Men! Dig into these walls, shatter these stones, and slay the maggots in their holes."

More rocs screeched and descended. Jeid growled and blew his flames again.

LAIRA

Laira filled the cave, a golden dragon. She sneered, beat her wings against the ceiling, and blew more fire out into the canyon. She heard the tribesmen scream, and a smile twisted her jaw. Even in dragon form, that jaw was crooked, shoved to the side, a reminder of Zerra's cruelty.

You are out there, she thought, blasting her flame. *The man who beat me, starved me, thrust into me in his bed.* She roared as her flames crackled. *Now I burn you. This ends here.*

Across the canyon, she glimpsed Jeid blowing his flames too. The jet emerged from a hole no larger than his snout. Within the canyon, the enemies died. Fire blasted against the walls, showered up, and knocked rocs down. Screams echoed and ash rained.

But the rocs kept coming, and Laira's flames were burning low. Soon her jet fizzled into mere sparks. Fear gripped her, and she growled and blasted out every last flame inside her. Across the canyon, she saw that Jeid and Eranor too were down to sparks. They would need time to rest and recharge.

But the rocs gave them no respite.

They kept diving into the canyon. Men leaped off and hid behind boulders where the fire could not reach. Archers rose from behind a dead roc, fired, and crouched down. One arrow slammed into the cliff side near Laira. A second entered the cave and grazed her cheek, and she hissed. She closed her jaw, waiting, sneering. Smoke plumed from her nostrils. When the archers rose again, she blasted what flames remained inside her. It was but a thin stream, but it caught one archer in the chest. He fell.

Requiem's Song

More arrows flew. Laira retreated from the exit and flexed her claws. Her foot stepped into the brazier, and she grunted and kicked the embers aside. Smoke rose around her. She had no fire within her—not until she could rest—but she could still fight.

"Enter and fight me!" she shouted. "Enter this cave, Zerra, and face me."

She snarled and raised her claws. Arrows flew into the cave, slamming into the walls around her. When she stepped back, they could not hit her. The tribesmen would have to enter, leaving their rocs outside.

And I will kill them, Laira thought, refusing to tremble, refusing to let the horror overwhelm her. She had killed men with her flames. Now she would kill with tooth and claw.

"You came here to die." She clawed the air. "Requiem is my new tribe. Requiem will be forged in fire and blood."

As she waited for them to enter, shrieks sounded above.

Laira whipped her head up and blasted smoke out of her nostrils. On the ceiling was a small hole, a vent for their brazier's smoke. Talons reached into the opening, scratching, cracking stone, widening the gap. Soon a roc head appeared, and its shriek echoed in the cavern, nearly deafening Laira. She cried out with the pain of the sound.

More talons dug above and debris rained. With a shower of dust, a chunk of the ceiling collapsed. Stones pelted Laira, cracking her scales, and she blasted what fire she could muster.

Through the dust, flame, and smoke, a roc crashed down into the cave.

Zerra sat upon it.

The chieftain stared at her and his lips—halved by his scars—twisted into a horrible smirk. He wore a breastplate beneath his fur pelts, and he pointed a bronze-tipped arrow at her.

Still in dragon form, Laira lunged toward him.

The arrow flew and slammed into her neck.

She cried out, the pain driving through her. Her neck stiffened. She felt ilbane flow through her, bitter and burning—a leaf's latex harmless to most but poisonous to dragons. She roared and tried to lash her claws. But the roc was quicker. Its talons drove into her chest, knocking her down.

She slammed onto the floor. The pain drove the magic away from her. She shrank, becoming a woman again. The arrow clattered to the floor, coated with her blood.

"Hello again, little Laira," Zerra said, staring down from his roc. He spat upon her. "You I will not kill, no. The other weredragons will die tonight, but you will return home with me. Do you think you suffered before? You will soon miss those days. I will make you suffer like no one ever has. Ashoor, grab her."

The foul vulture, dripping oil and shedding charred feathers, raised his talons over Laira.

She tried to shift back into a dragon, but she was too hurt, too weak. She swung the bronze sword Jeid had given her—a wide blade the length of her forearm—but the roc knocked it aside. The blade sparked against the wall.

As the talons descended, Laira scurried away. Clutching her sword, she stumbled into one of the tunnels.

She plunged through shadows, fell, and banged her hip. Her muscles felt stiff, her eyes puffy, her bones cold and throbbing. Grimacing, she began to crawl backward, leaving the cave and entering the network of underground passages. The burrow would take her under the canyon—to Jeid.

Light blazed as Zerra thrust a torch into the tunnel. She heard him laugh as he crawled in after her.

"So you will be caught like the maggot that you are." His voice echoed. "Maybe you would like another bedding here in the darkness before I drag you home. Yes, I do think that back in our tribe, I will take you every night."

Laira tightened her grip around her sword's hilt.

She kept crawling. Soon she would reach Jeid. He would help her. They would battle Zerra together. As the torch grew nearer, as he crawled after her, Laira kept scurrying. Her blood trickled and her head spun. The tunnel grew larger; soon she was able to run upright, though her legs would not stop shaking. Blood covered her cloak.

Stay alive. Keep moving. Soon you'll reach Jeid. Soon—

She slammed into stone.

"No. Stars, no."

The tunnel had collapsed; boulders blocked her way. She was trapped.

She spun around to see Zerra walking toward her, a torch in one hand, his sword in the other.

No fear. For Requiem.

Laira screamed and lunged toward him, swinging her blade.

JEID

The cavern collapsed around him.

Rocs clawed and bit, tearing at the opening. Stones crashed down. The ceiling cracked. The beasts, mightier than any animal that roamed the earth or flew in the skies, were tearing the canyon apart. Boulders slammed down behind Jeid, blocking his way deeper into the network of tunnels. He roared, down to mere sputters of flame, as the cave collapsed around him.

And so I fight in the open, he thought.

Stones pelted him. One slammed down onto his spine. More buffeted his neck, knocking him down. Jeid growled.

And so I fly out to death in fire.

He stretched his wings wide. He bellowed—a cry that shook the canyon.

"For Requiem."

He crashed forward, driving through the raining boulders, barreling past rocs. Clawing the air and lashing his tail, a copper dragon blowing fire, Jeid emerged into the canyon and sounded his cry.

"For Requiem!" His voice was hoarse, and blood coated his scales. All around the enemy flew, wings covering the sky, arrows filling the air. But beyond them a light shone; the sun was rising. "For a dawn of dragons!"

He soared, blowing fire, into a sky of talons and arrows.

A roc swooped toward him. Jeid clubbed it aside with his tail. A second rancid bird landed upon his back, and a beak crashed through Jeid's scales. Blood showered and he howled, flew backward, and slammed the roc into the canyon wall. The creature crashed down, but three more swooped at Jeid. He roared his flames and bit into rank flesh. Arrows pelted him. Jeid flew higher, grabbed a rider between his jaws, and bit down hard. The man tumbled down in two halves, entrails spilling like streamers.

Flame and blood lit the sky.

"Eranor!" he cried. "Laira!"

He could not see them. When he stared down, he saw that their caves had collapsed. They were trapped. Perhaps dead.

I killed them. I led them here. I called this a new home; it became a tomb.

Rocs slammed against him, shoving him down. He growled. His claws hit the canyon floor, and he shoved upward, wings beating, tearing through the beasts.

So I die with them.

He crashed through the sea of fetid birds, rose out of the canyon, and entered the sky. The trees burned across the escarpment. Red smoke hid the sky. Everywhere they flew—the rocs of the Goldtusk tribe. The arrows of riders fell like rain, slamming into him. One sliced through his wing.

I fly to you now, my wife, he thought, eyes rolling back. *I fly to you, Requiem.*

When he closed his eyes, he saw it above—the Draco constellation, stars of Requiem, wells of magic. He flew through blood toward the lights.

Heat bathed him.

Roars rolled like thunder.

Jeid opened his eyes and saw them there. They rose from the dawn, three dragons, blowing their fire.

"A dawn of dragons," he whispered, tears in his eyes.

With slicing claws and streams of flame, they flew into the battle, red and green and blue. Tanin. Maev. The Prince of Eteer.

Jeid joined his roar to theirs, and their flames wreathed together.

MAEV

She had wrestled in grungy town squares. She had fought in pits of mud surrounded by cheering tribesmen. She had swapped punches and kicks in rundown huts and cellars, and she had flown over a southern kingdom, battling demons. She was Maev, a lost woman, a fighter, a dragon of Requiem. And here above her home, above this new tribe, she fought the battle of her life.

This was also the battle of her death. The battle she could not win.

The rocs swarmed toward her, many times the size of demons, dwarfing even her dragon form. They clawed through her scales. Their beaks drove into her flesh. She kicked, bit, lashed her tail. She blew her flames, and her comrades fought with as much vigor.

But the enemy was too strong.

The arrows of their riders were too many. The bolts slammed into Maev, and she dipped in the sky.

"Requiem!" she shouted, hoarse. A roc swooped toward her, and she torched it. It slammed into her, burning, and she knocked it off. "Fight them, dragons of Requiem! We die in blood! We die in fire!"

Yes. She would die here. Maev knew that, and she was ready. She would die in glory, slaying them, so that for eras tribes and villages and distant kingdoms would speak of Requiem, would speak of the last stand of dragons.

I do not go gently into death, she thought, grinning as blood dripped from her mouth. *If I die here, I die taking down dozens of you.*

She whipped her tail, slamming its spikes into a rider. The man's armor caved in. She yanked back her tail, tugging the man off his roc, and tossed him against a second bird. The beast shrieked, and more flew from above, and more claws slammed into Maev.

She dipped in the sky, and her flank hit the side of the canyon. Boulders tumbled down, and her tail hit a tree. The oak crashed into the canyon, burying a man beneath it.

She heard Tanin cry in pain above, and his blood splattered her. He crashed down, three rocs upon him, plunging into the shadowy gorge. A boulder shattered beneath him. Ahead of her, Maev saw more of the vultures mob her father. They knocked Jeid into the forest above the canyon. Trees ignited and fell, and fire hid the world. She no longer saw Sena, but blue scales fell from the sky, pattering around her like small discarded shields.

And so here I fall, Maev thought. *Not in a distant kingdom. Not in a strange town. But here. At home.*

It was not a bad place to die.

She pushed herself up.

She emitted a roar and torched a swooping roc.

Claws lashing, wings beating, she soared. The sky was hidden behind feathers, blood, and smoke.

Let me die in the sky.

"Requiem!" she cried. "My wings will forever find your sky."

She soared into the cloud of rocs, crashing into them, smiling as she killed.

LAIRA

Their blades clashed together in the tunnel, bronze against bronze, showering sparks.

"I will kill you now," Laira said.

Zerra laughed. "I will show you no such mercy."

His sword swung down. She raised her own sword, and the blades clanged together. She thrust and he parried, and when his blade swung again, it cut her wrist. Her blood showered but she gripped her hilt tightly.

"Yes, bleed for me, harlot." Zerra spat. "Bleed like you bled into the crone's leeches. Bleed like you bled under my fists. Bleed like you'll bleed tonight as I bed you, as I toss you to my men. They will each take you in turn until you're too hurt to scream."

Laira sneered and swung her blade. "No. No more." She advanced, forcing him back. He was twice her size, his head nearly grazing the ceiling. She was small and weak, and ilbane ached in her muscles, but a fire burned inside her, and she attacked in a fury. She drove him another step back. "No more. Never again." Her voice rose in strength, and she barely heard the slur of her crooked jaw. "You will nevermore hurt me, Zerra. I am no longer the little girl you beat, enslaved, tortured, starved." She thrust her blade at him, and her voice rose to a great cry. "I am Vir Requis! For Requiem I slay you. For my people. For a dawn of dragons."

Her sword slammed into his, again and again, until she found an opening. Her blade sparked against his breastplate, denting the metal.

He only laughed. "Vir Requis? Is that what you call your wretched kind? This is nothing but a colony for the diseased. I will cleanse the world of my brother and his children, and I will shatter your soul. You have grown impudent, and I will enjoy breaking your spark of defiance." He thrust the blade. "When I'm done with you, you will eat dung and drink piss and thank me for it."

She tried to parry but he was too fast. His blade drove into her shoulder.

Laira screamed.

"Yes . . . scream for me."

He swung his sword again. She leaped sideways, hitting the wall. His blade nipped her thigh, and her blood flowed. She parried the next blow but wasn't ready for his fist. His blade in his right hand, he slammed a left hook into her cheek.

White light and stars exploded.

She swung her blade blindly

He grabbed her throat. She gasped, struggling to breathe. When she could see again, she found his face near hers, a smile twisting his halved lips. She tried to swing her blade, but he caught her wrist, pinning her arm to the wall. She struggled, kicking, but couldn't free herself.

"So deformed . . ." He thrust out his tongue and licked her crooked jaw—a long, languorous movement that left her dripping with his saliva. "So sweet. But not hurt enough. Not yet. Look at my wound, darling." He turned the burnt side of his face toward her, forcing her to stare at the grooves and rivulets. "Soon your whole body will look like this."

Still clutching her throat, he sheathed his sword and lifted his torch, which had fallen during the duel. He brought the flame near her cheek. She winced and tried to turn her head away but could not. She sputtered and blackness spread across her. All she could see was the fire. All she could feel was the pain. She closed her eyes for fear of them melting.

"We will begin with burning your face," he said.

She couldn't move her right arm; he held it pinned to the wall. She kicked hard, hitting his knee. His leg crumpled. They fell together and she grabbed a fallen stone. She sprang up, slamming the rock into his temple.

He grunted.

His fingers released her, and Laira gasped for breath.

She wanted to collapse. She wanted to simply breathe. Instead she lunged forward, swinging the rock again. A shard of granite the size of her fist, it drove into Zerra's jaw. She heard the *crack* as the bone shattered. Two teeth flew. His chin drove sideways with a sickening *crunch*.

He fell to his knees, clutching his face with one hand, and managed to lift and thrust his blade. She parried and swung her sword down. The bronze drove deep into his arm and thumped against bone. He screamed and dropped his sword. Laira kicked it aside.

She placed the tip of her sword against his neck.

"Beg me for your life," she whispered.

Suddenly she trembled. Her voice was hoarse. Her knees shook.

"Beg me!" she shouted.

He stared up at her, eyes baleful. He said nothing.

"You will die here," she said. "Beg for life."

He stared, silent, his jaw shattered. His arm hung loosely, slashed open; she saw the bone and tendons. He managed to slur, blood and saliva dripping down his chin.

"What . . . do . . . you want?" He coughed out blood and teeth. "To be a huntress? Tell me. Tell me what you want."

She shuddered. In the darkness of the tunnel, she saw her again. Her mother smiled at her, stroked her hair, and told her bedtime stories. Laira ran with her through the forests, collecting berries, laughing and speaking in Eteerian. She remembered joy. She remembered warm embraces, safety, love.

"You killed my mother," she whispered, tears in her eyes. "You shattered my life. What do I want?" Her breath shook and she bared her teeth. "I want you to die, you bastard."

She screamed as she leaned forward, driving her blade into his neck.

His blood dripped, and he gave her a last stare, then tilted over and lay still.

Laira stared down at his body, and she no longer trembled. A peace descended upon her.

"For my mother," she whispered. "For Requiem. For me. It's over."

She knelt, grabbed his hair, and lashed her blade again.

Her footsteps were slow. Blood trailed behind her. She stepped out of the cave into a canyon of flame and blood, carrying Zerra's severed head.

"Goldtusk!" she shouted.

She stood upon bloodied boulders. The dead lay around and beneath her. Arms thrust out from the debris, and gore painted the canyon walls. One rider lay whimpering, his organs dangling from his sliced belly. Dozens of rocs still flew above, and at least two dragons still lived. Maev writhed on a pile of boulders, blowing her last sparks onto a roc. Tanin lay slumped, lashing his claws, holding back a beast; arrows pierced his flesh. Laira had never seen these two dragons, but she knew them from Jeid's stories—his children returned to battle. She did not see the others.

"Goldtusk!" Laira shouted. She raised the severed head above her. "Goldtusk, hear me! I am Laira Seran. I was one of you. I carry the head of Zerra, your chieftain."

The rocs shrieked. All eyes turned toward her. The battle died down as they stared. Hunters hissed and tugged their reins, halting the rocs. The birds hovered, blasting Laira with foul air, billowing her hair.

"I am a child of Goldtusk!" Laira cried, voice hoarse. "I slew the chieftain. By the law of our people, I lead this tribe now. I am chieftain! I am Laira of Goldtusk, a worshiper of Ka'altei. I command you—land, dismount your rocs, and kneel before your mistress."

For long moments—the ages of the stars and the world, the rise and fall of kingdoms, the endless mourning in her heart—they merely hovered, staring. She stared back. She knew how she looked—a scrawny thing, broken, scarred, covered in blood. A wisp of a person, a hint of who she could have been.

But this is who I am, she thought. *This is me. These years of pain, this fear, this broken body—they made me who I am. This person was hurt. And this person is strong.*

She raised the head higher, staring, silent. All others fell silent too. She could hear the wind in the trees and the crackle of fire.

It was one rider—a gruff old man named Sha'al, a chunk of mammoth tusk still embedded in his chest from an old hunt—who landed his roc first. He dismounted, gave Laira a hard look, and then knelt before her.

A second rider joined him, a young man who had once tossed Laira a few nuts on a cold winter night. He knelt before her, sword lowered.

"Chieftain," he said.

A third rider joined him, then a fourth. Soon dozens of rocs landed in the canyon, cawing nervously. Their riders covered the boulders, kneeling before her, heads lowered.

"Chieftain."

"Chieftain Laira."

"Daughter of Ka'altei."

They spread across the canyon, kneeling in a great wave. Laira stood, staring upon them—her people. She looked to her side where Maev and Tanin struggled to their feet—her new family.

"Our war ends now," Laira said softly. She lowered the severed head. "Goldtusk and Requiem will forge peace. We—"

A grunt rose ahead, followed by a strangled cry.

Laira raised her eyes and her heart nearly stopped.

"No," she whispered.

Jeid stumbled forward across the boulders, back in human form. A young man—not a rider of Goldtusk but a foreigner in the robes of Eteer—walked behind, holding a blade to Jeid's throat.

SENA

He shoved the gruff, bearded man forward, holding a knife to his throat. Everyone stared at him. Everyone judged him. Everyone thought him a villain. Sena trembled and felt tears stream down his cheeks, and he pushed the knife a hair's width closer.

"Stand back!" he shouted. "Stand back or I slit his throat!"

This battle, like all of this autumn, had been a feverish dream. For so long Sena had languished in Aerhein Tower, chained, starving, mad with his thoughts, the demons flying outside his window to torment him. Since fleeing that place, he had found no solace.

They said the north would be safe, Sena thought, the blade trembling in his hand. *They said this would be a home.*

But here too people hunted his kind. Here great vultures, each larger than ten demons, slew dragons.

"I can't live like this," Sena whispered, voice shuddering, as they stared at him. "I'm a prince. I'm a prince!" His tears flowed. "I can't live in the wilderness, hiding in caves, hunted, hurt. Look. Look at the blood. Oh Taal . . ."

The dead spread around him. He saw scattered limbs blackened with fire, white bones thrusting from the torn flesh. A severed head lay before him. Globs of flesh and puddles of blood lay everywhere. A dragon claw had disemboweled a roc, and pink entrails spilled across the ground, wet and stinking.

A home? This was a morgue. This was a nightmare.

The burly, bearded man grunted in his grip. Sena held the brute tightly, pushing his blade closer against the skin.

"Be still!" Sena said. "Be silent! I will cut you."

Upon the boulders, Maev leaped up and glared. "Sena! You pathetic little snake. You foul piece of pig shite. I saved your backside from that tower. You hold my father now!" She hopped across a boulder, moving closer. "Drop your knife or I'll smash your head against the canyon wall."

"You will stand back!" Sena said, staring back at her. Tears burned in his eyes, and his legs trembled. He pushed the blade a little deeper, nicking the man's skin, and Maev froze. Blood dripped down Jeid's neck. "Stand back, Maev, or your father dies."

Ahead, a short young woman was holding a severed head. She had been shouting something earlier. Crouched in the forest among the dead, Sena had been unable to make out her words. The woman looked about his age, maybe older, but haggard and small, frail as if after a long illness. Her black hair was cut short, and her mouth was slanted, her chin thrust to the side. She stared at him, tilted her head, and approached slowly.

"Why do you do this?" she said. Her voice was vaguely slurred, perhaps due to her crooked jaw.

Sena glared at her, clutching Jeid. "I am a prince of Eteer! I don't belong here. I can't live in this place. I have to go home." A sob fled his throat. "If I kill a weredragon, my father will forgive me. If I bring him this man's body, his demons will sniff the weredragon curse. They will know I killed one. And my father, the king, will forgive my own curse. He will let me return to my palace. Maybe not as heir, but a prince again." His chest shook and he cursed himself for weeping. "I want to go home. I just want to go home. Oh Taal . . ."

The young woman with the short, black hair stepped closer to him. She raised her emptied palms in a gesture of peace.

"You are . . . the Prince of Eteer?" Her voice was soft, and she tilted her head. "You are Sena Seran, son of Raem."

He nodded, peering around Jeid's shoulder, keeping the knife in place. The bearded man was silent save for his gruff breath.

"And who are you?" Sena demanded. "Another one of this man's daughters who wants to crack my head?"

The young woman shook her head, and a tear streamed down her cheek. "My name is Laira."

Sena snorted. "I had a sister named Laira once. It's a name of Eteer, not this forsaken place. She was exiled years ago and—"

He froze.

Laira stared at him, eyes soft, and moved closer. She reached out her hands. "It's me, Sena," she whispered, tears falling. "It's me. Your sister. I'm here."

Sena lowered his head and closed his eyes. Sobs wracked his body.

My sister . . .

"Oh Taal. Oh righteous god of purity. What have they done to you, sister?" He looked at her through his tears. "We have to go home. Both of us. We have to kill the others so Father forgives us. I want to go home."

Laira smiled tremulously. She stepped across the boulders toward him, reached out, and gently touched his arm.

"We are home, brother. We are home."

A *clank* sounded below, and Sena realized he had dropped his knife. With a grunt, the bearded man moved aside, and somehow Sena was embracing his sister, crying into her hair. She was so short—the top of her head barely reached his shoulders—and he held her slim body, nearly crushing her.

"I'm sorry," he whispered. "Laira, I'm sorry. I'm sorry."

She looked up at him, smiling, tears spiking her lashes. She touched his cheek. "Hello again, dear brother. After so many years, hello again. I love you."

He embraced her tightly and they stood for a long time, holding each other upon the boulder, a sea of blood around them.

JEID

Another Vir Requis had joined them. His twin brother was dead. The Goldtusk tribe was Laira's to command. The world shook around Jeid, but he no longer cared.

He cared for only one thing now.

Back in dragon form, he dug through the rubble, tossing boulders aside. His eyes burned. He worked in a fury, unearthing dead tribesmen, a crushed roc, and puddles of blood. Boulders rolled around him.

"Help me!" he said. "Tanin, Maev!"

His children rushed forth, shifted into dragons, and dug with him. Their eyes were narrowed, their mouths shut tight. They were thinking the same thought as him, Jeid knew.

Eranor was missing.

Jeid ground his teeth. Last he'd seen his father, the elderly druid had been blowing fire from the pantry, the rough cave that was now buried under rubble. With a grunt, Jeid grabbed a great boulder—it was as large as a man. Tanin and Maev had to help, shoving against it, before it creaked and crashed down.

The entrance to the pantry, once a narrow cave barely large enough for a man to crawl into, lay shattered. Jeid tugged back stones, widening the opening, revealing the shadowy chamber.

"Father!" he called. No answer came.

His arms shook as Jeid shifted back into human form. He raced into the cave and felt his heart shatter.

Eranor lay in the cavern, in human form again, rubble upon him. The ceiling had collapsed, and a boulder buried the old man's legs. Blood stained his long, once-white beard.

"Father!"

Jeid rushed forward and knelt by the old druid. Eranor was still alive, his breath ragged. The old man managed to focus his eyes on Jeid and clasp his hand.

"My son . . ." His voice was a mere whisper.

Maev and Tanin rushed into the cave too and knelt by their grandfather. Tears filled their eyes.

"Tell me what to do." Jeid clutched his father's hand. "Tell me how to heal you."

Eranor smiled—an almost wistful smile. "This body cannot be healed. Do not weep for me. I am old and I've lived longer than most. I lived to see Requiem rise." He closed his eyes. "In my mind I can see it—a great kingdom of dragons. You will lead them, Jeid. Lead them to hope, to light."

"No." Jeid shook his head. "No, Father. You will lead us. Don't leave. Now is not your time."

"I fly now to the stars, my son." Eranor's eyes narrowed to mere slits. "Tanin. Maev. Come closer. Be with me."

They all crowded around him, holding on to the old man, tears in their eyes.

Eranor gave a last smile. "I fly now to the Draco constellation. I fly to those we lost. I—"

His eyes closed.

His breath died.

Jeid lowered his head, pulled his father to his chest, and held him close for a long time.

The last leaves of autumn scuttled across the hills, and the first snow began to fall, when Jeid buried his father. Wind fluttered his fur cloak as he stood above the grave. A third boulder rose here, a third tombstone coated in moss. By it lay the two other graves—the young Vir Requis who had lost his leg, a stranger and yet one of their family, and an older grave overrun with ivy, the grave of his daughter. Of Requiem.

Requiem's Song

"I don't know how many more will die for our tribe," Jeid said, throat tight. He clenched his fists at his sides. "But I will fight on."

He looked at the others who stood around him, faces pale, eyes cold. His people. His tribe. The ones he loved.

Maev had refused a cloak of fur. She stood in a simple tunic, her arms bare, displaying her coiling dragon tattoos. Snow frosted her golden hair. No tears filled her eyes, and as always, her bottom lip was thrust out in defiance. As always, bruises and scratches covered her. Yet Jeid knew that beneath that stony exterior lay pain, love, and hope. The young woman stared down at the grave, chin raised, a well of tears hiding behind stone walls.

Tanin stood at her side, his eyes red, snow filling his shock of brown hair. The tall young man wrapped his fur cloak more tightly around himself. His lips whispered silent prayers or perhaps goodbyes. The juggler turned warrior—now a man grieving.

I never wanted this life for you, my children, Jeid thought. *I wanted you to grow up in safety, a true roof over your heads, a life without fear, without pain.*

Perhaps this day he grieved for his children—for their life of exile and bloodshed—as much as for his fallen father.

The new members of his tribe stood here too. Sena—slender, his cheeks soft—stood wrapped in a cloak, pale with frost. He stared down at the grave, silent, thoughtful. Laira stood at his side, holding his hand.

You too are my family now, Jeid thought, looking upon them. *I will fight for all of you.*

He knelt and placed a single birch leaf upon the grave, securing it with a stone. His father had always loved birches, and it was the only gift Jeid had to give. The others followed, one by one, placing down their own leaves and stones. Snow dusted the gifts.

Jeid straightened and looked at his new people. Young. Afraid. Looking to him for guidance. He spoke softly as the snow fell.

"Thus, with leaf and stone, we say goodbye." The others stared at him, eyes large, lips tight. "Thus, with blood and fire, we defended our home. We fled a village, a tribe, a southern kingdom. All over the world they hunt us—the people they call diseased, the cursed ones they call weredragons. But we are blessed. We are Vir Requis, and our magic comes from the stars." He looked up at that sky as if, past the pale sunlight and clouds, he could see those stars. "For a long time, I called Requiem a tribe. Tribes move across the world, seeking safety, struggling to survive." Jeid shook his head. "Requiem will be no tribe. We will be a kingdom." He looked back at them, meeting their eyes one by one. "We will tell the world: You can no longer hunt us. We will no longer hide. No more will the children of Requiem hide underground, ashamed, afraid."

They nodded. Maev growled and raised her fist. Tanin punched his palm and sneered. Laira's eyes lit up, and she raised her chin, and even her brother straightened and gazed ahead with pride.

"We will stand proud!" Jeid said, his voice rising louder. "We are only five, but more will join us. Many more Vir Requis hide across the world, afraid, believing they are cursed. We will trumpet our cause and call our people home. We will raise a palace of stone, and we will tell all tribes and nations: If you hunt us, you will die. If you attack us, you will burn. Dragons will rise! The kingdom of Requiem will last ten thousand years."

"Yes!" Maev said. The young woman shifted into a dragon, beat her wings, and soared. She raised a great pillar of fire, and her roar pealed across the land. "Requiem! I fight for you."

One by one, the others shifted too. They took flight, roaring for Requiem.

Requiem's Song

Only Jeid remained on the ground, still in human form. He looked down at the graves, and his eyes stung.

For you, Father. For you, my daughter. For you, unknown warrior. For all those who've died.

He looked up at the sky, shifted too, and took flight. He joined the others. They hovered above the hills and valleys, and Jeid added his flames to theirs. Five jets rose, spinning and crackling with heat and light, wreathing together into a great column of fire, a beacon for hope, for life, and for a new home.

* * * * *

They flew through the day and night, five dragons no longer afraid, until they reached the great mountains of Dair Ranin. There their claws dug, cutting loose marble from the mountainside, a great round pillar they could not carry, but which they rolled across the hills and valleys upon a wagon of logs.

For long days they worked in the forest, carving, smoothing, sculpting, using both dragon claws and bronze tools. The rocs awaited them in the hills beyond, for here among these birches—here was holy ground, blessed with dragon starlight. Fresh snow covered the trees when finally their work was done. A great column rose between the birches, three hundred feet tall, its marble smooth and glittering like the snow, its capital shaped as rearing dragons.

They stood before the pillar, five dragons, dwarfed by the size of their creation. It seemed to Jeid that the pillar glimmered with inner light. A circle of marble tiles stretched around it, and birch leaves scuttled upon the polished stone. In the distance, rising above the forest, sunlight gilded the distant mountains.

"The Column of Requiem," Jeid said. He shifted back into human form and placed a hand upon it. "A beacon to draw our kind to this forest like a lighthouse draws in ships."

Laira shifted back into human form too. She held Jeid's hand and leaned against him.

"Requiem is a true kingdom now." She stared up at the pillar. "But we need a king." She looked at him and touched his cheek. "You vowed to lead us. Be our king."

The others gathered closer, also resuming human forms. They nodded, one by one.

Jeid barked a laugh. "King Jeid Blacksmith? Doesn't sound very kingly."

"It sounds bloody stupid," Maev said and spat.

Laira smiled and placed her small, pale hand against Jeid's wide chest. "You told us that Requiem will last ten thousand years. But Requiem will last for eternity. Give yourself a new name, not the name of a blacksmith but the name of a dragon. Become King Aeternum, a king whose song will echo through the ages."

Beside them, Tanin nodded in approval. "King Aeternum. I like it. Future generations might even think Jeid was noble, not a grizzled, gruff grizzly."

"The only thing eternal about Grizzly is his appetite," Maev muttered.

Jeid sighed and shook his head. Ignoring his children, he looked back up at the column. It soared past the treetops toward the clouds, and the sun fell upon the capital, breaking into many beams.

I hope you are watching, Father, Jeid thought. *I hope you are proud.*

Laira let go of his hand, stepped forward, and touched the column. She smiled softly and closed her eyes. When she sang, her voice—passing through her crooked jaw—barely sounded slurred to her but high and pure.

"As the leaves fall upon our marble tiles, as the breeze rustles the birches beyond our column, as the sun gilds the mountains above our halls—know, young child of the woods, you are home, you are home." She opened her eyes, smiled, and looked up at the pale clouds. "Requiem! May our wings forever find your sky."

Jeid smiled too. He repeated the prayer, a new song, a holy song—Requiem's song. The others joined in and their voices rose together.

"Requiem! May our wings forever find your sky."

ISSARI

The city-state of Eteer—center of a civilization, a light to the world—lay charred and crumbled.

Issari stood upon her balcony, staring at the destruction. Aerhein Tower, the prison which had once held her brother, lay fallen, crushing houses beneath it. Blood and gobbets of demon flesh covered the city domes, courtyards, and cobbled streets. Half the trees had burned, and ash rained across the balcony, remnants of the fire upon the palace roof.

"Two dragons came to this city," Issari whispered, the smoky wind invading her nostrils. "Three left. And here I remain, an heiress to a broken land."

The demons too remained, still marring her city. Dozens had died in the dragon onslaught. But Angel, their queen, still crackled in the underground, moving through the city sewers, nursing her wounds and blasting flame and smoke through sewage holes. Hundreds of her minions still covered the roofs, gardens, and streets, screeching and cackling. Hundreds of women walked the streets, dazed, holding their growing bellies; the spawn of demons festered in their wombs.

Issari winced in sudden pain. The welts on her back blazed with agony if she even breathed too deeply. When her father had returned to the city—only three days ago—he had beaten her, whipping her back until she bled.

"I left you here alone for a month," King Raem had said, voice cold. "I left you, my heiress, to rule this city, and I return to find it in ruins."

She had not wanted to scream. She had vowed to remain silent under his lash. Yet as he had beaten her, and as her blood had splattered the walls, she had screamed.

A sigh ran through Issari as she stood here now, gazing upon the hive of devilry and ruin. She raised her hand and gazed at her amulet. When she'd pressed it against Angel, it had embedded itself into Issari's palm. Her flesh had healed around the silver sigil—a slender man within a circle. She had tried to pull the talisman free but could not. It was a part of her now—as much as her heart. The silver gleamed softly, crackling to life as a demon fluttered by the balcony. She closed her fingers around the amulet, and its glow faded.

"Forever I will be a bane of demons," she whispered, though she did not know how one woman could fight so many. Even three dragons, blowing fire, had been unable to defeat Angel. How could she stop this? How could she save her kingdom?

She closed her eyes, trying to remember flying upon Tanin, the red dragon from the north. Like she did so many times, Issari again wished she too could shift. If she could become a dragon, she could fly north. To Requiem. She could join Laira, Sena, and the others. Her eyes stung, and Issari felt like she were the cursed one—lacking magic, plain, weak.

Do you like me like this, Taal? she thought. *Pure?*

She raised her head. Night was falling and the first stars emerged. The new constellation shone, shaped like a dragon. And for the first time in her life, Issari prayed to new gods.

"Please, stars of Requiem, if you can hear me, bless me with your magic. Let me rise as a dragon. Let me fly. Let me be strong."

She closed her eyes, took a deep breath, and tried to shift. She imagined herself as a dragon—beating wings, roaring fire. Yet nothing happened. When she opened her eyes, she was a girl again, only a slim thing in a white gown, her dark braid hanging across her shoulder.

She left the balcony and walked through the palace, heading down stairways and corridors. When Mother and Laira had fled, Issari had been only a babe, but she knew the stories. To this day, guards whispered how Raem—then only a prince—had found his wife and child shifting into dragons in the palace cistern. Since then, few had dared enter that dark, wet place, perhaps fearing that the miasma of reptilian disease still lingered there. But this evening, Issari needed to see that place—to think of her family, to imagine dragons.

She walked down a craggy tunnel and stairs, plunging into underground depths, until she emerged into the cistern.

It was a towering cavern, as large as the throne room above. Columns supported a rough, vaulted ceiling. Water rose taller than a man here, still and silent. A cold place, wet, secret, and dark.

Slowly, Issari began to walk down a flight of stairs toward the water. When she saw the shadow ahead, she gasped and froze.

Merciful Taal . . .

Ahead of her, half-submerged in the water, was a dragon.

Instinctively, Issari reached to her belt and clutched the hilt of her dagger.

She did not know this dragon. The beast was black and burly, his horns long. He had not seen her, and Issari quickly hid behind a column and peeked. The dragon stood still in the water; the only movement was the smoke pluming from his nostrils. Finally, with a grunt and shake of his head, the dragon began to shrink. His wings pulled into his back, his scales faded, and a man floated in the water, bald and shirtless.

Issari slapped her palm over her mouth to stifle her gasp.

It was her father.

Slowly, dripping water, King Raem stepped out from the pool. Issari pulled her head back, pressing herself against the column. If he saw her here, he would not merely beat her again; he would drown her in this pool. She crept deeper into shadows, waiting for Raem to climb the stairs and leave the cistern.

But she did not see him leave. For a long moment, she saw and heard nothing. Then a loud *crack* pierced the silence, followed by a grunt. A second *crack* followed.

Issari dared to peek around the column. Her father was kneeling by the pool, chastising himself with a belt. Welts rose across his back, much like the ones he had given her.

"Diseased," the king hissed. "Cursed. Shameful." With every word, his belt lashed again.

Issari stared in disbelief.

Her father. The man who had banished his daughter and imprisoned his son. The man who had murdered scores in the city, those he called weredragons. The man who had released an army of demons to purify his kingdom with blood and rot.

Her father . . . was Vir Requis.

Issari's eyes stung.

All those you killed, she thought, trembling. *All that you destroyed. All this pain, all this terror . . . because you are ashamed. Because you are one of them.*

Her amulet blazed in her hand; it felt like holding an ember. Issari took ragged breaths and raised her chin. She knew then. She knew what she could do, what she had to do. She knew that only she, here in this place, could save Eteer, could save Requiem, could return light to the darkness.

She drew her dagger.

Leaving her hiding place, she walked toward her father, daring not breathe.

He did not see her. He was still kneeling by the pool, chastising himself. Blood dripped down his back.

It will be just one more wound, Issari thought, staring at his blood. *Just one thrust of the blade.*

Her dagger shook and her heart thrashed, but Issari knew she had to do this. She would sin. She would murder again—like she had murdered the crone. She would save the world.

She reached her father—the man who had beaten her, tortured her siblings, the man who had to die—and raised her dagger.

With a sob, she thrust the blade.

Raem spun around.

The king gasped and raised his arms, protecting himself. The dagger sliced into his forearm, ripping flesh open. The blade scraped against bone.

Issari screamed.

Raem reached out, grabbed her wrist, and twisted. The blade clanged to the ground. A second later, the king's fist drove into Issari's chest.

She fell back, unable to breathe. She tried to suck in breath; horror engulfed her when she realized she could not. The pain bloomed through her.

"Father—" she tried to whisper.

He grabbed her. He twisted her arms behind her back and manhandled her forward, his blood dripping.

"You treacherous whore." His voice shook. "You worm that crawls with maggots. You betrayed me."

Issari managed a hoarse whisper. "You killed your own father. You unleashed demons upon this world. You are the traitor to Eteer. You—"

He clamped a palm over her mouth, and she screamed into it. He shoved her up the stairs, his blood leaving a red trail. When she fell, he dragged her. Her hip banged against each step. She tried to fight, to punch him, to kick, but could not. Another blow from his fist rattled her jaw. A slap sent her reeling.

"Father, please!"

Blood filled her mouth. And she knew that begging wouldn't help. She had stabbed him, almost killed him. Her life was forfeit.

I should have flown north with the dragons, she realized. *I should have fled. Now I will die here, alone, afraid.*

He dragged her down a corridor, past tall bronze doors, and into the palace throne room.

Once a place of splendor, it had been transformed into a hive of fire and brimstone. The porphyry columns, once pure and pale blue, now stank with serpentine demons that wrapped around them, oozing drool. Once a mosaic had covered the floor, featuring birds and dolphins. Now globs of rot hid the artwork, and demons rutted in the puddles, grunting in their passion. Once the throne had risen in a beam of light; now it rose from a mass of writhing creatures who bit, licked, and clawed one another. Angel herself now lurked here, clinging to the ceiling like a bat, drooling lava and hissing down at her minions below.

Issari gasped as her father tossed her into the chamber. She fell, landing in a puddle of rot.

"Demons of the Abyss!" Raem called out.

The creatures ceased their racket and turned toward him. One paused with another's leg between its jaws. Others froze, still linked together as they rutted. They stared, hissing, tongues lolling.

"Here lies a traitor." Raem pointed down at Issari. "She is yours to do with as you like. Mate with her. Eat her flesh if you like. Keep her alive for your amusement or kill her. But one thing I demand: Make sure she never leaves this chamber again."

With that, he left the hall and slammed the doors behind him.

Issari leaped up, raced to the doors, and yanked at the handles. Locked.

She spun around, pressed her back to the doors, and stared at the creatures. The demons approached slowly, grins widening. Angel detached from the ceiling, landed on the floor, and hissed like a viper. Her tongue reached out across the hall, an obscene tentacle longer than three men, to lick Issari's cheek.

Issari raised her hand. Her amulet, embedded into her palm, blazed to life.

"By the light of Taal!" she shouted. "I banish you. I—"

Angel spat. A wad of dark drool hit the amulet, hiding its glow. With a scream, Issari tried to rip the glob off, but it clung to her hand, black and sticky.

The Demon Queen leaped toward her, crossing the throne room in a single bound. She landed before Issari, gripped her cheeks, and hissed.

"What a pretty thing." She caressed Issari's hair with a clawed hand. "So fair. So fresh. So innocent. You will be mine to break. I will mate with you, and so will all in my hall. And when we are done, we will feast upon you." Smoke rose from her mouth, and she licked her lips. "You will live through it. You will watch as we devour your legs, then your arms, then slowly work our way up your torso, sucking up your entrails as you scream. But you will not die." Angel sneered, holding Issari pinned against the doors. "Not until I say you can."

Around them, the other demons howled, drooled, laughed, beat their wings, spewed their filth. Their faces spun, eyes red, mouths dripping.

Issari closed her eyes.

A dragon can defeat them. A dragon can blow fire. A dragon can fly away.

She took a deep breath, seeking a magic deep within her. She imagined herself growing wings and claws, rising, flying. Yet nothing happened.

Requiem's Song

The demons dragged her away from the doors. They slammed her against the floor, stretched out her limbs until they almost dislocated, and held her down on her back. Towering creatures like human vultures cloaked in red feathers leaned forward. Their beaks opened, full of serrated teeth. Worms crawled between their feet, as large as children; they were great leeches, Issari realized, like the ones Shedah had used but many times the size.

"Break her!" Angel commanded.

Issari closed her eyes again.

To shift is not a curse, she thought. *My mother could shift. My siblings can. Even my father shifted.*

She breathed shakily. For years, King Raem had preached of the evil of the reptilian curse. For years, Issari had feared the magic, thinking the weredragons poor souls to pity. But her father too could shift! It was not a curse. It was not an abomination unto Taal.

It was magic.

Issari took a deep, shuddering breath.

Wings sprouted from her back, shoving her upward.

She opened her eyes to see claws growing on her fingertips. Her body ballooned, knocking demons back. White scales, glimmering like mother of pearl, grew across her body like armor. Demons clawed but could not break through.

A white dragon, Princess Issari rose in the chamber, sounded her roar, and blew her fire.

RAEM

He stood in the charred rooftop gardens—the same place he had stabbed his father—stitching the wound his daughter had given him. His lips were tight, and sweat dripped down his face as he worked, sewing his arm shut.

The trees, bushes, and flowerbeds lay burnt around him. The broken lattices rose like blackened bones. Once this had been a garden of life, a place of solitude and peace. The dragons had come. The dragons had burned. The dragons had torn his life apart, torn his children from him.

Two of those children—Laira and Sena—now flew in the north, diseased creatures. His third child, his youngest, he had taught too well.

"Issari is like me," Raem said softly into the ashy wind. "A traitor to her father. And so she will suffer."

He violently thrust the needle into his arm, savoring the pain. He was sewing the last stitch when the palace shook. Dust flew. Bricks toppled into a courtyard below. Raem leaned over the roof's edge and sucked in his breath.

A white dragon crashed out of the palace doorway, shattering bronze and stone, and soared into the sky.

Raem stared, silent.

A cloud of demons burst out of the palace like black blood spilling from an infected wound. They began to fly in pursuit, but the white dragon turned and blasted fire. The inferno blazed across the demons and crashed into the palace, forcing Raem to step back into the charred gardens. Sparks landed upon him, searing his skin; he was still shirtless after his visit to the cistern.

When the flames died, he saw demon corpses upon the courtyard below. The white dragon was already flying toward the coast.

Light caught the dragon's palm, shining against something metallic. Raem knew that light.

An amulet of Taal.

"Issari," he whispered.

Before he could take another breath, the roof crashed open behind him. Through a cloud of rock and smoke, Angel ascended, shrieking. Claw marks drove down her stony chest, leaking lava. Rings of fire burst out from her.

"Your daughter!" she cried, voice a storm. "Your daughter is diseased!" She landed before him, wings knocking down charred trees, and clawed what remained of the roof. "You have forbidden me to leave this city, and now she flees. Send me after her!"

Raem was surprised.

Not surprised that Issari was a dragon.

Not that his city crumbled around him.

Not that his wound dripped, a failed assassination attempt from his dearest daughter.

Raem was surprised that, despite all these things, he found himself feeling remarkably calm, even casual.

He cleared his throat. "Yes, my dear Angel, it seems she is a dragon. And yes, I have forbidden you to leave this city."

The Demon Queen screamed. Her fire blazed, a great pillar upon the roof. The palace shook. Demons who flew above, balls of slime, burst under the sound wave of her scream, falling down in tatters.

"Send me after her!"

Calmly, Raem turned to look toward the coast. The white dragon was now over the water, fleeing north. A second beast was flying in the opposite direction, heading from the sea toward the city. As Raem watched, a great oily vulture—larger even than a dragon—flew toward the palace, a rider upon its back.

With a shriek, the roc landed on the palace roof. A Goldtusk hunter spilled off its back, barely landing on his feet. He was a tall, hirsute man with beads threaded into his beard. Three fingers were missing from his hand, the wounds fresh, and a gash ran down his chest. His skin was ashen, his eyes sunken. Blood stained his tattered fur cloak.

"I seek King Raem!" the man said, wavering, looking so weak he barely acknowledged the smoky, fiery Angel.

"You have found him," said Raem.

The hunter gripped Raem's arms. "The rocs . . . many dead. Zerra . . . slain. Laira, that maggot of a harlot . . . took over the tribe. The dragons have a kingdom now. Requiem, they call it. All is lost. All . . . lost . . ."

With that, the man collapsed. He breathed no more.

Raem stared at the dead man, at Issari who was barely visible upon the horizon, at the ruin of his palace, and at the panting, sneering Angel.

And he laughed.

His laughter seized him. He could not stop. Angel shrieked again, beating her wings, and Raem laughed so much he had to wipe a tear from his eye.

"Do you see, Angel?" he said. "Do you see the pain of children? Never breed, Angel. Never bear a child."

She ripped out a chunk of roof and tossed it aside. She lifted the dead hunter in her claws, raised him to her lips, and hissed.

"It is time," she said. "Time to eat human flesh. Time to grow. Time to kill dragons."

Raem looked down upon the city. He saw no living souls. All his people—once proud and strong—hid in their homes.

The dragons destroyed my city, he thought. *And so be it. Let blood fill these streets.*

He nodded.

"A thousand men and women I give to you. A thousand meals. Fly through the city with your demons, Angel. Feast upon them. Grow large. Grow strong. And then . . . then we fly north. To Requiem."

Angel howled in joy. Her jaw unhinged, her maw opening wide like a python about to swallow a pig. She stuffed the dead tribesman into her mouth, gulping him down, chewing, swallowing, until her belly extended like some obscene pregnancy. Her limbs grew longer. Her head ballooned. She laughed as she grew taller, sprouting to twice her old height, then growing even further. She spread her wings wide like midnight sails.

"Rise, demons of the Abyss!" Angel shouted. "Rise and feast upon the flesh of Eteer!"

She beat her wings, rising, ringed in fire, a woman of stone and lava the size of a dragon. From the palace windows and doors, they burst out, a thousand abominations of the Abyss. They spread through the city streets. They crashed through the doors of homes and shops. And they fed. And they grew.

Screams and blood filled the city of Eteer that day.

Raem watched from the palace roof, a thin smile on his lips.

Before him, the demons grew, extending like boils about to burst. Globs of flesh. Scaled creatures of hooks and horns. Unholy centipedes of many human heads and limbs. All rose before him, growing to the size of dragons. They hovered before the palace roof, swallowing the last bits of human flesh.

It was an army of darkness. It was an army to purify the world.

Upon the roof, Raem raised his arms. He shouted out for them all to hear.

"I have fed you, my children! And you have grown strong. Now we fly! We fly north. We fly to Requiem. We fly to kill dragons!"

They shrieked, howled, sneered, laughed, roared. Their voices rose into a single cry, a thunder that shook the city, that shattered towers, that sent burnt trees crumbling. Raem's mount—the twisted woman broken, cursed, and stretched into a bat—flew toward him. Once the size of a horse, the deformed creature was now as large as a dragon, and the blood of men stained her lips. Raem mounted the beast and stroked her.

Hiding the sky behind their wings, leaving a trail of rot, the demon army flew across the city and over the sea, heading to the land of dragons.

The story continues in . . .

REQUIEM'S HOPE

Dawn of Dragons, Book Two

NOVELS BY DANIEL ARENSON

Misfit Heroes:
Eye of the Wizard (2011)
Wand of the Witch (2012)

Song of Dragons:
Blood of Requiem (2011)
Tears of Requiem (2011)
Light of Requiem (2011)

Dragonlore:
A Dawn of Dragonfire (2012)
A Day of Dragon Blood (2012)
A Night of Dragon Wings (2013)

The Dragon War
A Legacy of Light (2013)
A Birthright of Blood (2013)
A Memory of Blood (2013)

Dawn of Dragons
Requiem's Song (2014)
Requiem's Hope (2014)
Requiem's Prayer (2014)

The Moth Saga
Moth (2013)
Empires of Moth (2013)
Secrets of Moth (2014)
Daughter of Moth (2014)
Shadows of Moth (2014)

KEEP IN TOUCH

www.DanielArenson.com
Daniel@DanielArenson.com
Facebook.com/DanielArenson
Twitter.com/DanielArenson

Printed in Great Britain
by Amazon.co.uk, Ltd.,
Marston Gate.